When He Loves

A Protector & Defender Romance
Book 6

Cynthia Eden

HOCUS POCUS
PUBLISHING INC

He's been in love with her since the day they met.

Love at first sight? Sure, you can call it that. Love, obsession, whatever. All Nash Quinn knows is that from the instant he met Delaney Daniels, he fell for her. Hard. Completely. And now...she's marrying someone else. A man who most people believe to be a prince charming, but Nash knows the guy is a real nightmare, and there is no way–*no way*–that he can let his Delaney go through with the marriage. Because as soon as she's married, she'll be dead.

So he has to kidnap the bride.

It's a dirty job, but someone has to do it. Nash rides in on his motorcycle, and when the priest asks if anyone objects, Nash steals the bride. Only...Delaney comes far too willingly. She jumps on the back of his motorcycle, and they ride off into the night...even as the groom gives chase.

She's in trouble, and the man who once shattered her heart is the only one who can help her.

Right before her wedding, Delaney found out just how dangerous and *evil* her groom-to-be truly was. Desperate and afraid, she'd sent a frantic text to her former best friend, Agnes, hoping for some miracle. She never expected her miracle to come in the form of Agnes's brother Nash– gorgeous, big, powerful Nash. He storms the wedding and carries her out into the night. Yes, she's heard the whispers about him. She even has secretly suspected that he might work for the government, but when she learns that big, bad

Nash is actually a spy...A *spy who just saved her from certain death*...everything changes.

The CIA wants to use her. Nash just wants to protect her.

He has to hide Delaney. Has to whisk her away and stay close to her every moment. But emotions and needs that Nash has held in check for far too long are pushing past his control. This is finally his chance–his chance to have Delaney, and Nash is not going to let her slip through his fingers again.

He'll be the one to put a ring on her finger. And to set a trap for her ex.

Another wedding? Sure, why not? When the CIA wants to nab her ex, Delaney is all-in on the plan. Even if that plan means traveling to Vegas, fake marrying the hot and brooding Nash, and risking everything to bring down a killer. She can do this...but, she may just lose her heart to Nash along the way. Her heart, and potentially, her life.

Author's Note: He's stealing a bride, and he will not give her back. Nash has been in love with Delaney for years, and he is not going to let anyone hurt her. He'll step from the shadows, he'll protect her, and he'll finally claim the woman who owns his soul. If anyone tries to get in his way, he'll show them just how dangerous a real protector can truly be...

Chapter One

It was going to take a miracle to save her.

Delaney Daniels tightened her grip on the bouquet of red roses as she ever-so-slowly made her way down the narrow aisle. Each tiny step made her feel as if she was walking straight to her doom because...she was.

Her groom waited about ten feet away. Handsome. Tall. Immaculate in his tux. His smile was warm and tender, and he utterly *terrified* her.

A few of the rose petals from her bouquet fell onto the white aisle runner beneath her high-heeled feet. The petals fell because her fingers shook so badly. Not like she could help the shaking. She was way too afraid. No way she could control herself.

A sweet little lady with wire-framed glasses played the organ. The church contained only a handful of people. It was supposed to be charming. Romantic.

It was not. It was horrifying. Gut-wrenching.

Her white high heels minced forward. *I am moving as slowly as I possibly can.* Still searching for a miracle. Still looking for some desperate way out of this nightmare.

The priest beamed at her. His right hand held the Bible, and his left hand motioned for her to come forward.

Oh, had she stopped advancing? And had she perhaps shaken her head in a *no* response to him?

She had.

Her groom—Kurt Henry Wellington, the *third*—lost a bit of his smile. His handsome face stopped looking quite so charming and became slightly more cruel.

I believed the lie right in front of me. Until it had been too late. Until she'd discovered the truth. Until she'd wanted to run away.

But there was no running from some people in this world. Kurt Henry Wellington was one of those individuals. A very, very dangerous individual. The man who wanted to marry her. The man who'd claimed to love her.

The man who *would* kill her as soon as the ceremony was over and he had her alone with him. Her honeymoon truly would be from hell.

"Darling?" Kurt's warm, deep voice.

She hated his voice. The care in it was a complete lie. Just like everything else about Kurt. *Lie, lie, lie.* But there was nowhere for her to go. The heavy satin of her dress trapped her. The train sliding behind her felt like a chain dragging her down. Down straight to her grave.

Kurt strode toward her. That charming grin flashed again. The grin wasn't for her benefit. It had to be for the few people watching. Strangers to her. Their ties were to Kurt, their allegiance to Kurt, not to her.

"Darling..." Kurt said the endearment again, and Delaney could not help but flinch. He'd eliminated the distance between them. Now, he stood right in front of her. He reached out and took one of her hands away from the quivering bouquet.

More rose petals trembled and fell. One rose petal landed on her dress, looking so very much like a blood drop that a shudder worked along her entire body. *Hello, foreshadowing.*

"You need to walk toward the priest," Kurt directed. "Now."

No, she needed to run for the exit.

But even if she got to the exit, there was nowhere for her to go. She had no car to make her escape. Kurt would catch her before she got more than steps away from the church. He'd hurt her. He'd make her come back.

"*Delaney.*" A warning note had entered his voice.

She smiled at him. Did it look like a tender, loving smile? Or a go-to-hell grin? And did it even matter? Voice low, husky, Delaney told him, "Go screw yourself."

His grip tightened on her hand.

She sucked in a quick breath because his grip was painful. She could practically feel the bones in her hand rubbing together.

"That's no way to talk to the man who loves you."

Only he didn't really love her. He couldn't. He'd just been using her all along. And this whole stupid setup at the church was a farce that would end in her death. What was she supposed to do? Go happily to her grave? Did he think she would just docilely accept her fate?

"Walk down the aisle," Kurt ordered her. "Say '*I do*' and then this will all be over for you."

Unfortunately, it would. Because as soon as he got her out of that church and away from the others, Delaney knew she'd be dead.

Instead of walking down the aisle, she instinctively took a step back.

He hauled her close. To the others, it probably looked as

if he was pulling her close in some sort of heated embrace. "I cannot wait..." Kurt began loudly. Then his head lowered and his lips feathered over her left ear as he finished, "To have you all to myself."

She felt something sharp stab into her side. As in, literally, a stab.

Delaney sucked in a breath.

Not a deep stab. A cut that had pierced her skin. A promise that more pain would come if she didn't follow his commands.

"That's a knife," he informed her. As if she had not already figured out that obvious fact. His lips brushed across her ear again. "Let's get the show moving, *now*."

He wasn't going to kill her right there. Not with the priest watching. At least, she didn't *think* that Kurt would kill her there.

"There are other people I can hurt," he whispered to her. "Do you want me to take out the people you care about?"

There weren't a lot of people on her list. That was one of the reasons why she'd been such easy pickings for him. Her parents were dead. No siblings or other close relatives. But she did have a few friends—

"I can make a phone call, and people will die."

She wet her lips. "I can't wait...to say 'I do' and spend the rest of my life..." That super short life. "With you." *You lying asshole. You sadistic creep. You—*

"Wonderful." He moved to her side. Kept the knife pressed against her, but he'd positioned her bouquet higher so that the roses hid the weapon.

The little lady playing the organ had stopped. But when Kurt nodded toward her, she began playing *The Wedding March* again. And Delaney began walking.

Her breath shuddered in and out. Her heart drummed far too fast in her chest.

When she'd been a teenager, she'd dreamed about her wedding. Even sketched out a dress that she'd love to wear. She'd wanted to carry daisies, not roses, and she'd wanted to be on a beach, with the waves crashing into the shore. She'd also wanted…

To marry a different man.

She and Kurt were directly in front of the priest. The knife still pressed into her side. A warning and a promise at the same time.

"Let's speed this along," Kurt urged as he sent an indulgent smile her way. "My bride is getting jittery."

Jittery. Oh, the lying ass. His *bride* was trying to figure out if she could be fast enough to swipe the knife and plunge it into his neck. His chest. Anywhere. His bride wanted to get stabby on him.

"Most brides do get nervous." A sympathetic nod from the priest. The overhead light gleamed off his bald head. "No need to fear."

Oh, there was literally every single need under the sun for her to fear the man beside her.

"This is the happiest day of your life," the priest added.

Nope. He was wrong on that count.

Her heart drummed faster because she had to find a way out of this nightmare. There had to be a way to escape. Something…

A loud and angry rumble—like a fierce growl—pierced the air just as the organist ended *The Wedding March.*

Delaney's head whipped toward the growl.

"Ignore it," Kurt ordered. "Just some idiot outside."

An idiot with a growling engine. One that seemed to be coming closer. Such a loud, powerful growl.

The priest cleared his throat. "Before me, I have two loving individuals—"

"How about we jump to the vows?" Kurt cut through the priest's words. "That good with you? Getting right to them?"

The priest frowned.

The growling was so strong now that Delaney could have sworn that the walls of the church were shaking.

"Uh...well..." The priest squinted at Kurt. "You're in a rush?"

The growling stopped. Just died away.

Kurt seemed to relax. "Can't wait to marry the love of my life."

Right. Sure. He said those words while he had a knife pressed to her side.

"Besides, like I told you, Delaney is jittery. Don't want her to suffer unnecessarily so let's hurry things along."

Miracle. I need a miracle. It would be fantastic if that miracle could come at any moment.

The priest asked, "Does anyone object to the marriage?"

"Yes," Delaney said, quite clearly and quite loudly, unable to hold herself back. *I object. He's a monster. I have to get out of here. I can't marry him. I won't.*

"Why in the hell would you ask that question?" Kurt snarled at the priest, his voice cracking over Delaney's.

"I..." The priest had a trickle of sweat running down his left temple. "It's normal to ask, part of the ceremony. I-I ask if there is anyone who objects to the marriage and then when there is no objection, we go to the vows and—"

"*I object.*" Deep, dark, dangerous. A voice that pierced straight to Delaney's heart.

At that booming voice, both Delaney and Kurt whirled toward the front of the little church. The doors had been yanked open, and a big, muscled, and glaring man in a black leather jacket stood with his legs braced apart and his strong hands fisted at his sides.

Fury hardened his handsome face. Rage charged his body. He looked deadly and scary and—

Like my miracle.

"Who the hell are you?" Kurt shouted.

"I'm the man stealing your bride." He stalked forward. Dark hair tousled. Faint stubble on his rock-hard jaw.

Kurt had let her go. When they'd both turned in surprise, he'd let her go and the knife wasn't pressing into her side, and this was her *chance.*

She grabbed for her dress's train, and Delaney surged for the powerful man charging toward her. But she didn't get far because Kurt grabbed her arm and hauled her back against him.

"What in the hell did you do?" Kurt gritted out.

She'd called a friend and begged for help. That help had just arrived.

Though I didn't necessarily count on the help arriving in the form of my ex. The big, bad, glaring badass storming toward her was Nash Quinn. The man who'd once owned her heart. Only to toss it away.

But beggars definitely couldn't be choosers. If her ex was her miracle, she'd take him in a heartbeat. Nash was there to save her ass, and she was running out with him.

As for Kurt...

"I'm not marrying you." She had a way out of this nightmare now. A muscled, beautiful, dangerous way out in the form of the furious man storming so quickly toward her and Kurt. *Safety.* "Get your hands off me."

Kurt shook his head. "I will *kill* you," he rasped, for her ears alone, "before I let you go to—"

"Hey, jerkoff, remove your hands from her."

But her hero didn't wait for Kurt to comply. Instead...

"*Duck, Delaney. Now,*" her hero ordered.

She ducked. Nash's powerful fist swung out, and it slammed into Kurt's jaw. Kurt stumbled back, and then he fell toward the floor. He crashed. Hard.

The priest gasped. The lady at the organ nearly fell off her wooden bench. And the men and two women in the pews—people connected to Kurt—froze.

"The wedding is *off*," Delaney told Kurt. The tall ceilings in the church made her angry words echo around her. She yanked off her engagement ring and tossed it toward Kurt. The ring and the bouquet. The rose petals fluttered in the air.

"Is that a *knife?*" Her hero had just noticed the knife on the floor. It had fallen when Kurt took the punch to the face.

No time for an explanation about the knife. The *guests* were shaking from their stupor, coming close, and she was sure some of them were armed because a few of those guys weren't *friends* of Kurt's. They were more like his evil henchmen.

"We have to get out of here, *now*." She grabbed for Nash's arm.

Once upon a time, Nash had been the star of her teenage fantasies. Technically, he was still the man who made far too many appearances in her adult dreams. The man who...

When she'd had those long-ago visions of a beach wedding, *he'd* been the groom in her daydreams.

Then, unfortunately, he'd gone on to utterly break and destroy her heart. After the breakup that had left her sobbing into her favorite chocolate ice cream, she'd planned to never, ever see him again. But, desperate times could call for some extremely desperate measures. She'd needed help. Her options had been limited. She'd had to text for emergency assistance and there had only been time to send out a cry for help to—

"Uh, Delaney?" Nash's deep, dark voice slid over her. Through her. "Is that creep in the front pew reaching for a gun?"

Yes, yes, he was.

Nash didn't wait for her to respond. He attacked the creep in the front pew. Nash drove his right fist at his target even as his left hand snatched the gun away and sent it hurtling beneath some pews.

The priest and organist ran.

As for Delaney—

Nash spun back toward her. "You coming with me?"

Uh, yes. "A thousand times, yes."

He grabbed her, tossed her over his shoulder, and hauled ass for the door. The train trailed over her head, falling over her upside-down self, and she fought to shove it out of her way. When she finally did get the satin and lace out of her way, she saw Kurt being helped to his feet. A groggy Kurt.

He staggered and pointed at her. "No!" Kurt shook his head. Almost fell again. *"Delaney!"* He lunged toward her.

But Nash was carrying her out of the open church doors. Fresh air hit her, and a wide smile curved her lips. Nash had gotten her out. Away from Kurt. She was bouncing along Nash's broad shoulder and then—

He lowered her in front of him. The satin and lace tumbled. Her breath heaved.

"You can't ride on my Harley wearing that damn thing."

And, for the second time in the last ten minutes, a man came at her with a knife.

Except the blade of Nash's knife didn't touch her at all. It *did* slice away her dress. He cut the bottom of the dress off her, leaving Delaney in a new, makeshift skirt that barely fell to mid-thigh.

"*Delaney!*" A bellow from the church.

She looked toward the open doors.

Kurt was trying to charge at her, but some of his friends-slash-henchmen were holding him back. For the moment.

"Let's go." She jumped over the discarded satin that had fallen at her feet. "Go, go, go!"

Nash stared at her with his amazing eyes—one blue, one brown. Both eyes glittered with his fury. "What in the hell is happening?"

Her side ached. Probably due to the stab wound. Or slice. Yes, she definitely preferred to think of it as a slice because a *slice* sounded way better than a *stab*. "How about we talk about everything once we are away? Okay? Good for you?"

His eyes narrowed. "Delaney…"

He saved me. Got me away from Kurt. She leapt at Nash. Grabbed his powerful shoulders and hauled him toward her. Her lips pressed frantically, desperately to his.

Nash stiffened.

"You just saved my life," she whispered against his mouth. "Now, if we both want to keep living, *we have to get out of here.*" Delaney backed away. Clutched his hand. "*Let's go. Please, please, please. Let's go. Fast. Now.*"

He climbed on the motorcycle. She jumped on, too, and locked her body behind his. The big, black beast of a bike snarled with fury when Nash started the engine. Oh, what a beautiful, dark, and growling sound. The sound of hope and freedom.

"Hold on," Nash told her.

Like she wasn't already doing that. Holding on for dear life.

The motorcycle leapt away from the church. She had a fast flash of Kurt's glaring face as he stood in the open doorway of the church, and wild laughter escaped her.

She'd just gotten her miracle. In the form of her ex-lover.

Fate could have such a twisted sense of humor.

Nash raced away with her into the dark, and she held on, well, as if her very life depended on him. Which, yeah, it did.

The man who'd broken her heart had seriously just saved her ass.

Chapter Two

He'd stolen a bride.

And he had no intention of ever giving her back. Delaney Daniels was *his*.

Nash Quinn knew his grip was far too tight around the handlebars. The Harley vibrated beneath him, and Delaney pressed every beautiful curve that she had against his body. She held him fiercely, desperately, as if she'd never, ever let him go.

Fair enough. I won't be letting her go again.

Walking into that church had been like walking straight into a scene from his worst nightmare. *His* Delaney. Marrying someone else. Standing in front of a priest, wearing a white dress, holding those blood-red roses with that creep in a tux getting ready to claim her as his bride.

The hell, no.

Especially because the intel that Nash had picked up about her groom—well, his intel indicated that the guy might as well be the devil. No way did the devil get to keep Delaney.

I'm keeping her.

He'd been afraid that he wouldn't get to Delaney in time. But he had. He'd stopped the freaking wedding and—

He steered the Harley off the road. Braked at an old, shuttered gas station.

"What are you doing?" Delaney asked, voice breaking around the edges. "Why are we stopping? Did you miss the part where we needed to go, go, go? Because I thought I was super clear on that point. If not, please allow me to repeat, we need to *go, go, go!*"

He killed the engine.

"Nash? Uh, Nash, this is the opposite of going."

He shoved down the kickstand and climbed off the bike. His body brushed against hers way too much during that climb from the Harley. He took two steps away from her. Then a third. Mostly because he needed a bit of space from the temptation that was Delaney Daniels. Talking while she had her body pressed against his was far too distracting. Breathing in her seductive scent was too distracting. Being close to the woman who'd haunted him for years was far *too distracting.*

"Nash, we need to be driving away. Super, super fast."

Stars glittered overhead. Moonlight. He'd deliberately chosen the darkest part of the lot to park his ride. The better not to be seen in case they were followed. And that brought him to his important question of... "You think he's gonna follow you?"

"Uh, yes. I do. One hundred percent. I think Kurt is going to run fast after me because he swore not to let me go."

Yeah, about that dick groom of hers...How should he break the news to her? *So, Delaney, the man you almost married is a psychopath.* That felt harsh. But it was true. *A murdering psychopath. And when I realized you were marrying him, nothing was gonna stop me from getting to you.*

"We are *still* not moving, and I just told you, he's going to come after me. As fast as he can."

His jaw locked. "Because he loves you so freaking much."

"What?"

Nash sucked in a breath. Then let it go. He'd sounded snarly and jealous. His bad. Unfortunately, he was snarly and jealous, and dammit, had she just gotten more beautiful over the years?

He was pretty sure she had.

As he drank her in, she hopped off the motorcycle and hurried to stand right in front of him. "Let me be very clear with you."

Great. She could be clear with him, and then he could break the news about the groom to her.

"Kurt Wellington doesn't love me at all." Her head tipped back. She was small. Always had been. Small. Delicate. *Breakable.* She barely clocked in around five-foot-three, while he was an easy six-foot-four. He outweighed her by a hundred pounds. Had, even when they'd been in high school. He'd been defensive line. She'd twirled a baton during halftime with the band, and one year that baton had been on *fire* because Delaney had wanted to—

"Just what did Agnes tell you?" Delaney asked as her hands went to her hips.

Ah. Agnes. His sister had been the one to aim him when he'd been hunting for Delaney. "She gave me your location. Said I had to stop the wedding." But, fun fact, that agenda item had already been on his list before he'd gotten the call from his sister.

"And that's it?" Her voice rose. "She just said for you to *stop* the wedding?"

His arms crossed over his chest. "Was there more?"

"Yes, a lot more!" Her hands left her hips to fly angrily into the air. "I wasn't sure if she got both texts. I barely had the chance to hit send on the second one before Kurt took my phone." Her breath shuddered out. "The first text *did* have the address of the church. I know that one got through. I heard the little *swoosh* as it was sent. The first text included the time and date for the ceremony. And it said *please stop the wedding*. But I sent a second text explaining why and..." Her shoulders fell. "She didn't get the second message?"

As far as he knew, nope, she had not. "Agnes didn't know why you wanted out of your wedding. Just said that you needed help. Agnes was too far away, she couldn't get here fast enough, so she called in me and my brother Ryan." One shoulder rolled. "I was closer than Ryan, so that's why I'm here." *I actually already intended to stop the wedding even before Agnes reached out to me, and I'm just trying to figure out how to explain all of this to you without causing a serious freakout.*

"So...what?" Delaney took a step back. "It was between you and Ryan and...you like, drew the short straw or something and had to come charging in?"

More like he'd come flying in as fast he could, breaking every speed limit possible, his heart in his throat as he prayed that he'd get to the church before Delaney said "*I do*" to the dangerous jerk who would never deserve her. "Uh, yeah." He sawed a hand over his jaw. "Something like that. You know, you could have just walked away from the guy. Probably a whole lot less dramatic than having me barge in and carry you away."

Headlights appeared on the dark road, slicing toward them.

Delaney hurtled her body at him. She shoved into him, surprisingly hard for someone of her size, and his hands automatically curled around her.

"Hide!" Delaney gasped out. "We have got to hide!"

His motorcycle was already pretty well hidden. And he'd been sticking to the shadows, too. She'd been the most visible, especially since she still sported half of a white wedding dress. He whirled fast, putting himself in front of her and caging her between his body and the brick wall on the side of the gas station.

The headlights rushed past them. The vehicle never slowed. Correction, two vehicles. No, three. They all blazed past the shuttered gas station.

"I bet that's him," she whispered. "Kurt said he wasn't going to just let me go."

"Guess he wants you very badly." Something Nash could understand. His hands were on her shoulders. Her scent—jasmine—teased his nose. "Guess he loves you, too." *The sonofabitch.*

"No, he doesn't love me." Very definite.

In the dark, he frowned down at her.

"He wants to *kill* me."

Nash's body stiffened. *Wait, hold up. Does she already know that her groom is—*

"Kurt wants to *kill* me," she repeated. "As in, if you hadn't come roaring to the rescue on your bike, I would have never lived past my honeymoon."

He didn't have a response. Mostly because there were some things he was not supposed to tell her. Confidential, classified things.

"You think I didn't *try* to leave him?" Delaney fired at him.

Every muscle in his body seemed to have turned to stone.

"I did. As soon as I found out the truth about him, I tried to leave. But Kurt chased me down. He caught me. He tied me up and locked me in a closet."

What. The. Fuck? Deadly rage burned beneath his skin. "He locked you in a closet?" *Holy hell. She knows exactly what he is. The intel we had on the guy was dead on.*

"I got free of the ropes. I managed to get my phone, and I texted Agnes. I know she worked as a Fed, and I thought she could help me. That she could come in with guns blazing only..." A faint click as she swallowed. "I guess she didn't get the second message. And instead of guns blazing..." Her voice trailed away. "*You* came to save me."

The night surrounded them. Her seductive scent filled his nostrils. And fury poured through every cell of his body. After a tense moment when the silence stretched far too long, Nash nodded. He forced his hands to release their too tight grip on her. And then he backed away. One step. Two. He spun on his heel and lunged for his motorcycle.

She rushed forward and darted around him to stand in Nash's path. "What are you doing?" Delaney asked.

"Going to kill a man." The first item on his to-do list.

"*What?*"

"The bastard put ropes on you? Locked you in a closet?" His teeth snapped together. "Dead. Don't worry, I'll make sure his death hurts. Count on it."

She pressed her hands to his chest, as if to physically stop him. "You can't do that!"

"If I'd known what the guy did to you when we were back at that church, I would have killed him then and there." Going back and taking care of the job was now mandatory.

Except, wait, the creep probably wasn't at the church any longer. Had he been in one of the three rides that just torpedoed past them?

"Nash! No!" Sharp. Confused. Delaney shook her head, and he saw some of the heavy locks of her dark hair fly over her shoulders. "You are a doctor! You don't kill people!"

His lips parted. But he didn't speak. Kinda because he wasn't sure what to say.

The last time that he'd seen Delaney, yes, Nash had *planned* to be a doctor. He'd been in medical school. He'd wanted to be a trauma surgeon. But...

Life had changed. *He'd* changed.

After two years of medical school, he'd followed the path to another calling. A calling that, ah, did make him highly skilled at killing. Turned out, he tended to excel in that particular area. But very few people knew about his real job. Not like you just made a habit of announcing that you worked for the CIA and that your job was to eliminate the deadliest criminals in the world.

And that job brought me to Kurt Wellington. A man with some seriously shady ties. A whole lot of suspicion was aimed at Kurt. Enough suspicion that, when Nash had realized Delaney was marrying the man—well, he'd had to act. *Can't let her marry him. Can't let her be hurt.*

Can't. Won't.

But he couldn't say those things to her, dammit.

It's a good thing Agnes called me. Though my sister has no idea I was already planning to stop the wedding. He'd gotten to the church so fast because he'd already been heading to Delaney. The minute he'd seen the surveillance photo of Kurt that had included a pic of his bride-to-be, the minute Nash had recognized Delaney's delicate features...

That was the minute when my world stopped spinning.

"Let's get back on the motorcycle, and let's get as far away from here as we can," she implored, her touch scorching through him. His black jacket hung open, and her fingers pressed to the dark t-shirt that he wore. One that was old and thin and, hell, yes, he could feel the heat of her touch through the fabric.

His body had always been far too sensitive, too attuned, to Delaney.

Once upon a time, Delaney had been his sister's best friend. She'd also been his not-so-secret obsession.

And now...now...

Stop thinking about what her touch does to you. The woman just told you that she'd basically been kidnapped and that her groom wanted her dead. "You need to contact the cops."

"I can't contact the cops here. They are on Kurt's payroll. That's why we have to get away. It's not safe here. Kurt will hunt me. If he finds me, he'll drag me back, and I'm afraid that he'll hurt *you!*"

Nash snorted. "Yeah, I'd like to see him try."

"I wouldn't." She pulled her hands away from Nash.

And why had she done that? He'd enjoyed her touch. Always had. Always would.

"I don't want you hurt at all." Definite, determined words from Delaney. "So how about you drive me out of this place? How about we just start driving and we don't stop until the sun is up? Then I can regroup, I can call Agnes, and I'm sure she can help me out." A brief pause. "I-I know you probably have your own life to get back to. I don't want to cause any more trouble for you than necessary."

Trouble? Walking into that church and seeing her poised to marry that jackass had completely wrecked his world. But now...

Now...

She's in danger. She needs protection. She needs me. "I'm the man for the job."

"Excuse me?"

He wanted to see her in the light. It had been far too long since he'd been able to drink in Delaney. Did she still have the sprinkle of freckles across her nose? Did her hazel eyes still sparkle and shift, seeming to reflect her mood? Become lighter, more golden when she was happy and a deep, turbulent brown when she was sad or angry? Did her dark hair still catch the light and reflect those nearly hidden, red highlights?

"The man for what job?" Delaney asked him, and then, he was pretty sure that she shivered.

Not that the night was particularly cold. It wasn't. They were up in the Blue Ridge Mountains, on a winding road in North Carolina, and it was late spring. The night was brisk, not cold, but she didn't have on sleeves, and he *had* cut off half of her dress.

He shouldered out of his jacket. Handed it to her.

She didn't take it. "What are you doing?" A suspicious question.

"Trying to keep you warm."

"I am warm."

"Then why are you shivering?"

Her chin notched up. A defiant motion he'd seen a hundred times in the past.

A soft sigh slid from him. "I stopped because you

needed a helmet." He hadn't taken the time to give her one at the church, mostly because the dumbass groom had been giving chase. Nash had also still been furious because the fool in the front row had drawn a gun.

"That's not a helmet. It's your jacket."

He was aware. Since she wasn't taking it, he put it on her. Of course, the jacket swallowed her, but that was the point. "The jacket is black, so you won't be as big of a target in the white dress." The heavier fabric of the coat covered the satin of her dress. He went back to the bike, bent near the saddlebag, and scooped up the helmet that he should have given her sooner. He returned to Delaney, slid it over her head, and tightened the chin strap. "You're not dying, Delaney." His head lowered toward hers. The visor of the helmet was up.

"I really don't want to die, Nash. And that's why we need to get out of here. We should cross the state line. I don't exactly know how far Kurt's reach extends, but getting over the state line feels like a good start. Then I can call Agnes, and I can get some Feds to help me out."

Because she didn't think he could keep her safe? Insulting. But, then again, she didn't know what he was capable of doing for her. "No one is hurting you." Not on his watch.

"And no one is going to hurt *you*, either," she fired back immediately. "I don't want you getting pulled into my battles. No sense in you getting hurt because you're being a good guy and helping out an old friend."

Her words had him frowning. "You're wrong."

She fiddled with the edge of his jacket. "About what?"

"I'm not a good guy."

Delaney laughed. Soft. Musical. Sweet. A sound that he'd never been able to forget. A sound that had haunted him because it reminded him of what he'd lost. "Of course, you're good, Nash. You're a doctor. You save lives."

No, he was a spy. And, on more than one occasion, he'd taken lives. They would get to that truth, but not right this second. He'd rather not have her more terrified than she already was. "And we were never friends."

She sucked in a breath and took a step back. "That hurts, Nash."

"You were a virgin, and I fucked you until you screamed for me. I don't think that qualifies as *friendship*." He'd fucked her on her nineteenth birthday. Right after she'd blown out her candle. He'd asked her what she'd wished for.

You.

She'd been all he ever wanted. No way could he hold back after that admission from her.

But, now, before him...

She retreated. Another fast step back.

Too bad for her, he wasn't letting her get away. Not this time. *Not ever again.* His hand slid out and curled around her wrist.

She hissed out a breath.

Immediately, he let her go. Because he knew the sound of pain when he heard it. "I...hurt you?"

"Damn right, you did." A fast response. "We *were* friends, you jerk. Don't ever say that we weren't! For a time, you knew me better than anyone else on the entire planet. And then everything changed. *You* changed." She pointed to the motorcycle. "Can we get going? Trust me, I am grateful for the save tonight. I seriously owe you my life, but I want to get out of here."

He climbed onto the motorcycle. She slid on behind him. Her hands curled around his waist as he got the engine snarling to life.

"And it was not very gentlemanly to point out the whole virgin and screaming part," she said, sniffing.

He laughed. "Sweetheart, I was never a gentleman." *But I am one damn fine killer. And I will keep you safe from the bastard on your trail.* "Hold tight," he told her, and then they raced into the night.

* * *

"You're falling asleep."

Her eyes opened. Groggily. Slowly.

"We're stopping for the night. It's either stop or tie you to my body so you don't fall off the bike, and I think the better option is to stop, don't you?"

She craned her head, trying to look around Nash and figure out where in the world they were.

VACANCY.

Her gaze caught the blinking, red sign near the glass window of what appeared to be a check-in office. An office of one seriously shady motel. *Shady* because rooms were advertised as being available for the night or for the hour.

"Where are we?" she muttered.

"Stay on the bike. When I go in, I will be able to see you every moment."

Uh...

He was already off the bike. Marching toward the check-in office. Her gaze darted around the lot. No one else was out. What time was it? It felt as if they'd driven forever, but she knew they'd probably only been on the road a matter of hours. Four hours? Five? And had they gotten out of North Carolina and made it to somewhere else that would be much, much safer for her?

He came back. Walking all casually and confidently.

He slid in front of her, and she tried to ignore the surge of awareness she felt every single time they touched. The bike revved to life, and she felt the vibration all through her body.

Yes, she'd been sleepy. How could she not be? She'd been close to collapsing, but she'd doggedly held on to Nash, and, fine, she was glad they were stopping. Even if their stop was taking them to a no-tell motel.

It was better than nothing.

They could rest for a few hours. Maybe she'd call Agnes when the sun rose. And then she'd go to the Feds, and she'd get help, and Nash could go back to his life.

She'd go back to her life.

He didn't pull the motorcycle in front of any particular room. In fact, he hid the Harley behind a large, green dumpster. And then he took her hand, holding her fingers in his bear-like grip, and led her to room number seventeen.

A light flickered on and off near the door to their room.

She swallowed as she watched him slide the keycard over the sensor to unlock the door. "Is this going to be one of those one-bed situations?"

His head turned toward her.

The light near the door came on.

She saw his handsome face. The strong lines. The chiseled jaw. The cheekbones that were to die for.

And those eyes...brown and blue...

The light flashed off.

"A one-bed situation?" Nash repeated carefully. He opened the door.

"Um. You know. The motel only had one room left. One room, with one bed. And because of that, we have to share..." She was rambling as she followed him inside.

He shut the door behind her. Flipped the lock. "Do you *want* to share a bed with me?"

"I wasn't talking about us, specifically. I was talking about things that happen in books and—"

He turned on the lights. "Two beds."

Illumination flooded the room, and she could see, yes, two beds. They appeared to be full-size beds. Maybe even queens.

"Didn't realize you wanted to share a bed with me." His deep, dark, sexy voice. "I could definitely have requested one king instead of two queens if I'd known."

"No!" Okay. Way too loud. She tried to tone down her volume. "This is fine. Really. I'm sure your...girlfriend would not approve of a one-bed situation anyway."

"I don't have a girlfriend."

And I don't have a fiancé anymore.

That did *not* mean they immediately jumped into one bed together. Nope, it did not. And if she hadn't just been existing on adrenaline and desperation, Delaney would not even be having the thought. She was just at the end of her rope. That queen-size bed near her was looking far too tempting.

Delaney shrugged out of her borrowed coat and carefully placed it on the back of a nearby chair. The lone chair in the room. She ignored the threadbare carpeting and the humming that came constantly from the sputtering air conditioning system as she made her way to the bed. "I think I am going to crash, and..." Her eyes closed in mortification. "Oh, gosh, I should have said this before." How could she have *not* said this before? Eyes opening, she turned toward him. "Thank *you—Nash?*"

Her words ended in a cry of surprise because he'd just pounced on her. For a big guy, he could certainly move quickly. He pulled her against him, and then his fingers dipped down her sides and...

"What are you *doing*?" Delaney gasped. Her hands swatted at him. "This is not a one-bed situation." They'd covered that!

"You're fucking bleeding."

She glanced down at herself. Now she could see the dark red that marred her white dress. "Oh, right. That."

"*That*? You were aware of *that*? Aware that you were bleeding, and you didn't say anything to me?"

It wasn't some massive amount of blood. But, yeah, it still didn't look good. "We needed to escape. Saying something about the knife wound didn't seem important at the time."

"Knife...wound?"

Her gaze shot to his face because those words had just been low and exceedingly lethal.

"He took a *knife* to you?"

Delaney nodded. "I told you, Kurt was going to kill me." She had told him that, hadn't she? The exhaustion pulling at her made things a bit hazy. "I tried to escape but—*Nash!*" For the second time in like, two minutes, she cried out his name. This time, she'd cried it out in shock and surprise because he'd lifted her up and was currently carrying her toward the super tiny bathroom.

They crossed the threshold of the bathroom. He lowered her until her heels touched the tiled floor.

"Strip," he ordered.

"Uh..."

"Delaney, take off the dress or I will rip it off you."

Chapter Three

Delaney let out a dramatic gasp even as she swatted at his hands. "You would *not*."

"Yeah, sweetheart, I would. In a heartbeat." Actually, a heartbeat had already passed. *There is blood on her dress. Delaney is bleeding. That bastard stabbed her.* Nash grabbed the bottom of the dress and began to yank it up. The fabric ripped and tore beneath his fingers.

"No! I don't have anything else to wear!" She backed away. Tried to, anyway, but there was nowhere for her to go in the tiny bathroom. "I'll take it off! I'll do it, jeez! Just give me second!"

And she did.

She put her hands behind her back. The zipper hissed as she lowered it. The dress sagged forward, and then it fell to pool at her feet.

Delaney was left wearing white stockings, white heels, white panties, and the most tempting bit of white lace for a bra that he'd ever seen in his life.

And, normally, he would have *loved* to just stand there and take in the perfection that was his Delaney but...

Blood. Blood covered her right side. It had hardened, and when the dress fell, he'd seen her wince as the dried blood had tried to cling to the fabric and to her body at the same time.

"Tell me that it's not terribly bad," Delaney whispered.

He couldn't tell much about the wound, not yet.

He reached for a towel. Then stopped. Dammit, he had to get some first aid supplies. She might need stitches. And there sure as hell wasn't going to be anything in that ancient bathroom that he could use that wouldn't be covered in germs. "Stay right here," he ordered.

"What?"

"I saw a first aid kit behind the check-in counter. I'm going to get it." He could grab it and be back in five minutes. Nah, three. Tops.

"No, I'm fine!" She grabbed for the faucet, turning and giving him a truly stellar view of her ass. "I just need to wash the blood away."

He wanted to treat the wound properly. No sense in exposing her to the risk of an infection. *"Delaney, stay here."*

She looked over her shoulder at him. "I'm sure it's okay." But her lower lip trembled. "He...put a knife in my side, Nash."

Fuck. "He's dead, Delaney." Correction, the prick *would* be dead when Nash got his hands on the guy.

A tear slid down her cheek. "He did it right in front of the priest. I...I stopped walking down the aisle, and Kurt came at me. He put the knife in my side—the tip of the blade, I felt it go into me."

Oh, but I will make his death hurt. "Why in the hell were you marrying him?"

She flinched. Squared her shoulders. Turned back to the sink.

But he could see her reflection in the mirror. See the second tear that slid down her cheek. Sadness tinted her face as she told him, "You don't know Prince Charming is a monster until he decides to let his dark side out to play."

Nash's muscles were already locked in fury, and he made sure not to let his expression alter at her words. Delaney had never understood the darkness that rested in Nash's own heart. He'd always tried to shield her from that part of himself. And eventually, he'd even walked away from her.

And missed her every damn day.

She yanked on the faucet, and water poured into the sink. "It's fine. I'm fine. Everything is *fine.*" A brisk nod. Another teardrop.

Things were not, in actuality, *fine,* and the woman had to know that. More like, everything was on fire.

But she nodded again and said, "I just need to wash away the blood. I absolutely do *not* need stitches. So don't even think of finding some shady needle to poke into my skin. The cut isn't that deep. I'm sure it's not and...*why do you keep picking me up?*"

He had picked her up. Turned her around. And sat her down on the edge of the sink. He stood in front of her.

"Oh, this countertop is not going to hold me." She bit her lower lip as she peered down at it. "I do not think we are talking quality craftsmanship here. I'm about to go flying to the floor."

"Stop."

Her long lashes fluttered. Delaney had dark and thick lashes. Full and gorgeous lips. And, yes, she still did have that faint sprinkle of freckles across the bridge of her nose.

"Stop what?" Delaney asked.

"You think I don't know that when you get extra scared

or nervous that you talk faster or that you throw out some joke? You always did that. Always tried to laugh it off when you were terrified of something."

She swallowed. "Excuse me for trying to find a bit of light in the darkness."

She was his light in the darkness. *Fuck me.* "This is such a mistake." He shoved back from her. Mostly because he'd been seconds away from kissing her.

She kissed me right outside of the church. He'd been so stunned that he'd frozen on her. When what he'd really wanted to do...*Lock my hands around her. Hold her tight. Kiss her frantically. Hungrily. Desperately. Never, ever let go.*

"What's a mistake?" Her big, deep and dark eyes—yep, the hazel had shifted more to dark brown—stared up at him. "Helping me?"

"Wanting to fuck you into oblivion. That's my current mistake." He shook his head. "I'd help you any day of the week. You need me, and I'll come running. Didn't I prove that tonight?"

Her jaw dropped.

"Stay here." He was pretty sure he'd given her that order before. But he wanted to make sure she remained in the motel room and out of sight. "I'm going to get the first aid kit. I'll be back in three minutes. *Three minutes.*" Maybe two if he hauled ass extra fast.

Her hand flew out to curl around his arm. "What if... what if Kurt comes while you're gone?"

"Then I'll beat the hell out of him." The way he should have done at the church. The way he would have done if he'd known that dick had taken a knife to Delaney.

He'd been operating in the dark. His only order from his sister Agnes had been...

Stop the wedding.

Something he'd already been planning to do before she called.

He pulled away from Delaney. Stalked out of room seventeen and made sure to lock the door behind him. In moments, he was back inside the small motel's office. The guy behind the counter was scrolling on his phone, humming and bobbing his head. Young male, with wild, puffy hair—blue in a few spots—and with the saddest wisp of a mustache imaginable trying to sprout across his upper lip. When the clerk caught a look at Nash...

The kid's Adam's apple bobbed. His eyes widened. "I know the room is shit, man. I tried to warn you. But there is no better room that I can offer. That is, like, it. And there are no refunds. Motel policy."

Nash slapped a fifty down on the counter.

The kid frowned. "What's happening right now?"

"I'm taking your first aid kit."

"My what?"

Grabbing hard for his patience, Nash pointed at the red first aid kit behind the counter.

"Oh, would you look at that?" Real surprise in the teen's voice. Hell, maybe he wasn't a teen. Maybe he was in his twenties, but he just looked helluva young. "Wonder when we got that?" the guy asked.

"I'm taking the kit," Nash said again. He slapped another fifty down on the counter. "And you are going to make absolutely sure that no one ever knows who stayed in room seventeen, got me? And if *anyone* comes around here before I check out, you alert me. Immediately."

The kid handed him the first aid kit. The clerk also made the money vanish in a flash, as if he'd just performed a magic trick. "Are you like, wanted for some crime or something?"

Nash stared at him.

"You're scary, man," the motel clerk told him. "And you're also not here. Not at this motel at all. Check. Understood." A sly wink. "I will tell no one. Never saw you. Don't know you."

Nash grunted. He'd deliberately kept Delaney out of the guy's line of sight. As far as Nash was concerned, no one else needed to see her. It was safer for Delaney that way. Armed with his kit, he hurried back to room seventeen.

Had Delaney followed orders? He entered the room, bracing himself to see her in those stockings and panties and the bra that made him want to get down on his knees and worship the woman.

Water was running in the bathroom. Nash could hear it. He locked the front door and hurried toward the sound of that water, only to draw up short when he realized that her stockings were on the floor near the bathroom's entrance. Her stockings and her high heels.

Nash stopped. Swallowed. "Delaney?"

"It's really not bad. I, uh, I cleaned away most of the blood. It's not deep. Not *too* deep, anyway." She moved into the bathroom doorway.

Sexy bra. Tiny panties.

Nothing else.

He almost lunged at her.

"See?" Delaney angled her right side toward him. "I got rid of the majority of the blood. It's just a cut. The slice was more a warning than anything else. If Kurt had wanted to kill me, he would have shoved the knife into my heart."

Kurt is dead. Dead. Dead.

"But he needed me alive until we were married. I wasn't

going to be useful to him as a dead fiancée. A dead wife is an entirely different matter." Her gaze fell to his right hand. "Oh, you have the first aid kit." She looked back over her shoulder. "It's really tight in here. You know, because...um, you're so big and, um..." Her head swung back toward him. "How about we just slap a bandage on me and call it a night?" She crept out of the bathroom.

"I'm not just slapping a bandage on you," he growled.

"Okay, Dr. Quinn."

He wasn't a doctor. His nostrils flared. "Come here."

She closed the distance between them. He yanked open the first aid kit and tossed it on the nearest bed. Antiseptic wipes were inside, and he snagged them first. His left hand curled around her waist.

Delaney sucked in a breath.

Immediately, his gaze flew to her face. "I hurt you?" He never wanted to hurt her. "I haven't even touched the wound yet!"

"No. You didn't hurt me." She licked her lips. "Just... sometimes, I forget what it's like when you touch me." She thrust back her shoulders, and the move just made her breasts all the more tempting. "Sorry, I'm good now. Go ahead."

I forget what it's like when you touch me. Yeah, they would be revisiting that statement. First, though, he cleaned the wound. He could see exactly where the tip of a knife had sliced into her skin, but, thankfully, the wound wasn't that deep. His jaw locked as he tenderly cleaned the cut and applied the antibiotic ointment that had also been inside his new kit. She was statue-still during his administrations, and when he finally pressed a bandage over her wound, Delaney released a slow breath.

His fingers lingered against her skin. "Why were you

marrying him?" *Him. Him and not me. You should have been marrying me.* But he'd screwed that dream up long ago.

"Because Kurt said he loved me."

But did you love him? She must have, right? To become engaged to the man in the first place?

"Kurt said all the right things. He did all the right things. He charmed and he lied and he had me believing that we could have a wonderful life together." A shake of her head that sent her hair sliding over her shoulders. "But he wasn't the right man. I knew it deep inside. I just didn't realize how much of a nightmare he was until..." Delaney stopped.

He waited.

She didn't say more. Just stood there, in her underwear, breaking his self-control breath by breath. Heartbeat by heartbeat.

"Delaney." A growl of her name. "Don't leave me in suspense." If she wasn't gonna talk, then he'd have to do it. But, damn, how was he going to break the news that he suspected her asshole fiancé was an international criminal? After what the man had done to her, Delaney *should* believe him, but then, once he started spilling about Kurt's crimes, Nash would have to tell her his own secrets and that was going to get extra messy.

"I saw Kurt kill a man."

"*What?*"

"I tried to stop him." Another shake of her head. "I couldn't. He just—he did it and he didn't blink, and I was screaming and lunging for Kurt's weapon, and I tried to help the man but blood was everywhere." She peered down at her own body. "That was when he locked me in the closet."

He tossed away the used medical supplies. Put the first aid kit near the TV. And he went back to Delaney.

The woman needs clothes.

He jerked off his shirt. Extended it toward her.

A frown pulled at her brows. "Why are you handing me your shirt?"

"Because if you keep standing in front of me just wearing your underwear, we're gonna have a problem," he rasped. Actually, they already had a problem. That would be the giant dick that was shoving toward her.

Her gaze darted down his body. Her stare widened, and then whipped right back up to his face. "You—"

"Have a hard-on for you? Always. Especially when you're practically naked in front of me. So how about you help us both out and you *put on the damn shirt?*"

She snatched the shirt from him, but when she did, his hand twisted, flipped, and caught her fingers.

"Nash?"

He could see the red marks around her wrist. Rope burns. "*Bastard.*"

"I..." The tip of her tongue darted to touch her bottom lip. "I need to put on the shirt, remember?"

He brought her wrist to his mouth. Pressed a kiss to the red marks on her delicate skin. "I will kill him for you."

A nervous laugh. "Doctors take an oath to do no harm, don't they? I hardly expect you to start fighting for me."

Oh, she had no idea. He'd fight for her until his very last breath.

He let her go. Watched as she pulled the dark t-shirt over her head. It fell down her body, swallowing her.

"Better?" Delaney asked him.

No, now she just looked like she was...*his.* Then again,

hadn't he always thought of her that way? Didn't he *still* think she belonged to him?

"I'm sorry, but curiosity compels me to ask this. How are you even bigger now?" Delaney questioned him.

His dick was bigger because she was there, right in front of him. His dick always got bigger when she was close.

"Your chest—your shoulders, your—" Her hand gestured toward him. "Do you work out every single moment or what?"

Before he could say anything, she turned and scampered toward the bed on the left. She dove under the covers and pulled them up to her chin.

"Forget I said anything," Delaney mumbled. "So the wrong time for me to say anything."

Nash figured that was his cue to stop the questions. Fair enough. They both needed to crash but, first, he took out his phone. Fired off a quick text. Short and sweet.

Wedding stopped.

"Who are you texting?" Delaney asked, voice husky.

"Agnes."

"Oh, good! Kurt destroyed my phone..."

His teeth could not clench harder.

"So I didn't have a way to contact her again. Thank you for letting her know that I'm all right."

Three dots appeared on the screen of his phone as Nash waited for his sister to respond.

Then...

What happened? From Agnes.

How to explain the situation? This was way more than they'd anticipated. This was—

Did she realize you still love her? Another text from Agnes.

Jeez. Could his sister not rip that particular wound open immediately? His fingers flew over the screen. *Her dick fiancé tried to kill her. This is a five-alarm situation. Will brief you in the morning.*

Three dots. And...

WHAT???

Then his phone was ringing because, of course, it was. Not like Agnes would ever wait for the morning to come. Sighing, Nash tapped the screen and put the phone to his ear. "I've got her." His eyes were on Delaney right then as she huddled under the covers.

"What did you mean he tried to kill her? Why? When? How?" A rapid firing of questions from his sister.

"Don't have all the details yet. I'm working on them."

"Working on them? *Working* on them?" Her voice rose several octaves. "What does that even mean?"

"It means I stopped the wedding. I stole the bride. And I have her in a safe location." Safe enough, anyway. The no-tell motel was hardly his dream destination. He'd be calling in some favors and getting a major security upgrade ready for them at the first opportunity. "The details on the dick groom will be forthcoming."

"Can't you get those details *now*? Because it's rather important, don't you think? Know what? Forget it. Just let me talk to Delaney. I'll get the details."

"No can do. She's in bed."

A pause. A long one. Then... "In *your* bed? Is Delaney in your bed, Nash?"

"It's not a one-bed situation," he informed her, remembering Delaney's words. "She's been through hell, and she needs her rest. You'll get an update tomorrow."

"We lost touch," Agnes said, voice sad. "After you and

Delaney and..." Her words trailed away. "I don't think she could be around me without thinking about you, so I wasn't surprised when she left town, too."

His jaw locked as his gaze drifted to the bedside clock. "I'm tired. It's been one long-ass day. I have to go." He didn't want to take a walk down memory lane right then. "Delaney is safe," he assured his sister. "I have her."

"And are you going to keep her?" Agnes asked. Typical Agnes. No BS. Just cutting right to the chase. "Or are you going to let her slip through your fingers again?"

He could feel Delaney's eyes on him. "I don't like to repeat mistakes. I tend to be a one and done kind of guy."

His head turned, and he caught Delaney's flinch.

Shit. Baby, no, I didn't mean I was done with you. He could never be done with her. He'd tried. That hadn't worked, and he'd basically wound up doing a long-distance stalking routine with her.

"I don't even have the groom's full name!" A cry from Agnes that shrieked in his ear. "Tell me his name, and I'll rip his life apart."

Nash knew the dick's name. He knew far more about the man than he should, and, until he got around to revealing that intel, he needed to play things very carefully. Lowering the phone, he tilted his head toward Delaney. "Agnes wants the full name of your groom."

"Kurt Henry Wellington," Delaney muttered. "The third."

Nash repeated the jerk's name.

"But I'm pretty sure he has a ton of aliases," Delaney added with a yawn. "Right before Kurt shot that man in the warehouse..."

What freaking warehouse? He would have to do a full

interrogation on her soon. Something he never imagined he'd do with Delaney.

"I heard the guy yelling, 'Typhon, I won't turn on you!' and begging him to stop. He kept calling Kurt this *Typhon* name over and over and then..." A ragged breath. "Bang. I thought it was a firecracker, and I wondered why there was a firecracker in the building. I ran toward the sound, and Kurt was firing *again*. I jumped in front of him—"

The fuck she had.

"But Kurt shoved me out of the way and fired more at the bleeding man. I tried to help the victim, I swear, I did. I rushed to him. Put my fingers on his chest to stop the blood flow, but he just kept saying *Typhon* over and over as he died right there beneath my hands."

Nash didn't even blink.

"What is happening right now?" Agnes huffed. "I can't hear Delaney's words clearly."

Oh, just a major clusterfuck was occurring. One that would now involve Nash having to call in some serious backup and potentially having to turn Delaney over to the CIA.

No, no, I won't turn her over. I'll figure this out. I'll stay with her. But he was going to have to update his boss. Stat. Keeping his voice flat, he asked, "Delaney? Where did you meet the groom asshole?"

"Milan. I was working in Italy when our paths crossed."

"When?"

"Six months ago."

Fucking fuck. Another confirmation that was like putting nails in a coffin.

"*Nash!*" While his voice had been calm, his sister's voice grated with intensity. "What is happening?"

"Classified," he snapped back.

"What? You can't be serious!"

Oh, unfortunately, he was.

"*Nash*." Agnes's tone told him she was on the verge of losing what little patience she possessed. Truth be told, his sister never had much patience, even on good nights. This was not a good night.

"Delaney is safe. I have her, and I will keep her." There. Done. "Talk soon."

"Nash!"

He hung up the phone. Tossed it on the edge of his bed but stalked toward Delaney. The floor squeaked beneath his feet, and he was aware of every single heartbeat and breath that he took.

She pulled the covers closer to her, tucking them beneath her chin. "Nash?"

He stopped right beside her bed. He wanted to reach out and touch her, but, instead, his hands fisted at his sides. "Say his alias again."

"I...Typhon?"

Dammit. "And you met him in Milan? Six months ago?"

She nodded.

Hell. She wasn't just a victim. She was a high priority witness.

"You know the name, don't you?" Soft. Worried. Her question hung in the air between them. "The *Typhon* alias. You've heard it before?"

Oh, unfortunately, he did know it. And she was giving him confirmation of something the CIA had needed for a long time. "In Greek mythology, Typhon was known as the Father of All Monsters."

Her head slid over the pillow.

"He was the worst of the monsters," Nash continued carefully. "The deadliest."

"Kurt isn't some Greek myth. He's an asshole, but just a man."

She didn't understand. "Typhon is an alias used by an international criminal, Delaney."

She sat up in bed, fast, pulling that cover up with her. "What?"

"He's a killer, a weapons' dealer, and the leader of a very dangerous and cutthroat syndicate." There was no time to soften this news. Not if she could directly testify to the fact that Typhon and Kurt Wellington were the same individual. That she'd witnessed Typhon murder someone in cold blood. The CIA had smoke and mirrors, they had suspicions that pointed to Kurt as being the wanted killer but Delaney...Delaney had been there during a hit. She'd *heard* someone call Kurt by that infamous alias. "Typhon is the father for them, their leader. He's been on the CIA's hit list for a very, very long time." If what she was saying was true, if she could provide direct evidence that tied Kurt to all of Typhon's crimes...

Game changer.

She stared at him, with her mouth hanging open just a bit. "Wait...no." A brisk shake of her head. "How would you even know this? How could you know anything about the CIA's hit list?"

Time to put his cards on the table. He'd thought this reveal could wait, at least until dawn. As usual, fate was not on his side. "I know because I'm not a doctor, Delaney. I'm a spy. I work for the CIA, and I've been hunting Typhon for a very long time."

And...

She laughed. Right in his face.

He stared at her.

Her laughter slowly died away. "Oh, crap." A whisper. Maybe a whimper. "You're not joking."

No, he was not. "Get some sleep, Delaney. You're safe with me." A vow. One made not just from her ex. Not just from the guy who'd loved her and lost her before.

This vow was from a trained killer.

A vow...from a spy.

Chapter Four

SHE DIDN'T KNOW HIM. AT ALL.

Not anymore. Delaney stared up at the darkened ceiling. She *should* have been asleep. She should have been exhausted, and she should have crashed from the adrenaline high and went straight to dreamland.

Only she hadn't.

Because Nash Quinn wasn't a doctor. He hadn't finished medical school and gone on to live his dream of being a trauma surgeon. He'd...become a spy?

In what world?

"You're not sleeping, Delaney." A growl from the bed near hers.

She rolled onto her side. She couldn't see much of him in the dark. He was just a big, shadowy form. "How do you know?" She'd been very, very quiet. And surely at least half an hour had passed? Maybe an entire hour?

Nash is a spy. A spy.

And her groom had been an international criminal.

And somehow, this utter madness was her life. She

knew because she'd pinched herself three times, thinking that she would wake up from this nightmare.

Turned out that she was awake.

"How do I know? You mean other than the obvious fact that you're talking to me right now?" Mocking. "Your breathing is too tense. Far too hard and fast. And you keep shifting around on the bed every three seconds. The rustles are a dead giveaway."

Their beds were so close together that if she'd reached out, she might have been able to touch him. She did not reach out. But she wanted to touch him, even as she might have been afraid of him. "You sent out some texts, after you got off the phone with Agnes." After his big reveal about being a spy. "Who did you contact?"

"People who can help us."

"People at the CIA?" Because he was a freaking *spy*. And her fiancé had been an international criminal. She kept circling back to those two important details again and again. And did *anyone* in this world not lie all the time?

"It's kind of a down-low sort of thing," he told her as his deep voice rumbled in the darkness. "Try not to announce my spy status to anyone, would you? It's a secret, one between me and you."

"And the people you contacted, the ones you texted."

"Yes."

"Because they are all after Kurt or Typhon or whatever ridiculous name he's using?"

"The criminal with the codename of Typhon is no joke, don't make that mistake. He's got a kill list a mile long. He's in bed with more major criminal players than you can imagine, and when it comes to the weapons trade, he is as dirty as they come."

Clearly, she had incredible luck when it came to picking men.

"What I don't get..." Nash muttered, seemingly more to himself than to her, "is why he wanted to marry *you*."

Well, insulting much. "You don't think he took one look into my eyes and lost his heart?"

"Delaney—"

"Because he didn't. Not even close. Though that was what he wanted me to believe. Instead, he was after me because of what he'd gain once he became my husband." The darkness was oddly comforting. Made it easier for her to talk. "I don't know how much you may have heard about me over the years..."

"I tried not to hear anything."

She swallowed. "Thank you for that. Really. Lovely." Talk about a brutal response. As if her heart had needed to be crushed any more than it already was.

His covers rustled. "Delaney, wait, that's not what I meant!"

"I left the US. Before my mother died, she wanted to reconnect with her father. They'd been estranged for my entire life. I'd never met the man, not until I left with her. I met him for the first time right before my twenty-third birthday." The first meeting had been brief. Awkward. Cold. "My mother got a villa in Italy. I studied design, worked on my master's, and the days passed." Slowly. "We spent more time with my grandfather. It became less awkward." But, still somehow, just as cold. "Then my mother got sick. She was in and out of the hospital, and before I knew it, she'd passed." And Delaney had just been left with the grandfather who felt like such a stranger.

"I'm sorry. Your mother was always kind to me."

Sorrow pulled at her. "She tended to be kind to

everyone. Which was why I never understood how she and her father had stopped speaking for so long. Then I met him. Got to know him and a lot became clear to me." Her chest ached. "He was a difficult man. Demanding. Controlling. And stupid rich."

"Excuse me?"

"Apparently, my grandfather didn't approve of my father. He'd told my mother that if she married him, he'd cut her off completely. Obviously, she married my father, and they had plenty of wonderful years together before—" Delaney stopped. She inhaled, then made herself finish, "Before my father was killed in a robbery at his garage." Her father had been alone there, after hours, when the robber broke in and shot him. A bullet in the head and one in the heart. The safe in the garage had been emptied. The killer never caught.

The grief had nearly destroyed Delaney's mother. And Delaney had felt like a walking ghost for weeks. Pain still pulsed through her when she thought of her father. He'd always had such a warm smile. Been willing to help everyone.

There had been no sign of forced entry at the garage, and the cops had thought that her dad might have let the attacker inside. Maybe her dad had believed the person knocking on the closed door needed help. He'd opened the door to help and been killed for his kindness.

Nash had gone with her to her father's funeral. Nash had been steady and strong when everything else had been falling apart around her.

"Delaney?" Nash's gentle prompt.

She realized the grief from the past had pulled her under. A few deep, long breaths, and she nodded. "Sorry."

Rushed. "I, um, I was talking about my grandfather, wasn't I?"

"You don't need to apologize to me. Not ever."

His words eased some of the tension in her shoulders. Delaney picked up her story, trying to keep her voice flat as she said, "My mother died." A long and painful battle with the bitch that was cancer. "Two years later, my grandfather died, and when he passed, that was when I discovered that I was in his will. His sole heir. He'd made that will on the day I was born. My grandfather kept his promise to cut out my mother, but he left everything to me." And by everything...

I don't know what to do with this new life. I don't know how to act. Who to be. "I wasn't ready for that world, or the predators that would come calling. My grandfather had land, property—*everywhere.* He owned so much property that, hell, he practically owned *towns.* And he died, and it all went to me, and I..." She sucked in a deep breath. Slowly exhaled. "Based on what Kurt told me when I was locked up in his closet, my grandfather's holdings are not all what you'd call legal."

Nash grunted.

"Maybe that was another reason why my mother fled Italy and didn't go back for so long." Delaney didn't know for sure because her mother had never revealed much about the past to her. "I know Kurt wanted what I had. He wanted everything that my grandfather left me. And I know when I die, as my husband, he *would* get it."

"What was he gonna do? Fake an accident for you?"

"He promised to drown me on the honeymoon. Such a tragic end for me. Kurt swore that he'd play the grieving widower perfectly."

"*Fucking sonofabitch.*"

Yes. Indeed. He—

She heard a creak just beyond the closed motel room door. Automatically, she stiffened. Her gaze flew to the door.

Just footsteps. Just someone going past to another room. Stop being so afraid. You're safe. You are—

A hand pressed over her mouth. "Do not make a sound," Nash ordered.

He'd moved in complete silence. And so *quickly*.

"Get out of the bed, Delaney."

She inched out of the bed.

But she could hear the faint *snick* of the door's lock. Nash grabbed her, he hauled her against his body, and they rushed toward the wall *behind* that door.

They reached the wall just as the door began to creak open. Inch by slow inch.

Nash pushed her into the corner. He stood near her, and she couldn't see anything because the door was in her way and Nash was in front of her like a giant, very protective shield.

The door slipped open a few more inches. The light from outside spilled into the room. As before, the light flashed on. Then off. On and then...

Nash slammed into the open door with all of his strength. The door went flying, and it rammed into the side of the man who'd just broken into their motel room.

The man let out a loud, pain-filled howl, one that pierced Delaney's ears, but the sound was abruptly cut off.

She heard the thud of flesh hitting flesh. A shudder worked over her.

The door shut. The lock clicked back into place. Nash flipped on the overhead lights in the motel room, and she saw him standing over the intruder. Her breath heaved in and out as she craned her neck to look down at—wait. Hold on. Was their intruder some teen? He looked maybe seventeen years old. Eighteen?

The long-limbed figure on the floor threw back his head. Lots of curly hair covered his head and part of that hair was blue. He swiped his hand over his face and smeared blood across his chin and cheek and a rather sad little mustache. The guy glared at Nash. "You dick!"

"You little shit," Nash snarled back. "Do you want me to kill you here and now?"

The intruder on the floor scuttled back, moving like a crab, and his frantic gaze jumped from the left, to the right, and then landed on her.

"Oh, no." Nash immediately moved to stand in front of her. "You don't look at her. Not even for a second."

"*He's coming! I already put in the call!*" A triumphant announcement from the teen on the floor. Only, maybe he wasn't a teen. Maybe he was older than he'd first appeared. She tried to ease around Nash in order to get a better look at the intruder.

"*I told him where she was!*"

Her heart sank to her stomach.

The guy was pushing up to his knees. Glaring at Nash. And when she peeked around Nash, the intruder's eyes immediately locked on her.

He smiled. "You look just like the picture he sent me. Knew as soon as this jerk requested two beds that he had someone with him."

She poked at Nash's back. "This is yet another reason why a one-bed situation is better."

"*Get your fucking eyes off her,*" Nash thundered, and

the lethal intensity in his voice sent a shiver skating over Delaney.

"You got the first aid kit," the intruder snapped. "That was another tip-off!"

Okay, if she was following along properly, the jerk on the floor had called someone to report that she was at the motel. That *someone* had to be Kurt. From the sound of things, Kurt had even sent the punk some picture of her? She and Nash really needed to get the heck out of there. ASAP.

"Made the call right after you got the kit," the intruder announced. "Gonna get paid 5k when they come to collect her." He pointed a shaking finger at Nash. "If I were you, I'd be long gone by then. No pussy is worth dying for."

Delaney was sure that she could feel the blood draining from her face.

"Trust me, hers is," Nash snarled right back.

Wait...*what?*

"No one fucking touches her, and you're a complete dumbass if you think that you're just gonna get some payment and get to walk away from this scene. They're gonna *kill* you, you jackass! Especially when they arrive and we are long gone." Nash spun back toward her. "Get your shoes. Get anything you need from this room. We're leaving."

She scampered past him and ran to snag her shoes. The intruder reached out for her, only to scream in agony when Nash caught his hand and twisted. *Hard.*

Someone banged onto the wall to the right. "*Trying to sleep, assholes!*" A disgruntled yell.

Delaney grabbed her shoes. She also ducked in the bathroom long enough to heave on her bloody dress because it was better than just wearing a *t-shirt*. And, besides, Nash probably needed his shirt. Double-timing it, she ran back to him only to draw up short when she found him still holding the intruder's arm in a twisted grip as Nash kept the younger man pinned on the floor.

"Uh, Nash?" Delaney extended the shirt. "You're gonna need this."

He glared down at the figure on the floor. "He sold you out. Sold *us* out, after I paid him for the first aid kit!"

"You only paid me fifty dollars for the kit! *Ow!*"

Nash had wrenched his arm even higher. "And fifty to keep your mouth shut. I want my money back, you little prick, because clearly, you did not hold up your end of the transaction."

The little prick began to sob.

Delaney cleared her throat. "Not to be difficult but..." She was still extending the shirt toward Nash. "How about we forget the cash and just get out of here? Not real sure how long we have before Kurt and his goons show up, and I would very much prefer to be gone by the time they arrive."

"Fuck." But Nash nodded. He also let go of the intruder's arm. "Have it your way." Then he drove his fist into the guy's face. Hard.

The intruder sprawled on the floor, groaning.

Nash took the cash in the guy's front pocket. "Mine."

Seriously? She grabbed Nash's leather jacket. *"Let's go."*

Nash pointed at the still groaning intruder. "Be smart. Get the hell out of here because you are playing way above your league." Then he caught Delaney's hand and hauled her with him toward the door. They ran for the hidden motorcycle, and she shouldered into his coat. He hopped on the bike first, even as he shoved a helmet toward her. She jumped on behind him, secured the helmet, and locked her arms around him right before the engine snarled to life, and they flew into the darkness of the night.

Except they didn't fly very far. In fact, they only flew a wee bit down the road. Toward a twenty-four-hour diner. Nash parked his motorcycle under some twisting trees and immediately hopped off the bike.

She blinked at him. "What is happening here?" She tried to balance on the seat.

"They know that we are on a motorcycle."

Um, they *had* been on a motorcycle. Now he was off it. She was still on it. And growing increasingly terrified. Shouldn't they be *driving away*?

"You're too much of a target on a motorcycle," Nash told her. "When you're behind me, they can just shoot you in the back."

A horrifying visual.

"We need a new ride," he declared even as he whipped out his phone and seemed to be texting someone.

"And where are we going to *get* a new ride?"

He shoved his phone into his pocket and pointed to the far right section of the diner's lot. Three vehicles waited there. A truck, an SUV, and a VW Beetle. "We're taking the SUV."

They were? "How?"

"I'm stealing it, of course."

Of course.

He was already heading toward it, so she scrambled after him. As they closed in on the vehicle, Delaney realized why he'd chosen the SUV. The driver had left the window partially rolled down.

A bad mistake.

Nash shoved his arm inside the open window, and a

moment later, he was wrenching the door wide for her. "Get in," he ordered her.

She scampered inside. Jumped over the console and settled into the passenger seat even as her heart raced. "I have *never* stolen a car before." Was it even okay for a CIA spy to do something like this? Wasn't stealing against the rules for law enforcement? For *everyone?*

"I get that you never have. And it shows." He was in the driver's seat. His hands darted under the dash, and she frowned at him because Delaney was certain he'd just insulted her.

But the engine sparked to life, and a wide smile curved her lips because, yes, she was a bit impressed with his hot-wiring skills.

He straightened in the seat, shoved the vehicle in reverse, and as he got them out of the lot...

"Down, Delaney!"

Down? Like, what did he want? Her, in the floorboard? Her—

He grabbed her shoulder and pushed her down. Because of the angle, she was halfway over the console and very close to his muscled thigh. Correction, partially *on* his thigh, and his dick was right in front of her face.

"If we're spotted, then I only want witnesses to see one person in the vehicle. Not two. No need for anyone to know about you."

This was awkward. Her hand pressed to his thigh. His really, really hard thigh. And she strongly suspected that his dick was getting bigger with every moment that passed.

Bigger, right in front of her face.

She should inch back across the console. Crouching in the floorboard was a way better option than her current position.

"Just a few more moments," he gritted. His hand was on her back.

His touch burned through her.

"*Almost there.*"

Okay, this was more than awkward. This felt like...

"Done." He gently pushed her back to her seat.

Her breath heaved in and out. "If you want me going down on you, just say so." She was far too aware of the burn in her cheeks.

"*What?*"

She gestured toward him. "You were, um—"

"Hiding you? *Protecting you?*"

"Getting aroused," she sniffed. She also put on her seatbelt. Because, you know, safety first. Or second, since the first thing had been hiding.

"*Delaney.*"

Her cheeks were flaming. "Your dick was about two inches from my face. You were getting aroused."

"I am saving your life! I stole a car for you! I am rushing into the night, *for you!* If you weren't with me, I would have stayed at that motel and fought those bastards."

She shook her head. "You would have been outnumbered."

He laughed.

Delaney did not. "I wasn't making a joke. Kurt would have come with backup." Her hand reached out and curled along his wrist as he gripped the steering wheel. "I don't want you getting hurt for me." More than just hurt... "*Don't you dare get killed.*"

"Aw, Delaney, you sound like you'd care if something happened to me. And here I thought all the emotions you'd felt for me before were dead and buried."

She snatched her hand back. Balled her fingers into a fist. "I don't want anyone dying."

"Of course, not." Gruff. "Not you and that tender heart you've always carried. You stop to help turtles cross the road."

She'd done that once. Fine, twice.

"You fret over every damn thing. I've even seen you pick up a bird with a broken wing and rush the thing to the vet's office."

Again, *once*.

Her head turned, and she peered out of the passenger window, staring into the night. "There's nothing wrong with showing some kindness."

"As long as the kindness doesn't get you killed, sure. Stopping to help a turtle isn't worth a freaking car slamming into you because you're in the middle of the road and the driver doesn't see you." Rage seethed in his words.

He'd just given a very specific example. Unfortunately, that had been an actual incident that occurred when she'd been sixteen. She'd been carrying a turtle across the road, and a truck had come barreling toward her. But... "You saved me," she recalled.

"I'm *trying* to save your sweet ass."

Her attention shifted back to him as her head angled his way once more. "I meant when I was sixteen. You saved me then." As if she'd ever been able to forget that day. The day of their first kiss. "You came flying out of nowhere, and you threw me off that road."

"I tackled you," he corrected. "Slammed you into the ground."

The ground on the side of the road. He'd tossed her there so that she'd be safe.

"Then you kissed me," she added. It had been her first

kiss. She had not told him that fact. You didn't tell the older boy you were trying to impress that you hadn't known how to kiss, that you'd only practiced against a silly pillow until he'd pressed his mouth to yours and shown you how it was really done. "Until that moment, I'd always thought you hated me."

Silence.

She swallowed. They were hurtling through the dark, he'd just stolen a car to keep her safe, and she was as twisted up for him as she'd always been. Her problem, not his. "Thank you," Delaney managed to say.

"What are you thanking me for now?"

"For helping me." But, "Even if helping me is putting you in danger."

He laughed. The sound was deep and rumbling and, yep, sexy. Most things about Nash were sexy, though. "My life is about danger," he confessed. "That's nothing new."

Because he was a spy. She was still trying to wrap her head around that new truth. Back at the motel room, when he'd attacked the guy who'd broken into her room, Nash had moved with savage strength and power. "Are you involved in lots of life-and-death situations?"

"You have no idea."

She'd take that as a yes.

"You can sleep," he told her.

Um, doubtful. Adrenaline poured through her body.

"When you wake up, we'll be at a safe house. I'd planned for us to head there at first light, but, seeing as how we were ratted out by the night clerk at our motel, our arrival at the safe house will just happen a little earlier than I originally anticipated."

A safe house sounded like heaven to her. "Once we are

there, I can talk to the authorities, and you can get back to your life."

"Sure." Flat. "My life."

She bit her lower lip. There was something else they needed to talk about. Oh, who was she kidding? There were a million things they needed to address. But one very big elephant in the vehicle was taking up a whole lot of space. "Nash..."

"Getting turned on by you is as natural as breathing for me."

She knew her eyes had just doubled in size. She'd been trying to think of a tactful way to bring up her reaction to him. A reaction that had not lessened in intensity, despite all of the years between them.

Every man she'd met since him had never compared. Nash had left too big of a mark on her.

"When we were pulling away from the diner and I pushed you down, that was probably not the best move," Nash admitted.

Her brows rose. "Do tell."

"Your mouth was close to my dick. You were on my thigh. No way my dick wasn't going rock hard in that situation."

Um, okay.

"But you are in no danger from me. I'm not going to jump you, Delaney."

It was suddenly way too hot in the interior of the vehicle. "I didn't say that you were."

"I get that you've moved the hell on from me."

Her hands fisted harder in her lap. Her nails bit into her palms.

"You were marrying someone else, for shit's sake. Trust me, I get it."

He did not get it. He had no idea how lonely she'd been. How much she'd ached for him over the years. How she'd missed the life that they could've had together. "It's been years. You're not the same person you were before. Neither am I." *Because you're a spy.* And that meant—what? That he lied for a living? That he lied as easily as he breathed? That he— "Have you ever killed anyone?" A question that blurted from her.

He cut a glance toward the rearview mirror. Automatically, she glanced back but only saw darkness behind their vehicle.

A heavy silence settled inside the SUV.

She cleared her throat. "Eventually, the owner of this vehicle will come out and realize that this ride isn't in the lot. The owner will call the cops. An APB will be put out for the SUV."

"I chose this vehicle because it was positioned with the others that belonged to the diner's staff."

How did he know that?

"Staff always park farther from the restaurant. Closer spaces are left for the patrons. Since it's a staff car, odds are the owner won't notice it's missing until his shift ends. That gives us some breathing room."

Breathing room, right.

"But don't worry, we'll take another ride before too long. We'll switch things up to make it harder for anyone to track us."

He definitely talked like he'd done this before. "What about your motorcycle? Don't you think the cops will find it?"

"Got that taken care of. Someone I know in the area will make it vanish."

She remembered him firing off a quick text after he'd

parked the motorcycle. "That's who you were texting? Your local contact?"

"Typhon is a very important individual. In fact, one of the most wanted targets out there, according to the agency. This is a big break—*you* are a big break."

How fantastic. "Yay me."

"What?"

"Nothing," she mumbled. Her eyes squeezed shut. "You didn't answer my question."

"Which one?"

The big one. "Have you ever killed a person?"

The SUV seemed to accelerate even more. "Do you really want me to answer that?"

Goosebumps rose onto her arms. Her eyes opened. Her stare slid to him. "I think you just did."

He grunted. "You were right when you said I am not the same person any longer." His gaze cut to her. "I won't make the same mistakes."

What did that even mean?

"I fight hard. I fight dirty. I lie. I steal."

Yes, obviously, because they were in a stolen vehicle at that exact moment.

"And, if it means keeping you safe, hell, yes, I'll kill. I won't hesitate. If that scares you, I'm afraid that's too bad." His stare was back on the road. His body tense. His voice hard. Deep. "I'll do whatever it takes to keep you alive. You picked the wrong man to fall in love with, Delaney. But I will protect you from him."

"I didn't love Kurt." There. Her deep, dark secret. "I tried, and I thought I should, back when I believed he was Prince Charming. I liked him." She liked the lie that he'd been. "But...love?" Love wouldn't have filled her with so much doubt.

"You were marrying a guy you didn't love?" More anger.

"I thought it would come, with more time. Didn't realize I didn't have time and that I'd have a watery grave waiting in my immediate future. This is certainly the kind of thing that will make a woman swear off relationships." She settled back against her seat and closed her eyes once more. "I needed something. Someone." How did she explain the hole she'd felt inside after her mother's and grandfather's deaths? The way she'd ached and grieved? And then... "Kurt swore he loved me. I was a fool for believing him."

"We're going to catch Kurt. We're going to lock him away. He won't hurt you or anyone else ever again."

We. Did he mean the CIA? "I'm sure that someone will be assigned to my case." Wasn't that how things worked? "You can deliver me to the safe house, to your friends, and then you can go on your merry way."

"My...merry way?" He seemed to choke on the words.

A yawn slipped from her. "Thanks for saving me," Delaney said, her words slurring just a bit. "But I know you don't want to be trapped with me any longer than is absolutely necessary. Drop me at the safe house and get back to the life that is waiting for you."

* * *

SHE WAS ASLEEP. He knew because her breathing had finally softened and eased up. She wouldn't be able to sleep long. He'd have to wake her when they switched rides.

You don't want to be trapped with me any longer than is absolutely necessary.

Delaney's words whispered through his mind again, and a faint smile tugged at Nash's lips. Oh, but she was wrong.

Dead wrong. Because he intended to be trapped with her as long as possible.

He'd been telling the truth when he said that he wasn't the same person she'd known before. He would *not* make the same mistakes. And he would absolutely not let her slip through his fingers again. Whatever he had to do, whatever rules he had to bend or just completely shatter, whatever it took—Nash was ready.

He would not lose Delaney again.

I will not screw up with her again.

Chapter Five

THE DOOR TO MOTEL ROOM SEVENTEEN HUNG OPEN. The lights blazed inside, and Kurt Wellington entered the small space with his gun drawn.

The beds were tousled. Covers rumpled. Two beds. Two people who'd clearly each been in a different bed.

The clerk at the motel hadn't been in the front office. He wasn't in motel room seventeen, either.

And neither is Delaney. Or the fool who took her from me.

Taking his time, Kurt searched the room. His men stood at attention, looking for any threat. Except there was no threat. There was no Delaney. His bride wasn't there. The only thing left...

Her stockings.

He found discarded, white stockings in the bathroom. Delaney's stockings. His fingers fisted around those stockings.

"Boss?" A tentative call from one of his men.

Kurt's hand flew out, and, still fisted around the

stockings, he slammed his fist into the bathroom mirror. The mirror shattered, and glass fell into the sink.

Everything with Delaney had gotten fucked. *Everything.* At first, things had been so easy with her. She'd smiled at him so trustingly and she'd looked at him...as if... as if...

As if she truly believed I was good. Some white knight to take away all her pain.

For a bit, he'd almost wanted to be that guy. The one she thought he was.

Only...

She'd seen him kill. Delaney should not have been in the warehouse that night. She should never have put herself between him and his target. After she had, there had been no more smiles from her. No more sweet stares of wide-eyed innocence. Instead, she'd looked at him as if Kurt was a monster.

Guess you finally saw me, huh?

He could have killed her then and there. It would have been smart to shoot her and dump her body with the dead man's but...

He'd hesitated. And he'd locked her in a closet. Thought that he could make her marry him. And maybe... maybe he'd even believed he could convince her to...

"Boss, boss, you're bleeding!"

His blood dripped onto the broken glass.

Convince her to love me? He'd threatened her with death. He'd fully intended to take all the wealth and the property that came with the pretty package that was Delaney. But, if she'd just fallen in line, if she'd just *loved* him no matter what, then maybe he could have let her live.

But now...

A long exhale came from him. "Find my runaway bride." He turned back toward the men. Kept the stockings in his bloody grip. "Kill the man with her and bring Delaney back to me."

Chapter Six

"HELLO, BEAUTIFUL."

Delaney stretched slowly in the feather-soft bed. Soft covers pressed against her, and a smile began to curve her lips.

"I hope you're having some incredibly sweet dreams."

Her eyes flew open as she finally registered that deep, male voice. Her gaze jumped from the ceiling to the bedside table to the doorway where a tall, hulking figure stood.

A figure who had his head turned away from her as he looked back through the doorway into the hall. A figure that was *not* Nash because she knew his massive body. A wild scream tore from her throat as she leapt from the bed and tried to scamper away from the man.

Where the hell am I?

The last thing she remembered was being in the front seat of a stolen ride with Nash and now, *now—*

"Easy." Strong arms wrapped around her from behind. "I was just coming to wake you up. Didn't mean to terrify you."

She could hear the fast thunder of approaching footsteps.

Her elbow shoved back against the man who held her even as she realized that his voice was vaguely familiar.

He grunted when her elbow hit him, but he didn't let her go. "Delaney, is this any way to greet an old friend—*ow!*" His hold tightened.

She let out a blood-curdling scream.

"Wait, Delaney, it's me and, *dammit, dammit, Nash, stop!*"

But, apparently, those thunderous footsteps belonged to Nash and he did not, in fact, stop. He grabbed the man who held her and slung him up against the nearby wall.

A framed black and white photo—appeared to be of a waterfall—tumbled to the floor.

And Nash, wearing jeans and a white shirt that emphasized his tawny skin and valiantly stretched over his bulging muscles, glared at the man he'd just casually tossed aside. "I said *wake her up*, asshole. As in, knock lightly on her door. *Not terrify her.*" Nash swung to face her. He sucked in a deep, shuddering breath. "I'm sorry. We both know that Ryan is always a bit of a dick."

Ryan?

"I am not." From the man straightening his dress shirt and rolling back his shoulders. "I am an incredibly charming, kindhearted individual. I knocked softly on her door before entering. I definitely did that. It's not my fault the woman snores like a freight train."

She sucked in a deep, gasping breath.

Ryan Quinn—*holy crap, that is Ryan!*—inclined his head toward her. He winked. "A cute freight train, of course. But I had no choice but to open the door and come inside. And then, did I *not* begin by saying that you are beautiful? I am sure I did. I said, '*Wake up, beautiful.*' Or, wait. Maybe I said '*Hello, beautiful.*' Something like that."

Nash growled at him. "I did *not* tell you to come in her room. I sure as hell didn't tell you to flirt with her."

Ryan's hands flew up in front of his body. His palms faced Nash. "Easy there, bro. Rein in that jealousy, would you? You're the one who sent me to her. If you wanted to wake her up and call her beautiful, then you should have done that job yourself. But, no, you probably didn't trust yourself to come in and find her all rumpled and sexy in bed and you—*Dude, I am messing with you! Do not dare take a swing at me!*"

Nash had just charged at his brother.

Because Ryan Quinn *was* his brother. She'd grown up with them both, and while Nash had barely tolerated her during their early teenage years, Ryan had always been kind. And generally charming.

Nash had been the reserved and growly one. Or he had been, until their first kiss. The kiss on the side of the road that had changed everything.

Now the two brothers were glaring at each other, and the tension in the room had notched up way too high. "Don't hit your brother," she rushed to tell Nash.

Both men swung their heads toward her.

"What? It's a fair request." Why were they staring at her with wide eyes?

Ryan cleared his throat. "I'm sorry, I hate to point out the obvious here, but you *do* realize you're wearing the remains of a bloodstained wedding dress, yes?"

She looked down at herself. Yep, she was still in the dress that would haunt her dreams. She wanted to burn the thing, as soon as humanly possible. Dried blood. Torn fabric. Hellish memories. Check, check, triple check.

"She was asleep when I carried her inside," Nash said, voice curt and a bit too biting. "Didn't think it would be *gentlemanly* to strip her while she was out cold. So I left the dress on her."

Ryan rocked back onto his heels. "Oh, yeah. That's you. The super gentleman. Not like you just didn't trust yourself with her so you probably dropped her in bed, snatched the covers up to her chin, and ran away as fast as you could. No, sir, not like that happened at all." He sucked in his cheeks as if fighting laughter.

"I can knock you out with one punch," Nash assured him.

"Yes, you probably can, but I do believe that Delaney said for us not to fight, so if you punch me, you'll just make her mad. If she's mad, then she'll be less likely to cooperate with us, won't she? And we will need her cooperation for when the boss arrives."

Cooperation. She latched onto that one word, and her brain finally started processing properly. Delaney blinked, and her gaze zeroed in on Ryan again. At first, she'd just figured Nash had called in his brother because he'd wanted someone he could trust at his side. But now suspicion simmered inside of her.

Ryan stood before her, dressed in an expensive, crisp blue dress shirt. A shirt that stretched at his shoulders and arms. Black dress pants. Gleaming, polished shoes. He and Nash were close in height, but Nash beat his brother in muscle span. Like Nash, Ryan also had dark hair, but Nash's hair was pitch-black. Ryan's eyes were a deep, dark brown. Sometimes, his gaze would appear warm, but other times, that gaze of Ryan's could be chilling.

Not brothers by blood, but by choice. She still remembered the day that Nash had first arrived at the

Quinn house. He'd been thirteen. She'd been two years younger, and so curious about the new member of the family.

Nash and Ryan had quickly become inseparable. One always watching the other's back and… "Oh, no." She had to voice her suspicion. "Are you CIA, too, Ryan?"

"Dammit!" Ryan glared at his brother. "You told her? You just seriously told the woman confidential information that we are supposed to take to our graves? The kind of intel that can't even be tortured out of us? You just *gave it to your ex?*"

She took that response as a yes. "Holy crap, you are." A shake of her head. "I remember when you joined the Marines but…" But after that, she'd been out of their lives.

"*You* just told her, dumbass," Nash growled back at him. "I didn't. And, shit, I have clothes for you, Delaney. Give me a minute." He stalked from the room.

Which left her alone with Ryan.

Ryan had rolled up the sleeves of his dress shirt, and she noticed the dark lines of one scary-looking tattoo on his forearm.

Soft laughter rolled from him. "That one's real," he told her, obviously catching her focus on the tat. "But you should have seen some of the ones I was sporting a few months back."

Her brows snapped together.

A sigh slid from him. "Delaney, Delaney, Delaney…just what kind of trouble have you gotten yourself into?" His arms fell to his sides as he began to advance toward her. "And are you seriously about to break my brother's heart all over again?"

Her jaw nearly hit the floor. "What on earth are you talking about?"

Ryan just nodded. "You are. I can feel it coming." A low whistle escaped him. "I think I should take over lead on this case. No way does Nash need to be doing the dirty work with you on this one."

"Dirty work?" Did it sound like she was strangling? It certainly felt that way to her.

"Um. I'll make the sacrifice. I'll play bodyguard, and Nash can go back to handling ops in Eastern Europe. Done."

Her head was spinning. And she was still in the stupid dress.

"So, I've got to ask. Did you know your groom was a psychopathic madman bent on being the number one criminal mastermind in the world when you said yes to him? Or did that big revelation come to you later?"

She blinked. "You are usually way more charming than this."

"Noted. Technically, though, I'm usually *pretending* to be charming." A shrug of one big shoulder. "But this time, we're talking about my brother. You pulled him into your nightmare, and I'm trying to make sure that he's not getting conned by a pretty face. Your groom is a sadistic criminal who has left a trail of bodies across Europe and the US. Let's completely understand one another. Nash will not be part of that trail."

One of her hands flew to her mouth. Her other dropped over her suddenly twisting stomach. "I think I'm going to be sick." *A trail of bodies?* Oh, God. Oh, no.

"Here. Fresh clothes. Toiletries. Everything should fit." Nash was back in the doorway. Filling it. Brushing his broad shoulders against the sides. He frowned at her. "Delaney, you okay?"

Nope, she was not. Delaney snatched the bag from him

and dashed into the nearby bathroom. She slammed the door shut. Dropped the bag and then she turned on the water and began splashing it on her too hot face.

A sadistic criminal who has left a trail of bodies across Europe and the US.

And she had been moments away from marrying the man.

* * *

NASH FROWNED at the closed bathroom door. He could hear the roar of the water from inside. Before Delaney had raced in and slammed the door shut, she'd looked far, far too pale. Her gaze had been terrified, and he did not want Delaney terrified. Ever.

He stomped toward his brother. "What in the hell did you do?"

"*Moi?*" All innocence, Ryan pointed to himself. "I just followed orders. I came in to gently wake our old friend, and…how was I to know that she would wake up screaming? Who could have predicted that response?"

"You scared her."

"Uh, yes, thus the screams, but that was not my fault!"

"I mean you did something to scare her when I went to get her fresh clothes. You said something while I was gone." The water was still roaring from the bathroom. Not just the sink, though. Had she turned on the shower, too? "What did you tell her while I was out of the bedroom?" He'd been gone for *moments*. How could his brother screw things up in mere moments?

But Ryan pursed his lips.

Hell.

He loved Ryan. Truly, he did. He'd literally taken a

71

bullet for the man before. He would kill for his brother in a heartbeat. Done. But Nash could still want to kick Ryan's ass, and he *would* be kicking that ass if Ryan had said or done anything to hurt Delaney.

Ryan ran a finger over the slightly crooked bridge of his nose. A crook that had come when they were younger and Ryan had caught their sister when Agnes fell out of a treehouse. He'd saved her and received a broken nose as a memento.

Ryan had a tendency to rub that slight crook whenever he felt guilty.

Hell. "What did you tell her?"

A grimace from Ryan. "I offered to step in as her bodyguard." His hand fell to his side as Ryan gave a brisk nod. "It's really the best option. You know the boss is coming in for a personal chat with her. Using her will be an opportunity that the agency can't pass up. Not like we can let Delaney just waltz off into the sunset."

Yes, he was aware of that. "You, as her bodyguard?"

"Yes, I mean, it makes the best sense." Ryan nodded. "She trusts me, she likes me, we don't have a messy past like you two do."

Leave it to Ryan to point out the obvious.

"Oh, wait, hold the thought," Ryan said. "My watch is vibrating." He tapped the screen of his watch. "Boss is approaching. How about we take this conversation downstairs, hmm? I'm sure Delaney will join us when she is done." He swung for the door.

Nash stepped into his path. "You did not."

"Did not...what?" Ryan squinted at him. "Please be way more specific with me."

"Oh, fuck. You did." He could see the truth in Ryan's eyes. "You said something to her about *our messy past.*"

"Dude. Would I do that?"

"Yes! Yes, you would." Dammit. "Did you say something about me that *made her sick?*" Because she'd definitely looked sick before she'd run into the bathroom. "Did you tell her about the missions I've worked?" Had Ryan told Delaney about the people Nash had killed?

"I'm not the one sharing CIA secrets. That is you!" An offended huff from his brother. "I think the sickness part came from when I *might* have mentioned that her groom was a psychotic criminal who'd left a few bodies across Europe and the US. But I mean, come on, some things needed to be said. Just because you were afraid to pull off the band-aid didn't mean I felt the same way. Better to just get that hard truth right out in the open so she fully understands the severity of the situation."

He grabbed Ryan's shirt and fisted it. "What *else* did you tell her?"

Ryan swallowed. His Adam's apple bobbed. "Our boss will be here soon. We should really get downstairs. Not like she enjoys being kept waiting. You know how Jez gets."

"*What else?*"

"I don't know…"

Uh, yes. He was sure that Ryan *did* know.

"I *guess* I *could* have said something about how I would do the dirty work on the case and stay close to her—"

"*You are not doing anything fucking dirty with Delaney. I'll be the one who is dirty with her!*"

"—because she is not going to break your heart again."

They both blinked as their words collided. Then Ryan squinted.

Nash let him go and shoved back. "You *told* her that she broke my heart?"

"You're ready to get dirty with her again?" Ryan

whistled. "See, this is why I have to take over. Pretty sure you're still at least halfway in love with her!"

Oh, there was nothing halfway about it.

"Bro." A slow shake of Ryan's head. "There is *fucking* the woman, and then there is getting *fucked over* by her." Blunt words.

And the bathroom door opened.

Because...

Sure.

The door opened, and they both whipped their heads toward the sound. Delaney stood in the doorway, hair wet, wearing jeans, white sneakers, and a soft, blue shirt. No makeup and with full lips trembling. Nash wondered just how much she'd overheard, and he found himself holding his breath.

But Ryan has one loud-ass voice.

"I've got a great idea." A broad smile curved Delaney's lips and never, ever reached her eyes. "How about neither of you become my bodyguard? Sound good? Fabulous." Her shoulders straightened. "I'd like to meet your boss, now, please. Thanks so much."

Nash sucked in a deep breath. "Ryan?"

"Yo, bro?"

"Get the hell out, now."

Ryan marched for the door. "Getting the hell out, now." He crossed the threshold and grabbed the doorknob. "Though, I feel duty bound to warn you that you should not do anything you might regret."

"Shut the fucking door."

Ryan did. Finally. His brother got his ass out of that bedroom. Nash was alone with Delaney. Alone with the woman he'd loved and lost so long ago. And maybe they needed to clear the air about that time. Maybe he needed to fess up and reveal some long-held secrets or...

"Fuck it." He surged toward her as she stood there, beautiful and brave and making him *ache*.

Even as her eyes were widening in surprise, Nash bent toward her. His hand slid under the curve of her jaw. He tipped her head back, and he bent down, and he tasted her.

I missed her.

Too many years had passed.

I craved her.

So many nights when he'd woken up, aching for her. Needing her.

I want her.

He couldn't let her slip from his grasp again. Whatever he had to do, whatever it took, whatever lines he had to cross, lies he had to tell, or rules he had to shatter, he would do it.

I won't let go.

Not the hell ever again.

Her hands flew up to curl around his arms. Her lips parted in surprise as she gave a little gasp against his mouth, and, yes, he knew this was the wrong time to be kissing her. The wrong time. The wrong place. The wrong everything.

But he didn't care.

He had her. He was kissing her. *I will be claiming her again.*

He thought she might shove him away. Maybe knee him in the groin and tell him not to touch her. She'd already been through hell and what he was doing—these were damn well not the actions of a gentleman.

But Delaney opened her mouth wider.

Her tongue met his. She kissed him back even as a moan trembled from her. She met him. Passion for passion. Lust for lust. Aching need for aching need, and his control snapped.

His hands flew down to her waist. His fingers tightened on her as he lifted her up, and her legs curled right around his hips just like they'd done in the past. A lifetime ago. And it was suddenly like no time had slipped away. Like it had just been yesterday when he'd lost his mind and taken and taken and *taken* her.

His dick shoved forward. He wanted *in* her. He wanted to sink into the paradise that was her tight core and feel her hot heaven clench around him. Nash needed to feel the ripples of her release. The wet, tight clasp of her body. He wanted her nails raking down his back and her body trembling for him.

He stepped forward. Locked her between his body and the wall even as he kept kissing her. Frantic. Desperate. His heart raced. His muscles tightened. His dick demanded.

Take.

Take.

Take.

"Yo!" A yell from the other side of the door that Ryan had closed not too long ago. "Do you *hear* me?" He pounded on the door again.

Nash wondered how long Ryan had been pounding.

"The boss just drove up with her guards. They are approaching the cabin right this minute. You and Delaney need to come downstairs, now. Let's get this show on the road." Another fierce knock.

Nash lifted his head.

Delaney's thick lashes flickered as her eyes opened. Her cheeks were flushed. Her lips red and swollen from his mouth. She looked as if she'd just been thoroughly kissed.

I want her to be thoroughly fucked.

Her breath came quickly, and her gaze searched his.

Dammit. "I should apologize," he began, voice rough, too growly.

She waited.

"But I'm not sorry I kissed you." Like he could ever be sorry for that. No way. Not in any universe.

"That's...not an apology."

"*I'm sorry I let you go before.*" There. A real apology. One he meant. "*I'm sorry it's taken me this long to find you again.*"

Her eyes widened. "Nash?"

"You're getting a bodyguard." One thing that was a nonnegotiable point in the upcoming meeting. And another nonnegotiable? "It's going to be me." Because no one would guard her body better.

No one knew her body better.

Every single inch. I know every inch of her. I've kissed her. Touched her.

And...

He was also more than ready to kill for her.

So, screw Ryan's offer. When it came to Delaney's protection, Nash would be the one in charge.

Chapter Seven

SHE DID NOT EXPECT JEZEBEL JENKINS.

Ten minutes after overhearing that Ryan feared she would *fuck over* Nash and that apparently, Nash should just *fuck* her, Delaney sat in the den of a wooden cabin. A cabin that, Nash had informed her, was nestled in Tennessee. A safe house with top-of-the-line security.

Delaney pressed her hands to the tops of her thighs as she forced her back to remain ramrod straight. Did it look as if she'd just been making out with Nash upstairs? Were her lips swollen? Her cheeks flushed?

She could have stopped him. Could have just said "no" and he would have backed off. Had she done that? Nope. Instead, she'd grabbed onto him as tightly as she could. Delaney had kissed him with every bit of passion inside of her.

She'd let her control vanish, and she'd given into the raw need that she'd always felt for Nash. Seriously, after all this time, shouldn't that need have faded some? But it hadn't. He'd put those big, strong hands on her, he'd put that wicked mouth on hers, and she'd practically imploded.

Desire had obliterated every other thought. She'd just wanted to kiss him. To pretend that her heart had never been shattered. That he still cared. That they had a chance together.

And then Ryan had pounded at the door. And she'd had to rush down the stairs to this meeting with...their boss?

Jezebel Jenkins had entered the cabin with two guards—both men who physically dominated Jezebel's petite frame. The woman appeared to be in her early sixties. Faint tendrils of gray showed in the darkness of her hair, hair that had been pulled back into a tight bun at the nape of her neck. The woman moved with the easy grace that you'd expect from a ballerina. And her stare? That darkness was ice cold.

Very few lines showed on her face. Only determination. Intelligence. Calculation.

She paused in front of Delaney. "Are you willing to die for your country?"

Delaney opened her mouth. That question had just come from absolutely nowhere.

"Her dying is not on the agenda," Nash snapped before she could reply. "Come on, Jez, she's a civilian. Let's get her the hell out of the line of fire and come up with a plan of action."

Jez cut her gaze toward Nash. "She *is* the plan of action."

Delaney did not particularly like the sound of that. She wet her lips and swore that she tasted Nash. *I should not have made out with him.*

But she had, and her body still ached. Her thighs trembled. *I had my legs wrapped around him. His heavy dick shoved against me. He wanted me as much as I wanted him.*

This was so not the time to be having those particular thoughts.

Jezebel's coal-black stare returned to her. "Your groom tracked you to the motel where you and Nash were staying. I have intelligence that indicates Kurt Wellington is desperate to get you back." She pointed vaguely to Nash. "The current orders are that Nash should be taken down. Shot on sight. Stabbed. Dismembered. Whatever." No accent entered her voice. No emotion showed on her face.

But plenty of emotions surged through Delaney. The strongest emotion was fear. Followed closely by rage. "Nash can't die!" Kurt had wanted him dismembered? What fresh hell was this?

"I'm not planning on dying," Nash groused. "Jez, you're trying to manipulate her."

"Am I the type to manipulate?" Jezebel asked with an innocent blink of her eyes. "How could you ever say such a thing about me? That hurts. Deeply." Small pearl earrings were the only jewelry she wore.

Ryan snorted at Jezebel's response. Then tried to smother a laugh.

Jezebel fired him a quick glance. "Does something amuse you? Is it the idea of dismemberment?"

He shook his head. "I was laughing because, of course, you don't manipulate. Not you, Jez. Why on earth would *you* do something like that?"

A nod from Jezebel. Her focus shifted back to Delaney. "Kurt Wellington wants you back, alive."

As to that..."I'm not actually under the impression that it's me he wants. I believe he is more interested in my inheritance."

"Because your grandfather's criminal operation would

be beneficial to him? Yes, I suppose that could be part of your appeal."

Oh, great. So was it just common knowledge now that her grandfather had been in bed with criminal elements? How come someone hadn't clued her in to this situation much, much sooner?

Had the CIA been monitoring her family? *Her?* And for how long? Worried and horrified, she darted a glance at Nash, but his stone-faced expression told her nothing. Stomach knotting, she concentrated on Jezebel once more.

"I certainly do believe that Wellington is interested in the benefits your inheritance would bring him, but I think more is involved here. I think..." Jezebel smiled. A wide, calculating grin that made a shiver slide down Delaney's spine. "I think we've found his weakness."

"No." Nash surged forward. "This is *not* happening. You can just forget it."

"What's not happening?" Delaney was lost in the conversation. Sitting on the couch was not working for her. Everyone was looking down at her, and she felt small and afraid and just—*nope*. Delaney jumped to her feet. "Will someone please explain to me exactly what is happening?" She didn't particularly want to revisit the "Would you die for your country" part of the conversation but some answers would be fabulous.

"Your fiancé is a very dangerous individual," Jezebel informed her. "If left unchecked, he will continue to kill, to kidnap, to trade weapons, to export drugs, and to just all around make the world a very dangerous place."

"Ex-fiancé," she corrected. "Ex. Super ex."

Nash was at Delaney's side.

Ryan watched them, his arms over his chest, as he leaned near the bookshelf to the right.

The two men who had accompanied Jezebel to the cabin—both tall, fit, wearing dark clothes and with holsters on their hips—waited near the doorway, bodies alert.

"You don't want to leave Wellington unchecked, do you?" Jezebel asked.

"No?" That felt like the right answer. "No." Better. Firmer. Because she one hundred percent did not want anyone else in danger. Kidnapped. Killed.

"Great. Then you'll allow him to find you, you'll monitor his business, and we'll gather evidence needed to prove conclusively that Kurt Wellington is, in fact, the criminal mastermind known as Typhon," Jez concluded with satisfaction. "It's an operation that I hope will be able to conclude within a few months."

What, what, *what*? "You want me to go back to him?" Back to the man who'd locked her in a closet, who'd stabbed her in the side, and who'd promised a watery grave for her honeymoon? Back to him?

No. She must have misunderstood Jezebel.

"Um." Jezebel watched her with an unblinking gaze.

Um was not a *no* answer.

Jezebel nodded.

Fear flashed through Delaney. "He'll *kill* me!" This was not the response she'd expected to receive from Nash's boss. She knew Nash had briefed Jezebel and Ryan on all the information she'd told him about Kurt murdering a man in front of her. She'd thought that giving her testimony would be enough to have Kurt locked away. Never in a million years had Delaney expected this development. "If I go to him, he'll murder me! There will be no intelligence gathering." As if she even knew how to gather data on him. "There will just be me dying!" Probably in a super painful fashion.

"I don't think so." Jezebel spoke with utter unconcern. "I believe he has developed an emotional attachment to you. If Wellington—Kurt—wanted to kill you, he could have just shot you while you were being carried out of the church or he could've had one of his men do the job. He didn't. You're alive so..." That calculating grin flashed again. "That makes you extremely useful to me."

Nash's hand closed around Delaney's wrist. "No." He pulled her toward him. Put her *behind* him. "We're not risking Delaney's life."

Good. Great. Fabulous response. She did not want her life risked. She wanted Kurt tossed in a cell, and Delaney wanted safety. "Can't I just file charges against him? Testify about the things he did? What I saw him do?" How could that not be enough?

"Sure, you can file charges." Jezebel's mild voice.

Delaney craned to see around Nash. To peer at Jezebel.

"And then he'll disappear into the wind like..." Jezebel snapped her fingers. "That. The man probably has at least a dozen passports, all with different aliases. He'll vanish long before law enforcement can get to him, and then he'll bide his time and he'll wait and he'll find a way to either eventually abduct you or to kill you."

Well, there was certainly no sugarcoating from Jezebel. "I'd prefer not to die."

"Um."

She'd also prefer not to go *back* to the man who wanted to murder her. "Going back to Kurt makes no sense to me." How did it make sense to anyone in that room? "He knows I ran away—willingly. I ran *to* Nash in the church. I couldn't wait to get away. You might believe I'm some weird weakness for Kurt, but that's just not true. Kurt has no weaknesses."

"I disagree." Flat. Then Jezebel cleared her throat. "Nash."

He was still standing protectively in front of Delaney, and she still was craning around his big body.

"Thank you for retrieving the asset," Jezebel said to him.

Oh, wait, was she an *asset* now? That sounded bad. Delaney craned a bit more about Nash so she could better see his boss.

"But I believe your work here is done," Jezebel continued with a regal incline of her head toward Nash. "You have a target on your head, courtesy of the scene at the church, so it is best if you are removed from the situation."

"No," Nash fired back.

"Yes," Delaney said at the same time.

He whipped around to face her. "What?"

Her heart nearly burst out of her chest, but Delaney said again, "Yes." Because it had to be said. He had to be protected. She did not want any target on his back.

"Yes—what?" he bit out.

"Yes, you should be removed from the situation." The words shook but she said them. "Thank you for saving me, but you can't stay with me. Not while there is a target on you." A target there because of her. This was one area where she and Jezebel were in complete agreement. "You should leave. Get really, really far away from me. As fast as you can."

One dark eyebrow rose. "You're serious?"

She was. Delaney nodded.

Ryan cleared his throat. "Already told you, I can take over bodyguard duty. Go, Nash. I'll watch over her."

From the sound of Jezebel's plan, no one would be watching over her. *The woman wants to send me back to*

Kurt. I may as well be walking to my death if I follow that plan.

Maybe Delaney should come up with her own plan. One that involved running...*by myself.* And not looking back.

A hum came from Jezebel. "You're dismissed, Nash. For your own safety, you need to leave the area. There is a case waiting in Berlin that can use your special skills."

That was it. Nash would be leaving. And maybe once he was gone, she could plan her own escape. She did have some resources and contacts that she could use. A few people—some slightly shady—owed her favors.

"The fuck no," Nash stated, very clearly. "We are *not* sending her back to that prick. Come up with another plan because if she goes back to Kurt, we will *never* see her alive again. We'll find her in pieces, the same way we've found some of his other victims."

Pieces? Delaney's eyes closed. Her chest ached. She had to remind herself to breathe.

"She's a civilian." Nash's voice edged with a thread of anger. "She can't handle him. That's like sending a lamb to infiltrate a lion's den."

"Well, there *is* another option, I suppose," Jezebel mused.

Her eyes flew open. "I would *love* to hear another option. One that does not involve me being found in lots of pieces. Though, for the record, Kurt promised me a watery grave. There was zero talk about being cut up."

For just an instant, she caught a glint in Jezebel's dark eyes. As if...as if...

She's definitely manipulating this scene. I don't think she ever intended to send me in undercover. She's trying to scare me. Why? Such an unnecessary tactic. Did the woman not understand that Delaney was plenty terrified enough? Additional scare tactics were not needed. Talk about overkill.

"If you don't want to go back to him, then you could lure Kurt Wellington out into the open. You could push him past his control, make him take risks that would cause him to be vulnerable, and allow us to trap him."

"Trap him," Delaney repeated. "Love it. I much prefer that plan." Jezebel should have led with that one. Except... "How do you want me to *lure* him?" A shake of her head that sent her now drying hair over her shoulders. "I mean, isn't he already hunting me? Do I just go out of hiding? Wave a red flag and shout, 'Come and get me' to him? Will that work for you? Sorry, but I'm new to the spy business and have zero clue about how this works."

"And she uses humor when she's terrified," Nash muttered.

"Guilty," Delaney whispered.

Jezebel pursed her lips. "A red flag will be necessary for Plan B to work."

Plan B. How many plans were stirring in the woman's mind?

"Before we get into logistics, though..." Jezebel began to slowly pace around the room. Her considering stare swept over Delaney. "Are we absolutely certain that you don't want to embed with Kurt for a time in order to acquire additional intel for us to use against him?"

"*She's not getting in bed with the bastard,*" Nash growled.

Jezebel blinked. "I believe I said *embed*. Not in bed."

"She won't be doing either," Nash threw back.

But Jezebel stared at Delaney. "The choice is yours, my dear. It's your life, after all."

Yes, a life she'd prefer to keep living. "I would really love to hear more about Plan B."

Jezebel's gaze cut to Nash. "In order for Plan B to work, are you willing to stay in the line of fire, Nash? Knowing how very much Kurt Wellington wants you dead?"

Ryan strode forward. "Told you all already, I'd be the bodyguard. I know everyone heard me. This is too personal for Nash. He needs to be removed from the situation, just like you said before, Jez."

"No one is removing me." Nash's voice was definite. "I'd like to see someone try." A dare.

Jezebel's eyes gleamed. "Last chance on this, Nash. You can walk out the door and be on a plane for Berlin within the hour."

"I'm *not* leaving Delaney."

Okay, he was going above and beyond. She poked at his shoulder.

He spun toward her. "*No.*"

"Nash, listen. I put a target on you. This is way more than you bargained for when you got the call from your sister about my wedding. It's too dangerous."

"Like Berlin *won't* be dangerous? Like my other cases haven't been dangerous?" His eyes glittered at her. "I'm staying with you. I can take the sonofabitch down and protect you at the same time. Done."

"Well, if that's your decision." Jezebel's smooth voice. "It will certainly work for Plan B."

Ryan swore. "Just spit it out already, Jez. What's the plan?"

Nash turned back toward Jezebel.

Jezebel's gaze darted between Nash and Delaney. "You two were involved, many, many years ago."

Delaney poked at him yet again. "You told her?"

His jaw locked.

"I excel at uncovering a person's painful secrets," Jezebel informed her as she paced in front of the sofa. "I'm incredibly resourceful that way." A delicate sniff. "I am quite sure Kurt will uncover your past association, as well. After all, he is rumored to be quite resourceful himself."

Okay, it almost sounded as if Jezebel admired Kurt. Scary.

"He *will* discover that the two of you were former lovers," Jezebel continued.

Delaney could feel the heat in her cheeks.

Jezebel stopped pacing and positioned her body about two feet from Delaney. "He'll think you called on your ex to rescue you. That will certainly piss him off. Hit him hard in his pride when he realizes your ex-lover carried you from the church."

An enraged Kurt was not a good thing.

"He wants you back." Jezebel straightened her already straight shoulders. "And he'll fight to get you back. We need to get him on our turf, though. Not just be running blindly as we throw a net to catch him. We have to get him into a situation that we control completely."

Where would that location be, exactly?

"He wants you back."

Jezebel kept repeating that point.

"He'll come for you. We have to make him step out and walk into the light. Make him pay for his sins. And what better place to pay, than in the city built for sin?"

Delaney was trying to follow along. She really, truly was. *Sin City.* "Vegas? Are you talking about Vegas right now?"

"Um." A nod from Jezebel. "When Kurt finds out that you

dashed off to Vegas in order to marry your ex, I think he'll come running to stop you. He'll be so enraged that he won't be thinking straight. He'll take unnecessary risks. Make mistakes."

Delaney took a step back. Then another one. "You *cannot* be serious." Was she still dreaming? Still upstairs asleep in bed? Because there was no way the woman was actually suggesting that Delaney and Nash run off to Vegas in order to get married.

"Kurt Wellington is an international criminal. We are lucky to have him on American soil right now."

Uh, Kurt was only on American soil because of *their* wedding. Normally, he resided in Milan, but he was an American by birth, just as she was, and he'd wanted them wed in the city where he'd grown up so long ago.

"He's disappeared. Vanished, according to my intel. But he is still hunting *you*. So when he finds out that you're heading to Vegas, I believe that he will head there, too. I believe he'll want to stop Nash from marrying you because Nash interrupted Kurt's own wedding to you."

"You..." Another step back. She was seriously considering running out of that cabin. "You want me to go to Vegas and marry Nash?"

"*Pretend* marry. We can fake the ceremony." Utter unconcern from Jezebel. "Or it can be real and we can just get it annulled later. Please, calm yourself. It's not like I'm asking you to fuck Agent Quinn."

Four frantic steps back.

Fuck Agent Quinn. Delaney fanned herself because she was flushed and way too hot.

"He'll come after you. I believe he will do anything necessary to stop you from marrying another man."

Delaney choked down the lump in her throat. "Will you

define 'anything necessary' for me? It would be super helpful if you could do that."

"He'll kidnap you. Attack Nash. Break laws." A shrug. "And we'll catch him in the act. Have *him* dead to rights. We'll have everything monitored and recorded, and there will be no chance of him escaping or worming his way out of a conviction."

"Provided you catch him in the act." Delaney hated the knots in her stomach. "Provided he doesn't succeed in, oh, I don't know, kidnapping me and possibly *killing* Nash."

"He won't kill me." Utter certainty from Nash. "And he *won't* take you from me."

"There is, of course, a Plan C, as well," Jezebel announced.

"Plan C," Delaney gasped out. *Am I in the Twilight Zone?* Plan C had to be better than the other two options, right? *Please, be better.*

Jezebel's expression hardened. She motioned toward the two men who stood near the door. They immediately shifted position, surging forward. "I take you into protective custody right now," Jezebel informed her. "My guards and I will spirit you to a secure location where you will stay for the foreseeable future while I assemble a team to track down Kurt Wellington. Once he is tracked down and apprehended—hopefully, without a major loss of life—then we will begin the trial process. Though, again, tracking him may prove impossible. Once he's aware that we are hunting him, I do expect him to vanish."

Right. Because of all the passports and his international, criminal connections.

Delaney's head hurt. "Let's think positively and say you do catch him. Then what?"

"The trial will be based purely on the testimony that

you can provide because there is no body for the man who was supposedly murdered."

"Uh, there is no 'supposedly' about it. Kurt murdered him! I saw the killing with my own eyes!" The throbbing in her head intensified.

"But there is no body, and it will be your word against Kurt's. Just as it will be your word against Kurt's regarding him holding you prisoner in a closet and him attacking you with a knife."

Jezebel had certainly been thoroughly briefed on a great deal of information. Nash must have updated the woman when Delaney had been sleeping. One hell of an update, from the sound of things. "I *saw* Kurt kill a man. I watched him commit murder with my own eyes."

"And do you know where the body is?" Jezebel asked her.

Delaney shook her head.

"Not having the body makes the case much harder to prosecute. We also don't know the victim's identity." A pause. "Do we?"

"I can describe him. Sandy brown hair, blue eyes, stubble on his cheeks. A scar sliding under this chin." She pointed to her own chin to show the spot. "I don't know his height because h-he wasn't standing. Medium build." Her hand fell. "He was scared. So scared. Begging to live and Kurt..." Delaney stopped. The memory of that shooting was far too vivid in her mind.

Jezebel advanced toward her. She reached for Delaney's hand. Lifted it. Stared at the marks on her wrists. "We should photo her injuries." Brisk. "Keep a log. Get a full statement. At the very least, we could try him for assault."

Assault. "And how long would Kurt serve if he was convicted of assault against me?"

Jezebel stared at her. "He's going to have a very, very good lawyer at his trial. And the trial is contingent on us actually catching him. As I said, Kurt will have plenty of passports and plenty of contacts so that he can vanish easily."

"Vanish..." Delaney pulled in a deep breath. "And just go kill someone else, somewhere else."

Jezebel let her go. "It's what he does."

"Unless I go back to him and gather evidence." The original option from Jezebel. Plan A.

A growl rumbled from Nash. "You're not doing that." Nash was adamant. "You go back to him, and you'll have no protection. He'll kill you."

"But...but Jezebel said—"

"Fine." Nash's eyes were filled with fury. "Maybe he won't kill you right away. Maybe you'll somehow manage— as a complete *civilian with no training*—to send us some intel that we can use against him. Then he'll figure out what's happening, and he'll make you vanish. Could be that he just kidnaps you. Could be that he takes you out of the country and there is no one that you can text for help. Because you've disappeared and even the CIA can't find you ever again. *I* can't find you ever again."

Yes, he made Plan A seem chilling. "Then I think I'll take what's behind door number two, please."

"What?"

She rolled back her shoulders. "Plan B." Her gaze did not waver from his. "Nash, will you marry me?"

Chapter Eight

"*Where is my wife?*" Rage twisted and heaved inside of Kurt Wellington. He should have been on his honeymoon by this point. He should have—*finally*—been fucking Delaney.

He'd played the patient boyfriend. He'd wined her. He'd dined her. He'd been the perfect gentleman.

Well, okay, *fine*, he'd been perfect until the end. But was it his fault that she'd walked into that gun scene? Not like the woman should have been there. He'd specifically *told* her that he would meet her later. How the hell could he have known that she wanted to surprise him? But she'd appeared, holding his favorite bottle of whiskey just when he'd been in the act of executing an asshole who'd *thought* Kurt would not find out about his betrayal.

She'd dropped the bottle. It had shattered. He'd whirled and *almost* shot her, but he'd stopped himself even as she'd rushed forward and tried to save the idiot who'd earned himself a ticket straight to hell.

Delaney had known nothing about the man she fought to save. Typical Delaney. Soft heart. Foolish choices.

She should have been married to me by now.

And, fine, he could see where he'd *maybe* overstepped by tying her up and locking her in the closet. But he'd just been trying to keep her in line. That was the same reason he'd used the knife in the church. Not like he'd stabbed too deeply. He'd barely broken the skin.

She left me.

It was driving him crazy. He wanted his gorgeous bride *back.*

Her and her fortune.

Delaney...something about her had challenged him from the beginning. He'd felt like she was holding part of herself back, and he'd been determined to break through every defense that she had. In his life, he'd always gotten everything that he wanted. Nothing was unattainable. But Delaney...a piece of her had just seemed to be right out of his reach.

Now he knew why.

Who was the bastard in the church, my love?

The man she'd run to. The man who'd fought for her. Tricky, tricky Delaney.

The man who will soon be dead.

The clerk from the motel had fled. But Kurt's men had tracked him down. The little shit was currently in the chair in front of him, arms tied behind his back. Blood dripping down his chin. Fear oozing from him.

If Delaney had been there, she'd probably be throwing her body in front of the kid, even though he'd sold her out. Probably trying to say that Kurt shouldn't torture him.

Kurt waved his hand, indicating that his man should punch the clerk again. Immediately, a powerful fist slammed into the jerk's jaw. His head whipped to the right.

But Delaney isn't here to beg me to stop. And I'll do

whatever it takes to get her back. An obsession was growing inside of him.

Hurt pride? Maybe. Because no one took what was his.

But...

More.

I will always get what I want.

"Stop! Please!" Blood flew from the guy's mouth. "I told y-you everything! He took her...left...*please!*"

Kurt began to circle his prey. "You said he came in alone at first, that he got the room for them?"

"Y-yes...Yes! He asked...asked for two beds. That's h-how I knew he wasn't alone."

So he's not fucking Delaney...yet.

"Big guy, dark hair, weird eyes."

Weird eyes? He stopped circling. "Weird how?"

"Different colors, man! Different!" His whole body shook in the chair. "One brown, one blue."

Interesting.

"I-I went in their motel room. I was just unlocking the door, trying to make it easier for you."

"You didn't make it easier, dumbass. If you hadn't done anything, they wouldn't have been alerted. Because of you, my bride got away."

The idiot's eyes were saucers. "That's why she was wearing that wedding dress? She married you?"

No, not quite.

"He was protecting her like crazy." The idiot licked his bloody lips. "You should have seen the way he looked at her. The man was clearly obsessed."

Kurt's body tightened. "Was he now." Not a question.

"He, uh..." The guy hunched his shoulders. "I don't want to get hit again..."

Kurt's eyes narrowed.

"But, uh, he said...said...I mean..." The motel clerk cleared his throat. "I told him that no pussy was worth dying for."

Kurt's hands fisted.

"But he, um, he said...hers was."

Rage nearly blinded Kurt.

You will die, you interfering bastard. I'll track you. I'll find you. I'll kill you.

Chapter Nine

"This is a shit plan," Ryan announced. "Granted, no one is asking my opinion, but, for the record, it is a seriously shit plan."

Nash turned to glare at his brother. "Thanks for the support." Delaney had been taken into another room by Jezebel. He knew Jezebel was in there, thoroughly interviewing Delaney and even getting pics of her wounds for documentation. The guards had gone inside with the women. Guards—other agents.

Tension rode him hard. He didn't like being separated from Delaney. For some reason, he felt like he had to keep his eyes on her.

"Maybe if you hadn't stopped to make out with her, then you'd be thinking with your head and not with your dick."

Okay. Enough. He bounded toward Ryan.

Ryan didn't even appear mildly intimidated. His brother simply quirked a brow. "Oh, come on. Don't deny the obvious. Her mouth was swollen and red when she came out of that bedroom, and her cheeks were flushed bright pink. She had the look of a woman who had just been thoroughly kissed while you looked like all you wanted to do was lock out the rest of the world and screw her senseless."

"Watch it," he warned.

"Why? I know you have never gotten over your obsession with Delaney. I know that you still sneak off to check up on her. I know that you even followed her to Milan a while back because you were worried about her meeting her grandfather."

Because he'd known exactly who—and what—her grandfather was.

Nash had met Delaney's grandfather years ago. When Carmello Ricci had come to the US. When he'd broken into Nash's apartment...*and told me to stay the hell away from Delaney.*

Delaney...

"Let me take care of her," Ryan said.

Uh, the fuck, no. "You'll keep your hands *off* Delaney."

"I did not say *let me fuck her*. Did you hear those words come out of my mouth? No, no, you did not. I said, ahem, *take care of her*. As in, I'll keep her alive. Count on me. I'll do whatever stupid cover Jez thinks we need on this mission. I'll be the big, bold, dangling bait that lures in our prey. You get your ass out of here. You get your ass out of the country. You just go."

His feet were rooted to the spot. "I'm not leaving her."

"Why the hell not?" Ryan demanded. "You did it before."

He caught himself just before he took a swing at his brother.

Ryan grinned at him. Smug. Annoying. As only a brother could be. "Ah, still a sore spot, isn't it? What have you been doing, bro? Living with regret all these years? Has it just been eating away at your soul? Do you wish with that hard, hard heart of yours that you could go back and change things?"

You have no idea.

"You never explained why you broke things off with her." Ryan rocked onto the balls of his feet. "Why you were hot and heavy one moment and leaving her the next, but I saw your pain. I know you *hurt* so I know she must have hurt *you*. Why the hell are you willing to risk so much for a woman who broke your heart?"

"You don't understand." Because he hadn't told his brother the truth. He hadn't told anyone.

Well, Jezebel knew. *And I think that's why she's doing this damn, crazy cover.* Jezebel Jenkins was cold, she was calculating, and she was also the best CIA training officer in the whole world. She'd helped Nash. Guided him after he'd talked to her years ago about Delaney's grandfather. Jez knew what a monster the man truly was.

Before Carmello Ricci died, Jez was working to bring him down.

Nash had been doing the same thing. Trying to rip apart the man's world. Not something that would ever be easy to admit to Delaney.

Hey, sweetheart, so I worked tirelessly to destroy the only family you had left in the world. I tried to send your grandfather to prison. I tried to annihilate his empire. I tried to leave you with nothing.

Also, by the way, the reason we broke up so long ago was because I traded you...I traded us...and I missed you every single day.

"Make me understand," Ryan demanded.

Nash opened his mouth.

A loud, blasting beat of music cut through the room.

"Dammit." Ryan yanked out his phone. "Agnes has programmed in more of her music." He shoved the phone to his ear. "This is not a good time."

Nash tried to suck in some calming breaths. No good. The breaths did not calm him. His gaze cut to the closed door on the right.

Jezebel is trying to help me. Trying to give me time with Delaney. Sure, sure, his boss was also trying to bring down Kurt Wellington because the man needed to be locked away in some dank, dark prison for the rest of his life but...

We don't have to fake some wedding. There are a hundred other scenarios that could work.

But only one that gave Nash back what he wanted most—Delaney.

"Delaney is alive. Delaney is being protected. And, no, I can't tell you more than that, sis, because this is a classified operation. When the dust settles, I'm sure Delaney will call you and update you on everything. Or, know what? Maybe she can come down and see you on that little slice of heaven you call home on the bay. But for now, I love you, sis, but *bye.*" Ryan hung up the phone and shoved it back into his pocket.

Music immediately began blasting again. Only this time, the music was coming from Nash's phone. The same grating tone. He pulled out his phone, and, as Ryan smirked at him, Nash put the phone on speaker. "Hello, Agnes."

"Ohmygosh. It is such a relief to speak to my *favorite* brother," she began.

"You are on speaker," Ryan informed her.

"I stand by my words!" Agnes immediately retorted. "Because a *favorite* brother doesn't hang up on you when you call him!"

"I am her favorite," Nash informed Ryan with a shrug of one shoulder. "She's not lying. Sorry if the truth hurts."

Ryan just sighed.

"I need to speak with Delaney," Agnes said. "The woman is not used to danger and drama, and she's probably freaking out. Someone needs to reassure her. I'm that someone."

Actually, other than the scream when Ryan had gone into her bedroom, she'd been pretty good and oddly controlled about things. Even handled the scene at the motel room with surprising calmness. "She's not freaking out."

Silence on the phone. Then, "Nash, may I *please* speak with my friend Delaney?"

Hell. He'd basically never refused Agnes anything since the day he'd met her. When he'd first come into the Quinn household, he'd been so scared his knees had knocked together. He'd stood there, bruises hidden beneath his clothes, and he'd waited for them to reject him.

Then a little fireball—seriously, Agnes's red hair had been bright back then—had hurtled toward him. She'd been all skinny legs and arms, and she'd thrown herself against him as she happily cried out, "*A new big brother! I will love you forever!*" And she had.

That was his sister, Agnes, though. Even as a kid, she'd loved with her whole heart, given herself completely, faced life at one hundred miles an hour. Generally, she was a tornado, and she got exactly what she wanted in this world.

"*Be firm,*" Ryan mouthed at him.

Because Ryan had the same weakness that Nash did. Nash nodded to his brother even as he had to force out, "Sorry, Agnes, no can do."

"*What?*"

"No can do." It was easier to say the second time.

Ryan gave him a thumbs up.

"Why can't I talk to Delaney?" Her voice had gone ominously low. "Do not tell me this is a classified situation."

That was exactly what he was going to tell her. "It's classified."

"Nash!"

Both he and Ryan winced.

"Don't worry," Nash assured her. "I will stay with Delaney until the danger has passed. I will do whatever it takes—"

"Even marry her," Ryan inserted in a very unnecessary and loud manner.

"—to protect her," Nash finished.

More ominous silence. Then, "Did Ryan say...*marry her?*"

The door to the right began to open.

"Got to go," Nash told Agnes. "I'll call you again when the case is closed. Until then...*classified.*"

"But—"

He hung up. He expected to see Delaney walking out of that room. Instead, Jezebel slipped out. She shut the door behind her. Her gaze darted between him and Ryan. "Gentlemen." A nod. "We need to talk."

His own stare shifted to the door. "Why is Delaney still inside?"

"Because I don't want her to hear this conversation." She marched past them. Her heels click-clicked on the floor. "Come with me."

With one last, lingering look at that closed door, he followed her into the kitchen. She spun as soon as he and Ryan entered. Her lips pressed together and the fingers of her right hand tapped against her thigh. "This could be quite the clusterfuck," Jezebel declared.

"I hope it's not," Ryan muttered. "Hate clusterfucks. They are my least favorite type of fucks."

Jezebel had her gaze on Nash. "You know what a big deal Typhon is to the agency. We've had suspicions about his true identity for a while, but never enough concrete evidence to act. Never possessed a good enough bait to trap him."

"I am aware." That would be why he'd called Jezebel as soon as he'd gotten Delaney tucked in bed upstairs. And, yes, side note, Ryan had been right about what had occurred in the bedroom. Nash had pulled the covers up over Delaney's body as quickly as he could and then he'd run for the door because lingering with her was so not a good plan. Not when his control was razor thin.

"We need him in custody." Jezebel spoke those words as if Nash and Ryan were not already completely aware of that obvious truth. "We need to catch him in the act of a major crime. Yes, I have Delaney's testimony. But a simple assault charge is going to be BS, *if* we could even get him in custody, and right now, the man is smoke. We need him to be brought into the open. I need evidence to nail his ass to the wall and conclusively link him as Typhon." She shook her head. "This will get messy. It will get dangerous. It will be—"

"A clusterfuck?" Ryan finished.

She didn't respond to that. "I chose Vegas because we have quite a number of agents embedded in the city. It's already an international hotspot. All intel I possess points to the fact that Typhon has major interests in two of the casinos there. Casinos that we think are tied to his money laundering and drug trade. He feels comfortable in that city.

His contacts there will let him know the minute Delaney makes an appearance, and you *will* make very public appearances."

Sure. They'd make a splash in Sin City.

"If he really did fall for the woman, then seeing and hearing that you two are romantically involved, that you are getting married, that will potentially push him over the edge." Jezebel's dark gaze had turned considering. "Maybe he'll get so angry that he comes for you himself. That would be the ideal response in this situation. We want to push him. Get him to come into the open. Get him to do the dirty work himself."

Ryan clapped. "Great. Hear that, Nash? You get Typhon coming to *personally* kill you."

He ignored his brother. "I can handle the danger." He had zero fears on that score.

"Can you handle the way you *feel* about Delaney?" Jezebel questioned him with a lift of her eyebrows. "Emotions make things messy."

"Damn straight they do." Ryan crossed his arms over his chest. "So messy."

As if Ryan had ever let his emotions get in the way of a case. The guy compartmentalized in his sleep.

"I know that this situation could be challenging for you, Nash," Jezebel added. Had that been a hint of concern in her voice? Maybe. Maybe not. "Your brother has already volunteered to be Delaney's lead bodyguard. I'm sure he'll make the sacrifice and be her groom, too."

"I've got it," Nash replied. "No sacrifice necessary."

Her gaze shifted to Ryan. "Will you go check on Delaney?"

Ryan did not move. "She's with your two guards. Don't you trust them?"

She smiled. "Will you go check on Delaney?" Jezebel patiently repeated.

Cursing, he spun and headed out of the kitchen. The door closed softly behind him.

Then it was just Nash and Jezebel. Her foot tapped. "I know you sacrificed a great deal years ago. You lost your relationship with Delaney."

He swallowed. "That intel remains in the vault. You swore on that. Whatever was sacrificed, whatever was lost— we don't speak of it." Because talking about the past changed jackshit. He still wound up without Delaney.

"Right." A nod. "Do you see this as your second chance? Is that what you're thinking?"

Sometimes, there were no second chances in this world. "You're the one who came up with the plans. A, B, and C."

A faint smile tilted her lips. "And you're the one volunteering to be the new groom."

Yes.

"But I have to know first, before we proceed even a single step, *can* you protect her? Will you be able to shut off your emotions when necessary and get the job done?"

"You really need to ask that question?" He kept his voice low because, knowing his brother, Ryan would be struggling to overhear their conversation. He'd shut the kitchen door, but Nash hadn't actually heard the sound of his brother's retreating footsteps. "I shut my emotions off before." *I broke her heart.* "I will do whatever it takes to succeed with this mission." Very careful wording because...

I have my own mission.

And it focused on getting back—reclaiming—the woman he'd lost before.

But, hell, yeah, he was also going to lock away Kurt

Wellington. The prick didn't get to threaten Delaney, hurt Delaney, and escape into the night.

Nash believed in multitasking. This time, he was determined to get the woman and lock away the sadistic criminal mastermind. Really, was that too much to ask? He didn't think so.

"That's what I like to hear," Jezebel praised. "Because you may be called upon to make some tough choices in the coming days. You have to remember, above all else, you are CIA. It's not just about protecting one person. We have global work that must be accomplished."

Not just about protecting one person.

Ah, Jezebel should really know him better than that. Because when it came to one person in particular...*There is nothing I will not do for her. No risk I will not take.* But he smiled at Jezebel. "You can count on me, boss."

She grimaced. "I feel like I should be alarmed."

Yeah, you probably should be.

"But let's get this case rolling, shall we?" A determined squaring of her shoulders. "Time is rushing past, and we have a sadistic criminal that we need to catch. So let's start implementing our trap."

In other words, let the games begin.

* * *

THE DOOR to the small study opened. Delaney's gaze had been locked on that door for the last—oh, ten minutes? Fifteen? And when she saw Nash fill the doorway, relief flooded through her.

"Everyone but Delaney—get out," Nash ordered in a tone that brooked no argument. "Jez has instructions for you all." He entered the room, stepped to the side, and jerked his hand toward the door.

They filed out. The two guards who'd come with Jezebel—uh, guards or agents—didn't even spare Delaney a second glance. But Ryan did. He'd come in moments before, looking extra tense and broody.

A broody Ryan worried her.

Ryan's watchful stare raked her. "Remember what I told you."

Yes, she would remember. They'd just had a very fast and heated conversation. She tried to give him a reassuring smile. In response to that smile, he locked his jaw. But he walked out, too, and Ryan pulled the door shut after himself.

So that left her alone with Nash. Alone with a Nash who—like Ryan—seemed extra tense. Nash also appeared even more grim and dangerous than before. A heavy silence filled the space. Nerves crashed through her body, and she waited for him to say—

"Marry me."

Oh, but those were words that she'd once dreamed that he would say to her. How many times had she hoped for those words? Unfortunately..."No."

Shock flashed on his face.

"I'm going to marry your brother," she mumbled.

And Nash's shock was replaced with rage.

Chapter Ten

I'm going to marry your brother.

Her words echoed in his head. No, no, she was *not*.

"It's really the better choice," Delaney added, sounding miserable as she twisted her hands in front of her body. "Ryan explained the situation to me, and you are needed more in Berlin, and he said you didn't want to be forced to stay with me, so, you're not. You can leave. You are free to hop on a plane to Berlin and forget all about me. You've already done more than enough."

He spun on his heel. Yanked open the door. "*Ryan.*"

His brother rushed toward him.

And Nash clocked him with a punch in the jaw. Just like that, his brother was on his ass. "*Stop trying to help.*" Nash slammed the door. He whirled back for Delaney.

Her lovely mouth was hanging open.

"There are other agents who can handle the operation in Berlin." Plenty of them. "There is only *one* agent who has a documented romantic history with you." He took a hard step toward her. "Only one agent who can play the desperate and determined, former lover who came running so that he could stop your marriage ceremony." Another hard step. Her wide eyes were on him. "Only one who was consumed with jealousy and had to steal you away." She'd backed up against the edge of a big, wooden desk in the room. There was nowhere else for her to retreat. So he eliminated the last bit of distance between them. He leaned forward, slapping his hands down on the wood on either side of her. "Only one who wants his second chance. Who will do anything for it."

She wet her lips. That sexy, pink tongue. Those full, plump lips.

"That's our cover story." His gaze lingered on her mouth. Because, yeah, he wanted her mouth. He wanted her. "That's our back story. It fits perfectly. Much better that way. Less chance that Wellington will realize that he's walking straight into a major trap. He won't know that I'm CIA. He'll just know that I'm the man who took you away from him." He finally yanked his gaze up. Locked his eyes with hers.

"Our cover story," she repeated. Her head tipped back as she held his stare.

"The cover story will have to look very, very real," he warned her. "*We* will look real. You won't look real with Ryan or any other random agent because you won't be comfortable with them putting their hands on you." *I won't be comfortable with them putting their hands on you. I will want to break those hands.* The same way he wanted to break Kurt Wellington's hands. "Kurt will know how you act with lovers. So he won't buy the bait if you look too stiff. With me, you won't—"

"He doesn't."

His brows shot up. "Doesn't what?" She'd lost him. And he'd been trying to sell his case so hard.

"Doesn't know how I act. Kurt and I were not lovers. So he doesn't know how I act with a lover."

His hands pressed *harder* to the desk. "Don't tell me what you think I fucking want to hear. *You were going to marry him.*"

"Why would you want to hear that?"

Because he was *insane* with jealousy. Because the thought of Kurt touching her, fucking her, made him want to rip the man apart.

"Why would it matter to you at all?" Delaney asked.

He leaned in even closer to her. "It matters because I've never been able to stop thinking of you as mine." Even as he said the words, Nash knew he'd crossed a major line.

A shake of her head. "I'm not—"

Aren't you? Because I never stopped being yours.

"I'm not lying to you. We didn't have sex. I'm not going to say that we didn't—didn't kiss, didn't do other things but—"

His mouth took hers. Slammed down onto hers and devoured, and he should not have done it. He should have held onto his control but ever since he'd gotten her back—*I want her back, I needed her all this time*—he'd been on a razor's edge. And he didn't want her thinking about someone else's kiss. Didn't want to hear about someone else kissing her or touching her. Nash wanted to obliterate everyone else from her memory.

He wanted to kiss her.

He wanted to give her pleasure.

To claim her. To take and possess her. Forever.

Her hands were on his chest. Soft. Light. One hand over his heart. *The heart that has belonged to her for years.* Her lips had already been open when he took her mouth. His tongue thrust inside, tasting the sweetness there, desperately needing it. He knew how dangerous he was, knew that he needed to pull back, and Delaney was the only thing holding him in check.

Holding him in check even as his need for her pushed him to the edge.

His hands flew to her waist. He lifted her up. Sat her on the edge of the desk, and he stepped between her spread legs. His hands remained on her waist. He didn't want to let go. The others were just beyond the closed door, and he didn't care.

Delaney mattered.

She'd always mattered.

Her tongue slid against his. Her body shuddered in his grasp. He wanted, he needed, he—

Her mouth pulled from his. Her breath came too fast.

"*This* is why I'm the man for the job." He had to say the words. Had to make her understand that no one else was going to do. "You react to me, and it's *real*."

A shiver slid over her body.

I react to you, and it's consuming. He swallowed. "It's not going to be the same with someone else. Kurt will see the lie. He'll smell a trap and think you went straight to the cops."

"I *did* go straight to the cops."

No, you ran straight to me. She hadn't known he was CIA.

"I called Agnes because I knew she was a Fed." Whispered.

Technically, Agnes was a *former* Fed. Currently, his sister was a small town sheriff hiding out with her very dangerous husband. But this did not seem like the moment to reveal all those details. "Next time, you call me."

Her long lashes flickered. "You hated me. I couldn't call you."

Had she thought about calling him? He would have come running in a heartbeat. Would always run to her. "Hate never enters the equation when I think of you." Never had, never would. "Maybe you hate me, though." Hadn't he feared that? The love she'd once felt for him must have turned over the years. Twisted. That was what betrayal would do. Twist and destroy.

She pulled in a quick breath. "I didn't even have your number. I didn't know where in the world you were."

"You'll always have my number from here on out. You need me, you call, and I'll come running."

"Nash...why?"

Because it's you. Because it's always been you. "I'm the best agent for this job." Safer words to say. "I will fit better with you because we have a history. Our bodies know each other. That works for us." He stared down at her beautiful face. "You won't react this way to someone else." *Damn well not to my brother.* "We need to put on a show, and, together, we can do it."

He'd said the wrong thing. He could see it in her expression. The minute the words slipped from his mouth, Nash knew he'd made a colossal mistake.

"A show. Right." She dropped her hands. "Because nothing you feel for me is real."

Screw that. "Touch my dick and you'll feel how *real* my desire is for you."

"Lust."

Yeah. He had plenty of that. But when it came to Delaney, there was so much more involved.

"Lust is fleeting. It doesn't last." She rolled back her shoulders.

"Really? That's weird. Pretty sure I've been lusting after you for years. Do tell, though, because I'm curious, when will it stop lasting? When will it finally end?" Because he was thinking he'd still want her when he was ninety.

Before Delaney could reply, a fist pounded into the door. "Jez is leaving! She has to get the trap in motion." Another hard bang of Ryan's fist. How many times would Ryan interrupt? "Before she goes, Jez has to get Delaney's consent. That means *Delaney* has to get her sweet ass out here and say what she's going to do."

She's not going to fake marry you, Ryan. That's one thing she will not be doing.

Nash realized that he still had a grasp on Delaney's waist. His fingers flexed against her. "I will keep you safe. I will play the lover who could not let you go." *I am the lover who could not let you go.* "I want you to trust me. I am the man you need for this job."

"I don't want you to get hurt."

He laughed at those fun words. "Sweetheart..."

She flinched.

"I've been hurt plenty. Hell, a few months back, I took a bullet to the side while I was protecting my sister. Before that, I got a knife to the stomach." A shrug. "Danger, risk, being hurt? That's all part of the job. None of that shit scares me."

A little furrow appeared between her eyebrows. "You were supposed to be a doctor. How did that change? How did *you* change?"

He looked down at his hands. Once, they had been all about healing. These days, they were far too good at killing. "I will keep you safe. I will help you to trap the man you were going to marry. And then..." His words trailed away.

"Let me guess. Then you'll walk away once more? Just vanish? Go off on another secret CIA mission and I'll never see you again?"

Not exactly. More like...*Then I'll keep fighting for you. I'll keep protecting you until the day I die, and I will do whatever it takes in order to convince you to fall in love with me again.*

Because she'd loved him once before. Surely, he could get her to love him again? Maybe?

She still wanted him. There was no missing the response of her body. And he could use that physical desire. He would use *anything* and *everything* in order to reclaim her.

But it was probably better not to say all of that, not yet. He was still just trying to get her agreement for the case. Having him pose as her lover would work for Nash in so many ways.

One, he'd get plenty of up-close and personal access to Delaney. The closer they were, the more chances he'd have to win her back.

Two, he seriously was damn good at protection. He fought hard, dirty, and didn't hesitate to kill. Three necessary requirements in a CIA operative.

Three, he would stop Kurt Wellington. Nash had a personal interest in the man's utter and complete downfall. *You don't ever take a knife to Delaney. You don't lock her up. You don't terrify her.*

Four—

More hard pounding on the door. "What are you two waiting for in there? *Christmas?* Jez needs confirmation, STAT. And if Delaney isn't consenting to Plan B, then that means she has to choose another option. I'm thinking Plan

C. She goes to a safe house, and she's well guarded until this is over."

If she chooses that plan, then I'll make sure I'm in that safe house with her.

Nash stepped back. Jez hated to be kept waiting, and a pissed Jez tended to make the world worse for everyone. His hands slipped from Delaney as he turned away. His steps were silent as he advanced toward the door.

"I choose you."

Hell, yes. Her words rolled through him.

"I'll tell Jez that *I choose you*."

And I will always choose you, sweetheart. Always. Never again would he walk away from her. He didn't care what threats were hanging over his head. He would not give her up.

Never. Again.

* * *

"You're sure about this?" Jezebel asked her.

No, she was not sure. She was terrified. Her body trembled. Her heart raced. She wanted to turn and run and go as far and as fast away from danger as she could and yet...

Delaney's gaze cut toward a watchful Nash. He'd vowed to keep her safe. Staying with him was far better than walking out of that door with Jezebel and being handed off to agents that she didn't know or—even more terrifying—trying to go undercover with Kurt? No, no way. She did not have the skill set for that kind of job, thanks so much. Lying had never come easily to her.

"I'm sure." Too bad the words didn't sound confident. "Nash will play the role of my, um..." *Boyfriend* didn't sound right. Neither did *lover*. Way too intense. So—

"Fiancé," Nash supplied. "I'll be the new groom. We'll spring the trap in Vegas."

Her gaze lingered on him.

Staring straight at her, Nash added, "She'll marry me."

"Pretend marry," Delaney corrected because that was an important distinction to note. "I'll *pretend* marry you."

He merely lifted a brow.

"And we'll catch the ex," Jezebel said. "Though, be warned, this mission will contain plenty of danger. We'll do everything possible to mitigate the threats to you, but Wellington is a sadistic killer. No variable can be controlled one hundred percent. Knowing that, realizing the risks, you are quite certain you do not want to simply take my offer of the safe house and vanish?"

Delaney curled and uncurled her fingers. "You need more evidence against him or else Kurt stays free. He keeps hurting other people." *And he'll stay out there, hunting me. I don't think he'll stop hunting me.*

"Yes." No sugarcoating from Jezebel. "He'll keep killing until we stop him."

"Then I can handle the danger." No, she could not. But she was certainly hoping Nash could step up on that score. "I will help to stop Kurt." There. Done.

"Excellent." A wave of Jezebel's hands toward the two guards who seemed to be her constant shadows. "We're going to make sure the trail of stolen cars can't be traced to this location."

The stolen cars. Right. Nash had been busy swapping out rides on their trek to the safe house.

Jezebel crisply continued, "I'll get Hans to switch out the vehicle that is here now, just in case you need to make a quick getaway."

Hans?

The man to the far right—the one who had dark blond hair and frigid, green eyes—nodded and stepped toward the door.

Had to be Hans.

But, ah, a quick getaway? "You think it's possible that Kurt will find us here?"

"Doubtful, but possible. We'll have eyes on the drive leading to the cabin. Both Nash and Ryan will stay here with you until we're ready for transport to Vegas. There is no reason to think you will not be secure here for the time being." One well-manicured finger tapped her chin. "Consider this your calm before the storm. Go ahead and get in practice time with Nash. Develop your cover. Get into the mindset of lovers who've finally been reunited after too much time apart. Make it believable." She turned for the door. "Screwups can be fatal."

Well, that was terrifying.

And Jezebel was gone. Gone with her guards. Shutting the door softly behind her. Leaving Delaney with Nash and Ryan.

"You'll be safe here," Ryan assured her.

A chill skated through her.

"It's a CIA safe house. Great security at the perimeters. Agents outside. Agents..." Ryan gestured to himself, then to a silent Nash. "Inside, too."

Right. *Safe.*

"It would take some serious firepower to get past all of us." Ryan sent her a reassuring grin. "So, how about we all grab some very late breakfast and relax a while? Then you two can, uh, get to work on that practice session Jez mentioned."

She could feel heat lance her cheeks. But her chin

lifted. "Breakfast would be great." She was *starving*. "And after that..." Her head turned toward Nash.

He watched her. Still silent. Still intense. Still a bit scary.

"I'd like for you to teach me how to kill a man, please," she said, very, very politely.

"Fuck me," Ryan breathed.

Nash's eyes narrowed.

"If you won't show me, then maybe Ryan can." Someone would be teaching her some tips to help save her life.

Nash advanced toward her. Slow, stalking steps. She held her ground, refusing to back up.

"I know basic self-defense," she said.

He kept advancing. He was almost on her.

"But that self-defense didn't do jack for me before. In case we're separated, in case Kurt gets too close, I want to know some fast and dirty tricks. I want to know how to stay alive." That hardly seemed like too much to ask.

But Nash shook his head. "That's not what you said, sweetheart."

Each time he said that particular endearment, she flinched.

"You've got to work on that." His sharp gaze had, of course, picked up on her reaction. "Got to be used to terms of endearment. Got to be used to my hands being on you."

His hands closed around her shoulders.

She shivered.

His jaw locked. "We'll practice me touching you, we'll get our cover role down and then..."

"Then you'll teach me—"

"How to kill?" Nash finished. "It's really not as hard as you think."

And, in a flash, there was a knife in his hand.

It *hadn't* been there a moment before, but it was there now, and fear flooded through her because the last time that she'd been near a man with a knife, he'd pushed it into her side. She could suddenly feel the ache in her body, and she broke from Nash's grasp.

A muscle flexed along his jaw. "First step is gonna be... *you have to stop being afraid of me.*"

So said the man with the knife.

"Yeah." Ryan cleared his throat. "Anyone else want some eggs and toast? I think I'll get breakfast going." He turned away. "Gonna be one long-ass day."

She didn't move from her spot. Neither did Nash. Delaney was far too conscious of the knife in his hand.

As she faced off with him, Delaney realized an extremely important fact. *I don't know him. Not anymore.* She'd known the man who wanted to save lives. This man was a stranger. "How many people have you killed?"

Many people had been unnerved by his gaze. Scared. When they'd been younger, she'd heard the whispers that circulated. It wasn't just that his eyes were two different colors. It was that his stare could appear so cold. So hard.

Except...

It hadn't ever seemed particularly cold to her. Not until that moment.

Not until...

"Don't ask questions that you don't want answered." Just that quickly, the knife was gone.

What was he now? A freaking magician pulling sleight of hand? "I want a knife," she blurted.

He shook his head.

She nodded right back at him. "Yes, yes, I do. I want a knife so that I can defend myself."

A long sigh slid from him. And then his hand was extending toward her. The knife was back—seriously, he needed to stop just magically producing weapons out of thin air—and he offered it to her, handle first.

Her fingers shook, but she reached for the knife. It was a light weight in her hand, and the blade gleamed.

"You know the problem with having a knife on you?" Nash asked.

Uh, no, she did not. Because having a weapon was better than not having one.

He moved in a blink, coming right at her, and she didn't even have time to scream. One moment, she held the knife, and in the next instant, he'd grabbed her, yanked her against him, and *he* had the knife.

He'd moved helluva fast. He'd spun her so that her back was to his stomach, one strong arm anchoring her at the waist, and his other hand—the hand that held the *knife*—pressed the blade to her throat.

"If you have a knife, it can be taken from you. Used against you." His breath blew along her ear. "If you're not planning to use it, if you're not ready to kill and you hesitate, that hesitation will just make you easier prey."

Ryan popped back in the room. "Forgot to ask, does anyone want..." He pursed his lips. "There is a knife at Delaney's throat."

She was aware of that fact.

"*Why* is there a knife at Delaney's throat?" Worry tightened his features.

"Because she wanted a knife." She felt the rumble behind her as Nash spoke. "And I needed her to know that weapons can be taken away easily and used against a person. She has to be prepared for that to happen. Has to know that Kurt and his men—they are gonna be a hundred times more used to violence than she is. So just saying she wants to know how to kill—all that will do is *get* her killed."

She grabbed at his arm. "Thanks so much for that lesson. It's not particularly *helpful*."

He moved the blade away from her neck.

She elbowed him.

Immediately, Nash spun her around. "You staying alive *is helpful*." His head lowered toward hers. "You want someone dead? I'll do it. I'll kill for you. Believe me, you don't want to carry that shit on your soul. You let *me* carry it for you."

Ryan whistled. "So, I was seriously just going to see if anyone wanted pancakes. I'd seen a box of mix in the kitchen earlier and wanted to come back and mention the option. Pancakes. Who wants pancakes?"

She did not look away from Nash.

His eyes were on hers. Their noses practically touching. Tension thickened the air between them.

"How about I just make pancakes for everyone?" Ryan asked to *no one* in particular. "Sound good? Great. You two kids keep practicing that sexual tension and reunited-lovers bit. Great job so far. Stellar." He stomped away.

Nash remained exactly where he was. So did Delaney.

"You can't be with me every single moment." She hated the stupid, continued tremble in her body, but she hated the tremble in her words even more. "So how about instead of trying to scare me, you actually help me? Let's assume I can actually hold onto a knife for longer than five seconds."

"Can you?"

"Stop being a dick! *Help me!*"

"*I fucking am. I will kill for you in a heartbeat.*"

"I need to protect myself! I need to be able to—"

He stepped back. His nostrils flared. "You will only have time for one or two slashes, if you're lucky."

Unfortunately, she'd never been particularly lucky.

"Strike first. If you're looking to completely incapacitate a person, you'd want to focus on the brain stem or the spinal cord."

Nausea rolled in her. She choked it down and made herself listen.

"But those hits will probably be too difficult for you to make. Your attacker will be coming straight at you, so you need to hit *fast*."

Not like she wanted to hit slow.

"The femoral artery is good." His left hand dropped to a point near his inner thigh. "That will give you massive blood loss. Along with that blood loss, your vic will feel a fast drop in blood pressure and probably a loss of consciousness, all within a matter of moments." His right hand—the one still holding the knife—rose toward his throat. "You can also go for the carotid artery. Always a winner."

"You're trying to terrify me. Unnecessary. I'm plenty terrified enough."

"You'll get covered in blood in those hits. And if you don't succeed in actually incapacitating your target, you'll be screwed."

She got that.

"You can go for major tendons." A quick movement of the knife over his body. "If you're on the ground and have the access, your attacker's Achilles tendon is a good target. Knocks out the person's mobility fast." His eyes glittered. "Of course, let's not forget the ribs."

"No." Hushed. "Not like we want to forget those."

"With a knife to the ribs, you can cause serious injury,

maybe even kill your attacker. You can puncture organs, start internal bleeding..."

She wet her lips.

"But you aren't going to have much time. The people that Kurt sends after you will be bigger, stronger, and one hell of a lot more used to handling weapons. You'll probably only have one go at it." If possible, his hard jaw went even harder. "Which is why *I will be with you.*"

But what if he wasn't? No way could he be with her every moment. And he'd been describing how she should attack. Except, what if she wasn't attacking? What if she was being attacked, and Nash was not there? "Next lesson. How do I *defend* against a knife attack?" Her gaze dropped to his knife. "If you were to come at me right now, what should I do?"

"A real knife attack doesn't happen in slow motion. It will be fast and brutal. Stabs that keep coming and coming, and you are probably not going to be able to stop them."

"Not the visual I want." But then again, she'd hated all the visuals so far. "Give me something to work with here, Nash." A plea.

"Your attacker is going to overwhelm you." Blunt. Brutal. "They'll start slicing and won't stop until you're immobile."

"Fantastic. I get one slice, but my attacker gets to keep coming and coming?" Did that seem fair? Delaney did not think so.

His dark lashes flickered. "You're gonna need to use whatever the hell is close in order to defend yourself. You're not gonna be able to grab the knife out of your attacker's hand like I did with you."

"Well, why not? You made it look easy."

"You just, hell, you barely had your hand on the damn

thing. I took it. You won't be able to do that. No way you rip the knife away from an attacker. So grab what is nearby, instead. A lamp. A picture. A pot. A freaking pan. Whatever you can find, use it. Your attacker is probably gonna be bigger, so he'll have one hell of a lot longer reach than you. You have to watch the space between you and him. Try to keep him as far from you as possible."

"Okay, so distance. Distance is key. And utilizing whatever the heck is close by. Got it."

"He'll stab and slash repeatedly."

More horrific visuals.

"There won't be time to get away after the knife starts coming at you."

"Not like I just want to stand there while he stabs me. Should I run? Fight? Try to block the blows?"

"I always try to take control of the hand wielding the attacker's weapon. If I break his fucking hand, not like he can keep coming at me with a knife." A curt nod. "You want a summary of what to do if some creep is coming at you with a knife?"

Yes, she did want one. Hadn't she *asked* for one?

"Fine. Stay the hell away from the attacker. Keep as much distance between you as possible. Use anything around you as a weapon. Destroy the attacker's hand that is holding the knife." A pause. "Don't get stabbed. Because it would really piss me the hell off."

"Not like it would thrill me, either." *Don't get stabbed* was the most obvious advice ever. Delaney glowered at him. "Fun talk."

"*Pancakes!*" A bellow from somewhere close by. Probably the kitchen.

The bellowing interruption was good because she could use a bit of distance between her and Nash. A break to eat might be just what the doctor ordered. She began to walk toward the sound of Ryan's bellow.

But Nash stepped into her path. Nash, who'd already made his weapon vanish again. "We'll work on self-defense."

"Promise?" Because she needed to feel more in control. As it was, she felt completely powerless in her own life.

His hand lifted. His fingers brushed over her cheek.

She flinched.

His stare hardened. "And we're working on that, too. You have to look like you *want* my touch."

Oh, screw it. "I do want it." Blunt. Bold. Pride destroying. "That's the problem."

Shock flashed on his face.

She skirted around him and fled for those promised pancakes.

"*Too many.*"

That low growl stopped her in her tracks. Frowning, Delaney glanced back.

"You asked me how many people I've killed." He looked down at his hands. "Too many." He turned his hands over, staring at his palms. "My hands have been covered in blood." He peered back up at her. "Can you handle that?"

She backed up a step.

"That's what I thought." His lips pulled down. "I'm not the boy you knew, and I am worried that the man I am will terrify you."

Chapter Eleven

"'Can you handle that?' Wait, wait, wait. You seriously said that shit to her? Those actual words? After Delaney admitted that she still wanted you?" Ryan sat on the cabin's front porch as darkness surrounded them. "Why would you do that? *That* is the time when you close in with charm and skill. When the woman says she wants you, you grab the opportunity. You don't send her running while you try to scare her away!" A disgusted shake of his head. "Talk about shooting yourself in the foot. No wonder she was edging away from you all day long."

Nash stared into the darkness. They were in the mountains, at the end of a long, lonely, snaking bit of road. A million stars glittered overhead, and a million insects seemed to chirp from the woods around them. "I was trying to be honest."

"Oh, great. *Why?* Because you want to watch her slip through your fingers again? That's your current goal?"

He turned to glare at his brother. "She thought I was a doctor. You get that? When I rushed into that church and took her out, she had no clue about what I'd become. When she sees me now, she still sees *him*."

"Him who?" Ryan stood and stalked toward Nash.

"The dumbass kid she knew before!"

"Uh, hate to point out the obvious, but you are that dumbass. From where I'm standing—which is basically right in front of you—you're even more of a dumbass now than you were then because you said the woman you are obsessed with, the woman who basically ruined you for everyone else—you said she confessed to still wanting you."

Why had he overshared that with Ryan?

"And then you said, let me paraphrase here..." Ryan's voice dropped as he growled, "'Oh, great. Delighted you want me. And by the way, I kill people for shits and giggles.'"

"That is *not* what I said. I told her that I'd killed *too many*—"

"Her ex is a psychotic killer! Why in the hell would you basically tell her you are the same as him? Newsflash. We are not the same. You and I target international monsters. People with victim sheets that stretch for miles. Serial bombers who are intent on chaos and destruction. Every target has been carefully researched and screened. We know that we are targeting monsters. Apprehension is the goal, but sometimes, those pricks try to take out others on their way down and we have no choice but to use deadly force. Did you explain all that to her?"

No.

Ryan sighed. "You're sabotaging yourself because you're afraid to take what you want so desperately."

Dammit. Ryan was...

Right.

His brother was also not done. "In one breath, you say

that only you can protect her. And then, in the next instant, you try to push her away. Hello, whiplash. Make up your freaking mind. Either you're all in with her or—"

"I'm *always* all in with her." His hands had fisted. "I just wanted her to know what she was going to get with me." Because if he had her again, then he could not walk away.

"You know what, bro? How about you *keep* some secrecy in your romance? Because right now, the goal is to keep her alive. Not make her want to run from us because she thinks that we're bad guys, too."

"Maybe I am bad for her."

"You're the woman's number one protector at the moment. Because you repeatedly volunteered for the job. Your ass had better be good for her." Ryan rolled back his shoulders. "We're supposed to head out at 0600 tomorrow. I'm about to go crash. I *will* be taking the downstairs bedroom. I'm assuming you'll be in the room right next to your lady?"

He assumed correctly. Nash turned to walk inside.

"There are no guarantees." Ryan's voice. Low. Far more serious than normal. "I don't like this case. I don't like this setup. I don't like that our asses just sat at this cabin all day long. If Kurt Wellington truly is Typhon—"

"He is," Nash returned. "Delaney said that he was specifically called by that name."

"Yeah, well, if he *is* the infamous Typhon, then you know he has serious reach. He has eyes everywhere. Maybe even in the CIA. And the stolen car you boosted was hauled off a little too late for my liking. Hopefully, those agents ditched it far, far away, otherwise, we could be tracked. Hunted too easily." His gaze swept the darkness. "I don't want to wake up to any surprises tonight."

Neither did Nash. "I'm going to check on Delaney." She'd gone to bed an hour before.

"Yeah, you do that. While you're checking on her, how about you try to say sweet, gentle, soothing things? Let's keep all references to being a killer on the down-low, shall we? Great plan. Fabulous talk."

Nash flipped off his brother as he marched back into the cabin.

And as he headed for the stairs that led to her room, Nash tried to figure out sweet, gentle, and soothing things to say to Delaney.

Unfortunately, he didn't tend to be an overly sweet, gentle, or soothing type of guy.

* * *

THERE WAS someone standing beside her bed.

Blearily, Delaney blinked her eyes as she tried to adjust to the darkness. She could definitely see a tall, shadowy form beside her bed and...had Ryan come into her room again? Because that shape did not belong to Nash. Not quite big enough. What did Ryan want this time? What was happening—

A hard hand slapped over her mouth.

"We have to hurry up!" A low rumble. "Those jerks on the porch won't be out there for long, and the men we disabled in the woods could get loose."

Fear blasted through her. She began to struggle but more hands grabbed for her. More hands—because there wasn't just one guy in her bedroom. There were *two*. One on each side of her bed. One with a hand slapped over her mouth. One with his hands on her arms to hold her down.

No, no, no. She twisted and heaved, but they were yanking her out of the bed.

"Tie her hands! Slap some tape over her mouth! Or just knock her out!" A whispered snarl. "We have to move! *Hurry!*"

Her legs kicked out, but she couldn't reach her attackers with her feet.

A soft rap at her door. "Delaney?"

Nash's voice.

Nash!

The door creaked open. Light spilled into the room. "I'm sorry to wake you but we really need to—*get the fuck off her!*" A roar.

Because the light had hit the bed. It had hit her. Her attackers. Nash lunged across the room. He grabbed one man—the jerk who'd been holding her arms—and Nash *threw* him into the wall. With her arms free, Delaney reached for the nightstand. He'd told her before to use anything close as a weapon, and she snagged the square alarm clock and slammed it in the face of the man who was *still* trying to keep his sweaty hand over her mouth.

She hit him with the alarm clock once, twice, and when she went for the third hit, Nash was there. He caught the attacker by the nape of the neck, spun him around, and drove his fist at the man's face.

Delaney scampered out of the bed. Her breath was heaving, her body shaking. *Weapon, weapon, weapon.* The man who'd been tossed into the wall was weaving as he stood next to an open window.

Open window? I'm on the second floor! Those men had scaled the cabin in order to get to her?

She flew across the room and slammed her hand into the light switch. More illumination flooded the room. Nash was still beating the hell out of the man near the bed. As for the one near the window...

They are both wearing ski masks. Both big. Dressed all in black. Their clothing would have let them blend with the darkness outside.

The man near the window was reaching under his shirt, and she realized that—oh, no. Oh, crap. *He has a gun!* He was going for a gun in a holster beneath his shirt, and he was looking straight at Nash's unprotected back.

"No!" Delaney screamed, and she charged at the attacker. She threw the alarm clock at him. Because, yep, she'd still been clutching it. The clock slammed into his chin.

Swearing, he angled toward her. Correction, he angled and aimed his gun at her.

"*No, don't!*" A yell from his partner. "*We're not supposed to shoot her!*"

But it was too late. The gun was pointed at her, and Delaney was sure he was pulling that trigger.

Except a bullet didn't hit her. Nash did. He slammed his body into hers, and she crashed into the floor.

"Run, run, run!" A wild order from one of the men.

She didn't even know which intruder had given that order.

"Shoot him and run!" The shrieking order came again.

Shoot *him?*

Nash shoved his body up. "Stay down," he barked at her.

They weren't planning to shoot her. They were going to shoot *him!* He needed to stay down. She and Nash were both too exposed. She needed a weapon. She needed to help. To fight.

Nash heaved away from her. He rushed at the man with

the gun. The guy who couldn't seem to decide what the hell he should do. Before the masked man could fire, Nash drove his body into the would-be shooter's. A hard, powerful hit. Nash's shoulder collided with the guy's chest, and the intruder went hurtling back.

Back toward the window.

He hit the window once. Tried to aim his weapon at Nash.

Nash drove into him again.

The attacker went through the window.

Halfway through the open window, halfway through the glass because the top part of the window shattered as the man's body heaved through it. Delaney screamed as she watched him topple out of the window and fall into the night.

The intruder's partner chose that moment to try and run past her. Still on the floor, she acted on instinct. Her hand flew out and curled around his ankle, tripping him. He toppled toward the floor. His body hit with a jarring impact.

He rolled and tried to kick at her fingers.

Delaney snatched her hand back.

Only for Nash to catch the guy's kicking foot in his hand. "You don't attack a lady." Nash twisted the foot he held. Hard.

So hard that the intruder screamed in agony and Delaney was pretty sure that Nash had just broken the man's ankle.

And then...

Nash kicked the guy in the dick. "And you sure as hell don't break into her bedroom in the middle of the night!"

Footsteps thundered outside of her bedroom. Then Ryan appeared in the doorway, a gun in his hand and his face twisted in fury. "What the hell?" His gaze took in the scene, fast. The man writhing in pain on the floor. Nash's enraged form. Delaney crouched nearby. The rumpled bedding. The shattered window.

Ryan did a double take. "What did I just miss?"

"Get downstairs," Nash ordered him. "See if a dead man is outside."

Ryan blinked at him.

"About seventy percent sure I just killed the bastard," Nash snarled.

Ryan shook his head. "Bro, that is not sweet. That is not gentle. That is *not* soothing."

Nash glanced toward Delaney.

No, there had been nothing gentle about Nash. He'd flown into her room like an avenging angel. He'd kicked ass and taken names and been awesome.

She staggered to her feet and rushed to him.

"Delaney, go to my room. It's the one right next to this one. Get the handcuffs out of the black bag at the foot of my bed."

She paused, mid-rush. "You have handcuffs in your bedroom?"

The man on the floor tried to lunge at Nash.

Nash knocked him back down with a fast upper-cut. "*In the black bag at the foot of my bed.*"

Right. Right. Right. She spun and ran into his bedroom. After a frantic glance, she saw the black duffel bag at the foot of his bed. Her hands grabbed for it, she unzipped it and...Wow.

Guns in holsters. Knives. Rope. Duct tape. And, yes, sure enough, handcuffs. Swallowing, she reached for the handcuffs and tried to ignore the fact that it looked as if the man had some sort of kidnapping or murder bag at the ready. A bag that also contained at least three passports and an extremely thick, curled-up wad of cash.

"*Delaney!*" Nash shouted.

Her fingers tightened around the handcuffs as she raced back to him. As soon as she entered her bedroom, the horror scene was the same. A masked man writhing in agony. Nash glaring down at his prey. Broken glass from the window scattered on the floor.

Nash took the handcuffs from her. He rolled the intruder over and slapped the cuffs on him with fast and brutal movements. "You made the worst mistake of your life," Nash told him. "You should have never come for her."

Her breath sawed in and out. "Did Kurt send you?" she asked the intruder.

Nash yanked the guy to face him.

"I'll never tell you, bitch!" the man spat. His hands were cuffed behind his back.

Nash yanked off the ski mask that had been over the guy's head.

Delaney nodded. "Hello, Jacob." She'd thought that she recognized that screeching voice.

"*You know him?*" Nash demanded.

"Yes. Jacob works for Kurt. I'd often see him around, skulking in the shadows."

"Well, well..." Nash began.

"I'm not saying a fucking word!" Jacob blasted. "And you're both dead! Dead! Do you hear me? *Dead!*"

"Those were actually quite a few words that you just *said*." Nash yanked Jacob up and brought him in so that they were nose to nose. Nash had to lean down toward Jacob, though, because the other man didn't match his height. "And those were the *wrong* words to say. Because I get deeply pissed off when someone threatens the woman I love."

The woman I love.

She shook her head. An instinctive denial. Nash didn't love her. He did *not*.

Get a grip, woman. The declaration isn't for you. He's playing a role. This is the cover story for this insane mission. Now suck it up and stop freaking out.

"Delaney!" A thunderous roar of her name. Coming from outside. Outside as in—outside of the cabin. "*Delaney!*"

She hurried toward the window, dodging the broken glass. Most of the glass had flown outside of the window, but there were still quite a few chunks on the bedroom floor, and her feet were bare. Not like she wanted to get sliced.

Carefully, she poked her head out of that window just a bit.

She could see two shadowy forms on the ground. One standing. One crouching. The standing one had a gun pointed at the crouching figure.

"Good news!" Ryan called to her. "He's still alive."

Ryan was the one with the gun.

"Alive," Ryan continued in his loud and chipper tone. "For the moment. But pretty soon, I'm thinking the idiot will be wishing that he hadn't survived the fall." Ryan shook his head and told the man, "You have no idea who you just fucked with."

A shiver slid over her. Delaney eased away from the window. She wore only a thin t-shirt, panties, and a pair of cotton shorts. All of the clothes had been waiting in the room for her. The clothes had been fine while she was sleeping, but now Delaney felt way too exposed. She glanced back over her shoulder at Nash. His face was locked into tight, angry lines. His stare blazed with fury. And he had a knife to Jacob's throat.

So, important point to fully understand—the Quinn brothers were decidedly dangerous and not afraid to kill. At all.

"You came for her?" Nash barked at his prey. "You broke into her bedroom? You were trying to hurt her?"

Jacob's eyes had swollen to the size of saucers. "Who... the hell...are you?"

Nash smiled, and it was the coldest, scariest smile she'd ever seen in her life. "I'm the man who is going to marry Delaney."

Another shiver shook her body. She grabbed a nearby robe and jerked it on.

"And I am the man who will kill anyone who tries to hurt her. So guess what's about to happen to you?"

She wasn't the only one shaking. Trembles ran over Jacob's body, too.

"You stalked the wrong woman," Nash informed him. "You stalked *my* Delaney."

Her arms curled around her stomach. She'd never, ever seen Nash this way. Cold and terrifying. Deadly and intense. The CIA operative.

Not the boy who'd loved her. The young man with the dreams of being a trauma surgeon. This man...this man...

"*Are you ready to die?*" Nash asked Jacob.

A sob broke from her.

At the sound, Nash's head whipped toward her. His gaze collided with hers. And whatever he saw on her face made his jaw go even tighter.

"Get out of the room, Delaney. *Now*. You don't want to watch this."

This? Was he about to kill Jacob? No, Jacob was cuffed.

He wasn't attacking any longer. She scrambled forward and grabbed Nash's arm. "Don't kill him." His muscles were rock hard beneath her touch.

"He would have killed *you*. In a heartbeat. He deserves exactly what he gets." Brutal, arctic words. No give at all in his fierce expression.

"No!" An impassioned cry from Jacob. "I wasn't gonna kill her! The orders were to retrieve Delaney! Kurt wants her back. He is desperate to get her back. I was never gonna kill her." His gaze swung to Delaney. "I wasn't. I wasn't gonna kill you, I swear. I just—you want to do what Kurt orders, understand? If you don't, bad things happen. He gave the order, and I had to follow. It wasn't personal."

When a hard hand had slapped over her mouth and terror had threatened to rip her apart, it had certainly felt personal.

"The order was to retrieve you. I-I got lucky. Talked to a guy who'd had his car stolen at a rest stop, and he had a tracker on it that led here. I was just gonna take you back!" His words tumbled out, one after the other, in a frenzy. "I was just gonna bring you back to him. I wasn't gonna kill you! I swear it!"

Fear nearly swallowed her whole. "Did you tell Kurt that I was here?" The last car they'd stolen had been at the rest stop. So that one had gone straight to the cabin. She'd been so tired then that she barely even remembered what the car looked like.

"Told the boss...told him I was following a lead. Didn't want you to escape and th-then have to explain to Kurt when I didn't have you." His Adam's apple bobbed. "He d-doesn't like f-failure. You don't want to disappoint the boss."

"Too fucking bad," Nash snapped. "Because he's about to be getting a whole lot of bad news. The man is going to have a life of disappointment waiting." His head cocked to the right. "You weren't supposed to kill Delaney. Kurt gave that order. Got it. Good to know." Flat. "But what did he say about me?"

Jacob licked at the blood dripping from his lips. "I-I... *don't kill me!*"

That hadn't been an answer. Delaney's stomach twisted.

"What did Kurt Wellington say about me?" Nash repeated, tone ominous.

"You're an...open target." Squeaking words. "The sooner y-you're in the ground, the better."

Delaney shook her head. Hard. "No."

But Nash laughed. "If he wants me in the ground, Kurt's gonna have to come and do the job himself."

That was exactly what the CIA wanted. The whole reason Jezebel had instituted her big scheme. They wanted to catch Kurt in the act. Not just of trying to abduct Delaney and get her back. *They want Kurt to try and kill Nash. To go after an operative.*

Ice poured through her veins.

"For someone who wasn't gonna say a word, you sure as hell just spoke plenty," Nash added.

Jacob's breath shuddered in and out. "*Don't kill me!*"

Nash smiled at him.

Ice poured through Delaney's veins. That smile chilled her to the core. *Who is this man?*

"I've got big plans for you, Jacob." Nash's flat response. "Very, very big plans."

Jacob whimpered.

Chapter Twelve

"You were not sweet. You were not gentle. You were not soothing." Ryan shoved his hands into the pockets of his pants. "I'd say that you were probably more terrifying, aggressive, and way too deadly. Those were not the descriptors that we were going for in that scene."

Nash watched as three operatives from the CIA shoved Jacob Brown and Lowell Vail into the back of a van. Those two attackers were about to vanish. The CIA—in the form of Jez—would grill them. Jacob and Lowell worked directly with Kurt, and if she could get them to provide evidence to tie Kurt to being Typhon, Jez would do it. The woman was truly a master when it came to interrogation. And flipping suspects. In exchange for their lives, she'd get them to roll on their boss. She had a way of convincing even the most hardened criminals to cooperate. With the right leverage.

Once upon a time, Jezebel had been a ballerina. She'd grown up in France, the daughter of a South African mother who'd married a French artist. Jezebel had always moved in the highest of social circles. Subterfuge had been her name and her game long before she'd entered adulthood. Being a ballerina, she'd been able to travel the world. She'd wined and dined the upper echelons, and she'd been stealing their secrets with every casual meeting.

She'd once confided to him that Josephine Baker had been her hero while growing up. And if Josephine had been able to work as a spy, well...

Jez had been sure she could get the job done, too. And she had.

Jezebel Jenkins was not her real name. She'd once told him it was the name she'd chosen. He had no clue what her birth name actually was. Jez had changed her identity over and over.

People underestimated Jez because she was physically fragile. *Just a dancer.* How often had she told him those were the words she'd heard? *She's just a charming dancer.*

A dancer who had brought down some of the worst criminals in the world.

"Jez will get intel from them. Hell, you already had that little Jacob jerk spouting off constantly. Even if the other one doesn't break," Ryan mused, "that one will." He turned his head and surveyed the woods around them. "We've got additional agents out there now. No one will get past them for the rest of the night."

They were just supposed to stay in the cabin until dawn. After it had already been compromised.

"You should go in and try comforting Delaney." Ryan's voice was mild. "I'm sure she's quite shaken after tonight's events."

"You mean after waking up to find two guys who wanted to abduct her?" Nash's words were gritted from between clenched teeth. "Or from watching me beat the shit out of Jacob because he'd terrified her? Which one of those events do you think left her the most *shaken?* Oh, and let's not forget the fun moment when I threw a man out of her window." Ryan had been right. He definitely hadn't been sweet or soothing or—dammit. *Not charming. So very far from charming.* Instead, he'd been deadly and vicious. And he'd seen the fear in Delaney's eyes when she looked at him.

"Probably all those events did it," Ryan drawled. "Waking up to find attackers by her bed had to be frightening. Then seeing you in your deadly glory probably sealed the deal. Not like it had to be an either-or situation."

Hell. He needed to go inside. "She's afraid of me."

"No." A very long and drawn out *nooooo.* "I'm sure she's not."

Bullshit. Ryan was lying. "She's *terrified.* I saw it on her face. In her eyes. If I go in there and try to touch her now, she'll probably flinch away from me."

"Well, you're gonna have to do more than just touch her." Ryan slapped a hand on his shoulder. "You're gonna have to marry her. So man up and get in there. Unless, of course, you changed your mind and you want me to take on the role of groom."

"*I'm marrying her.*"

"Pretend marrying," Ryan corrected. "You're pretend marrying."

Nash didn't speak.

"Pretend marrying," Ryan said again.

And, again, Nash did not speak.

"Unless you want a real marriage?" A careful question from Ryan. "Is that what you are trying to tell your big brother?"

Their birthdays were literally a month apart. But Ryan still liked to toss out that big brother bullshit every now and then. It brought him joy.

"Huh." From Ryan when the silence just kinda stretched.

Hell, yes, I want to really marry her. It is what I've always wanted. But you don't always get what you want in this world. A painful, bitter truth.

"You usually tell me every secret you have." Ryan's voice was low. Considering. "You're my brother, and there is no truth that I haven't given to you. No matter how painful it is, I've always told you everything about myself."

Nash's jaw hurt because his teeth were clenched so tightly.

"You never told me why you walked away from Delaney before."

He hadn't been able to tell anyone.

"At first, I thought she'd done something to break your heart. So, yeah, I was an asshole to her back in those days."

"Delaney never did anything wrong." Gritted words.

"You just stopped loving her?"

Never.

"Uh, huh. Thought so." Still low. "I hate that I was an ass to her back then. But my loyalty is always to you, without question."

Dammit. Ryan was being *nice.* Such a bad sign. "Give your loyalty to her. Give your protection to her. If this shit goes sideways before we can secure Wellington, do whatever it takes to save Delaney."

"*You* save her. You're the groom. Not me." He let go of Nash's shoulder. Stepped back. "Had to be something pretty big. That's what I figured, anyway. For you to give up the woman you loved? Must have been major. What was it? Did someone threaten you? Threaten her?"

How about threaten everyone in my world? But he held

those words back. No point in saying them. The past would not alter.

"Everything about you changed when you separated from her."

Ryan wasn't wrong. Nash had changed. Because he'd needed to change. He had to become someone a whole lot stronger and a whole lot tougher in order to protect the people he cared about in this world.

"Hell," Ryan groused, "I joined the CIA just to keep watch on you. *You* were the one to start hunting killers first."

While Nash had been in college and med school, Ryan had been a Marine. *Semper Fi* had been his life. *Always faithful.* Yeah, that was his brother. Ryan had always been at his side. Always watching his back. And as for Nash...

I had to protect him. I had to protect my family. I had to protect Delaney.

Sometimes, to protect someone, you had to walk away. Even if it meant cutting out your heart and bleeding the fuck out.

"The CIA operative inside needs to leave with the van," Ryan muttered. "We can't keep him waiting any longer."

The van was about to pull away, and, yes, there was an agent inside. From here on out, Nash was gonna make sure that Delaney had a guard with her. He'd wanted to personally see Jacob and Lowell get their asses loaded into the van.

And now, he was going back to Delaney. Even if she feared him.

She definitely feared him. *Oh, baby, just wait until you find out that we are going to have a one-bed situation for the foreseeable future.* "Still think I should aim for sweet and soothing with her?" Nash asked.

"Nope. Too late. That ship has sailed."

Yeah, it had.

"Just try to be less scary, would you?" Ryan advised. "Maybe you could aim for semi-charming?"

Impossible. "You're the charming one." He squared his shoulders.

"And which one are you?" Ryan wanted to know.

I'm the one who will kill to protect Delaney.

Chapter Thirteen

"You'll be sleeping in my room," Nash announced.

He'd just stalked back into the cabin. The intruders had been taken away, though she was pretty sure the assailant who'd gone through the window had needed to be *carried* away due to his broken leg.

Lowell Vail. Delaney had recognized him, too. Both intruders had been on Kurt's payroll. Their presence just reinforced the fact that Kurt was not going to let her walk away. He would keep hunting her. Hunting Nash.

"Did you hear me?" Nash strode toward her as she perched on the edge of the couch. "My room."

Her head tilted back. "Considering that there is a huge hole where my window should have been, yes, I did figure that I would not be sleeping in that particular bedroom tonight." She tapped the couch cushion near her. "But there is no need to sacrifice your bedroom. I can sleep right here." *If* she slept. "The couch is perfectly fine." Adrenaline pumped through her veins, and she was terrified that, even if she did sleep, she'd just wake up to dark shadows near her. Shadows who wanted to take her away.

Nash eyed the couch. Then the floor. "If you insist on sleeping in here, then I'll bunk on the floor next to you."

"Why would you do that?" She craned to look toward the front door. An agent had been inside with her while Nash and Ryan made sure the intruders were secured. An agent who'd given his name as John Doe. Sure. Whatever. But John Doe was gone, having stepped out just as Nash entered.

"Because you're not going to be away from me again," Nash said in his deep, rumbling voice. "Where you sleep, I'll be sleeping. No one is going to sneak in and try to take you. Not happening."

Her stare whipped back to him. He could not be serious.

Nash nodded. "I believe you would call this a one-bed situation."

She jumped to her feet. "You sleeping on the floor is not a one-bed situation!"

"One couch? Is it a one-couch situation?"

"Nash! Stop!" She wanted to touch him. She was afraid to touch him. She was afraid of everything. Her arms crossed over her chest. "I heard the orders you gave. There is a semi-army of agents surrounding the cabin now. No one else is going to get past them."

"No one should have ever gotten past the exterior agents—or past me—in the first place."

She swallowed. "You were outside..." Delaney began.

He stepped closer. "I wasn't close enough to you. That mistake won't be made again. When you sleep, I'll be right next to you."

"But—"

"It's a done deal. So we either bunk down here, with you on the couch and me on the floor, or we go upstairs and sleep in my bed."

Despite her previous words, the couch was not, in fact, fine. The couch was lumpy. Old. Narrow. And she didn't want him on the floor. But the idea of being in bed with him set off all kinds of alarm bells. "How big is the bed?"

His eyes narrowed. "How terrified of me are you?"

Her chin notched up. "That is not an answer to my question."

"Fine. You answer my question, and then I'll answer yours."

The front door squeaked. Her head whipped toward the sound. Ryan crept inside, wincing. "Sorry. Feels like I just interrupted something." He pursed his lips. "You guys want to take this upstairs? I'd really like to crash on that couch. It's a more central location than the back bedroom that's down here on the first floor, and, if I'm on the couch, I'll be able to spring into action faster from this location. Should, you know, any would-be kidnappers or killers make an appearance."

If Ryan was taking the couch, then she didn't really have a choice. Brisk, determined, she nodded and began walking for the stairs. The robe she wore swirled around her feet. She'd grabbed the robe right before the other agents arrived. The soft, white cotton robe skimmed her ankles and fell all the way to her elbows.

As she mounted the stairs, she was far too aware of Nash following behind her. She could feel him. Warm. Strong. Determined.

Her eyes were up, focused ahead. She reached the

landing, then turned to the right. Her fast footsteps led her past her room, and Delaney only paused when she was at the bedroom that had been designated for Nash.

"Queen-size bed," he told her. "So it will be a tight fit."

She wet her lips. He'd finally answered her question. Was she still supposed to answer his? Truth be told, she'd really love to avoid a response to his query. *How terrified of me are you?* Delaney reached for the doorknob and swung open the door. Her fingers hit the light switch.

The covers were still in place. The bed made. Unlike her, Nash had never gone to sleep.

And it was, indeed, a queen-size bed. Given Nash's massive proportions, it was certainly going to be a tight fit, as he'd said.

She made sure the belt of her robe was extra snug as she made her way across the bedroom. Delaney hauled back some of the covers and slid as far to the right side of the bed as possible. Practically hanging off the edge.

Nash watched her. Again, she *felt* his stare.

"You didn't answer my question," he said. His fingers slid over the light switch.

Darkness.

But the floor creaked, and she saw his shadowy form moving around the room. He went toward the window. Peered out.

"I don't, uh, remember your question," she lied.

"How much do I terrify you?"

"Oh, right, that question." She blew out a long breath. "On a scale of one to ten? Is that what you're asking?"

More creaking of the floor. And then the bed dipped. He'd just slid onto the mattress.

Her shoulders tensed.

"You planning to keep that robe on all night?" Nash murmured.

"There's barely a few hours left of the night. And I'm cold."

"You're afraid. Of me."

Yes. So, about that scale. "Maybe a two." A whisper. But, she'd lied. "Or...maybe a nine." Still not true. "Ten," she confessed, miserable.

"Fuck." Anger pulsed in the word.

She flipped toward him because he was beside her in bed. "Well, what do you expect? How do you expect me to feel? You are putting your life on the line! You are fighting men who want to *kill* you!" He was mere inches away. It would be far too easy to touch him. "You don't seem to care about the risk to yourself. You act like the danger doesn't matter. Or, worse, that you *like* it. So, yes, that terrifies me! You shouldn't like danger. You should run from danger the way a normal person does. The way I want to run!"

"No, Delaney. *No.* I mean—you're terrified *of* me. Of. Me. Not for me."

She had a death grip on the covers.

"I saw the way you looked at me when I was taking those intruders down." Gruff.

"You were relentless." She would never get those images out of her head. The way he'd just launched at Jacob. The way he'd tossed Lowell through the window. "You attacked brutally."

"And you're afraid. *Of* me."

Was she? "Yes." A stark truth that hung in the air between them.

Nash cursed.

She sprang toward him, and Delaney kissed him.

Super huge, super terrible mistake, but she did it.

Because while she might fear him, the fear didn't stop her from wanting him. Nothing had ever stopped her from wanting him. She'd wanted him when she was a lovesick teen. She'd wanted him when she'd been an impassioned college student. She wanted him now, when she was a desperate and afraid adult.

There just had always been something about Nash.

Her lips pressed to his. It was a quick, clumsy kiss. Exceptionally low on the skill and seduction level. She'd just done it to prove a point. Fear didn't stop her. But he...

His hand curled around her hip. "Do it right," he growled against her mouth.

Her lips parted.

His tongue thrust inside. A hungry, desperate moan pulled from her lips even as wildfire seemed to ignite in her veins. Her breasts ached, her sex yearned, and she could all too easily imagine stripping off the too hot robe and ditching all the clothes she wore beneath it. Climbing on top of him. Feeling that long, hard dick of his pushing between her legs.

Nash had been the one to teach her all about pleasure. To set her expectations so high in the bedroom that no one else had been able to match him. No one else had come close.

Unfortunately, Nash had also been the one to teach her about pain. As he'd shattered her heart into a million, itty-bitty pieces.

His hand grabbed the belt of her robe. He yanked it loose, and then his fingers slid inside the robe. He caught the edge of her t-shirt. His hand slid under the t-shirt. His warm, callused fingertips touched her skin.

She jerked at the contact.

"That's gonna be a fucking problem," he rasped against

her mouth. "You kiss me and you fear me and you *flinch* when I touch you." Nash began to withdraw his hand.

She caught his wrist. She pushed his hand back against her. "I flinched," a whisper against his mouth, "because when you touch me, I feel it in every cell of my body. Heat surges all the way through me. When we are skin to skin, I want to forget the years between us and just give in to the need that burns inside of me. A need for you that just won't stop." A stark, painful truth.

But...

They shouldn't. They should not have sex right then.

They. Should. *Not*. There were a million reasons not to go too far. And...

So much need. Craving. Wanting. Longing.

"You like for me to touch you?" Nash's low, deep voice.

She nodded. He could see that gesture in the darkness, couldn't he? He'd always had such strong vision in the dark.

"Prove it." A dare.

She eased away from him, but she still held his wrist. She could still taste him on her tongue.

"Let me touch you." Hard words from Nash. But, somehow, they held the ragged edge of a plea. "*Just touching*. Not fucking, Delaney. Let me just touch you."

What were they doing? Why did it feel as if everything was already out of control? Because it was? Her body was too tense. Her nerves on edge. She should not say... "Yes. Touch me." But she did. All husky and breathy and such a mistake.

But she said the words.

Because it was Nash. In bed with her. Not a dream. A reality. And with the madness around her, she wanted to grab tight to him. Correction, she *had* grabbed tightly to him. She still held his hand.

"Show me where you want my touch." That deep, dark, tempting rumble again.

She bit her lower lip. And she eased his hand down.

"*Delaney.*" A savage snarl that held hunger and desire.

She pushed his fingers under the elastic edge of the cotton shorts that she wore.

"Fuck, baby, fuck."

His big fingers eased under her panties. He pushed down, moving his hand between her thighs. His right hand was between her thighs, and his left shoved the covers out of his way as he edged ever closer to her.

She eased back onto her pillow. Stared up at the dark ceiling above her. His big hand was between her legs. His thumb stroked her clit. Slid over it again and again. Dragged over it.

"You're getting wet for me."

She bit her lower lip harder. She *was* wet for him. It was so easy to get turned on for him, when it had been hard with others. Almost as if he'd marked her body. Trained her to respond quickly to him.

"I'm fucking rock hard for you. You breathe, and I get this way."

She was breathing quickly. Her body had tensed. He was strumming her clit, over and over. Possessive, commanding strokes even as one finger pushed inside of her.

Her head tipped back against the pillow. She stopped biting her lower lip as a moan slipped from her.

"You are so fucking *tight.*"

He eased his finger out. Pushed it back in. Dragged his thumb over her clit.

Her legs had stiffened. Her sex seemed to hunger. To

need. Empty and it wanted to be filled. She wanted him inside of her.

His finger sank into her again. "So tight." That wicked thumb didn't stop strumming her clit. "Let's get you to take two." Another finger worked inside of her. Stretching her. Sending surges of pleasure pulsing through her.

Her eyes squeezed shut. Her body was on a razor's edge.

The covers rustled. His left hand yanked down her shorts. Her panties. And then he was between her legs. She didn't see him, Delaney kept her eyes closed, but she could feel him.

"You're wet and you're hot, and you're going to come for me, aren't you?"

Yes, she was. She could feel her orgasm bearing down on her. Closer and closer. All from a touch. Those wicked fingers, working her. Owning her.

"I like touching you with my hands, Delaney. I like feeling your heat. Your softness. Your desire." In and out, his fingers went. And that thumb never stopped as he caressed her clit. "But I like touching you with my mouth, too."

Her eyes flew open at his words. Too late. His mouth was already *on* her. She looked down, seeing the shadowy darkness of his head and hair. Seeing him between her spread thighs even as she felt the warm, wet lick of his tongue against her clit.

There was no stopping. There was no holding back. She was too desperate. Too at the end of her rope and too *hungry* for Nash. She didn't push him away. Her hands grabbed onto him. They sank into the thickness of his hair even as her hips slammed up against him.

He licked and sucked, and he had her twisting and heaving beneath him.

He worked her with his tongue. His fingers.

Those fingers were sliding into her even as he tasted her and kissed her, and the feel of his wicked, skillful tongue on her clit was too much for her.

She climaxed. *Hard.* A sharp cry burst from her lips as the orgasm ripped through her. A heaving, surging release that pounded and pounded through her body. Pulsing and quaking. Firing her veins with pleasure as she struggled to catch her breath.

A release so powerful that she screamed for him. So good that tears leaked from her eyes. So intense that her whole body quivered.

Pleasure. Pleasure with Nash.

Her breath heaved in and out.

Footsteps thundered. *Outside the bedroom.* Footsteps that were coming up the stairs. Footsteps that were flying toward them. Toward their room.

Nash's head whipped up. "Fuck!"

She blinked at him.

He lunged from the bed. Nash paused only long enough to throw the covers over her, and then he rushed for the door. He ripped it open.

She yanked those covers to her chin. Through the open doorway, she had a sudden, fast image of Ryan's frowning face.

Oh. My. God.

"I heard screaming," Ryan began.

She *had* screamed. Oh, no. Delaney yanked the covers over her head as embarrassment swallowed her whole.

* * *

"GO AWAY, RYAN."

"But I heard screaming—oh." Ryan winced.

Nash glared at him. Nash jerked the bedroom door completely closed behind him. No need for Ryan to even peek inside that room.

Ryan tugged at his collar. "I would like to point out that there was an attack here not too long ago."

Nash crossed his arms over his chest.

"So when I heard a scream, I naturally bounded into action. Like the heroic individual that I am."

"Go away, Ryan."

"How the hell was I supposed to know you were—uh. *Shit.*" Ryan spun on his heel. His steps hurried toward the stairs, but then he paused. Glancing back, Ryan asked, "Does this mean you're getting a second chance with her?"

He had no idea what it meant.

I can still taste her. She came apart for me.

"If it's a second chance, don't screw it up."

"Working on that," Nash muttered as he watched his brother vanish down the stairs. He didn't go back in the bedroom, not until he couldn't hear Ryan's footsteps any longer. Then he turned back, opened the door, and slipped inside.

Darkness still reigned in the bedroom. But his eyes had always adjusted easily to the darkness. He made his way to the bed, pausing to ditch his shoes and socks. To toss away his shirt and jeans. Wearing only his boxers, he slid into the bed.

A mound of covers waited to the right. Delaney, bundled up. He stared at the mound. Wondered what to say.

The covers mumbled, "Is he gone?"

"Yeah, sweetheart, he is."

The covers slowly lowered. Delaney turned to peer at him. "I'm not afraid of your touch."

She'd gone molten beneath his hands. Certainly hadn't felt like fear.

"I don't respond the same way to other people that I do to you." A stark confession from her.

Good. I don't want you ever responding like that to anyone but me. "Same," he said. It was true. He'd never wanted anyone the way he wanted her.

Nash could feel her eyes on him. "You should get some sleep," he said. "0600 isn't far away. You need to rest up before we put on the big show."

The covers rustled. He grabbed a sheet. Part of the comforter. Hauled them over his body.

"Nash...you didn't..."

"No, I didn't." His dick was heavy and aching, and he would love nothing more than to drive into her and erupt. To feel her tight heat clenching around him as he pounded his way to paradise.

But this time was going to be different. He was going to be different. This time with Delaney wasn't about a quick fuck. It was about forever.

"Do you want to?" Soft. Husky.

The hell, yes. He pulled in a breath. "I will want you until I die."

"Then...why...?"

Why was he holding back? Clinging to his self-control with bare-knuckled desperation? Excellent question.

"Why did you leave me?" Delaney asked. "If you still want me, if you wanted me then, why did you throw us away?"

Fuck. The million-dollar question. A secret he'd buried. And if he opened his mouth, if he revealed all to her now, it would hurt her more. He didn't want to hurt Delaney any more than she'd already been hurt.

Bullshit. You're just afraid if she hears the full truth, she'll run from you. Open your damn mouth and tell her. Tell her.

The silence had stretched too long. He knew it. Could feel it ticking past as he tried to find the right words. But there were no right words in this situation.

"I will never, ever throw you away," he swore softly. "I plan to stay by your side. I will help apprehend Wellington. I am not going to leave him out there. I will not let him hurt you." A promise that he meant to the depths of his soul. "I..." *Fuck.* "I missed you." Even softer. "I thought about you every single day." The nights had been the worst. How many times had he reached for her, but Delaney had not been there? "I want another chance." There. Done. Said. "I can prove that I won't ever let you down again. I can prove that I am the man you need now." No threats would take him away. He wouldn't be forced from her side again.

But she said nothing.

His heart seemed to squeeze in his chest. "Delaney?" Her breathing had changed. Softer. Steadier. He didn't move at all as he strained to listen to her, and Nash realized that she'd fallen asleep in their bed. He'd waited too long to speak.

He angled his body closer to hers. "I didn't want to leave you." Whispered. "It was like cutting out my own heart. But lives were on the line. People would have gotten hurt. Killed." Back then, he hadn't possessed enough power to fight back. Now, he did. Now, he'd fight like hell and never, ever stop. "I watched you over the years. I had to find you. Just *see* you every now and then. And when I'd see you with another man, it took all of me not to annihilate the bastard." What did that say about him?

That I could never fully let go. That I always thought of Delaney as mine.

He still thought of her that way.

He wanted to reach out and touch her, but Delaney needed her rest. The coming days would not be easy, but he would get her through them. They would stop Wellington.

And Nash would finally marry the woman of his dreams.

Even if the wedding was just pretend.

Chapter Fourteen

JACOB AND LOWELL HAD NOT CHECKED IN. KURT should have gotten a call or a text from those two idiots hours ago, but there had been nothing.

He stared at the rising sun. His men knew better than to leave him hanging.

They all knew that the last thing they ever wanted to do was disappoint him. Disappointments could be fatal. Correction, disappointments *were* fatal.

"What do you want to do with him, boss?" A growling voice broke into his thoughts.

Kurt's gaze slid toward the man still tied in his chair. That blue hair hung in the clerk's eyes. His face was swollen. Lips busted. "You weren't very helpful, Charlie," Kurt told him.

Charlie Murphy. Twenty-two years old. Thief. Drug dealer. No family. No friends who gave a damn about him. It had been so easy to learn everything about the punk. Some people just could not handle pain.

Charlie whimpered. "I told you...told you everything that I knew."

Yes, he actually believed that the younger man had done just that. Unfortunately, Charlie knew shit.

Kurt studied him, frowning. "You understand who I am, don't you?" Charlie hadn't just been a clerk at the hotel. Charlie had been a distributor. His youthful appearance had let him blend with the teens in the area, and Charlie had been passing his drugs off for years.

Charlie was far more industrious than he appeared.

Charlie's head tipped back. His eyes met Kurt's, just for a moment, before his gaze darted away. As if he was too afraid to hold Kurt's stare for long.

Good. Kurt enjoyed invoking fear in others. One of his favorite things to do. Everyone had to enjoy a hobby.

"I-I know," Charlie whispered.

"Right. That's why you sent in the tip about Delaney. You were in the network who knew I was searching for her." The drugs Charlie distributed? They came from Kurt. "You wanted to impress me, didn't you?" He stalked toward Charlie. "I am not impressed."

"Oh, God." A desperate gulp.

Kurt assessed his prey as he began to plan. "You have two choices. Either die right here..."

"*No! Please, no!*" Frantic shakes of Charlie's head. "I will do *anything, just don't kill me! Don't!*"

Ah, fabulous. That was just the kind of positive, enthusiastic talk that Kurt liked to hear. "Or you do exactly what I say. You follow every order I give with no questions."

Charlie's head stopped shaking.

"I know all about the skeletons in your closet, Charlie. With one phone call, I could have you locked away. There are lots of cops who see the value in working with me." A pause. "Or I could just kill you here and now."

"No, No, I can follow orders, I promise! I can!"

Good. "I want my wife back." Not his wife, not yet. But, soon, she would be. "And you are going to help me get her."

Charlie scrunched his face. That young, currently battered-looking face. The guy looked like such a victim.

And Delaney had such a soft, soft heart. He'd originally approached her while she was working for the charity she loved so much in Milan. In truth, he'd found it fucking hilarious that the granddaughter of Carmello Ricci had been intent on *helping* people. Especially when Carmello destroyed lives with a snap of his fingers every single day.

Priceless.

"How am I gonna get her?" Charlie wanted to know.

Kurt smiled at him. "Don't worry. I'm working on the plan. Though, I do have to warn you, you may need to suffer more in order for it to work."

Charlie whimpered again. That pathetic, weak whimper.

"That's the spirit," Kurt praised.

Chapter Fifteen

THE WEDDING MARCH WAS PLAYING AGAIN.

Delaney stood at the end of the aisle, her hands clenched in front of her. This was it. In rapid-fire time, she'd found herself ditching one groom and, now, she was in Vegas. Preparing to walk toward another groom. Preparing to head down the aisle and marry Nash Quinn. Correction, *fake* marry him. Because the marriage wasn't supposed to be real.

So why did it feel so real?

No long, satin dress this time. No veil. No train. No roses that would drop their petals and look like blood as she headed down the aisle. In fact, she had no bouquet at all. She wore jeans and a blue sweater. Sneakers.

As for Nash, he waited at the end of the aisle. Jeans. Battered jacket. Tousled hair. Looking big and bold and sexy. His eyes were on her. Locked hard. Glittering. Waiting.

The music kept playing.

She kept not moving. Way too frozen.

"*Ahem.*"

Her gaze darted to the right.

Ryan widened his eyes. "Is there a reason we haven't taken a single step yet? Just, you know, curious."

*We. A reason we...*Because he was walking her down the aisle. He was also acting as their witness. Signing the paperwork.

And he was currently shoving daisies into her hands.

Blinking, frowning, Delaney peered down at the daisies. "Where did you get these?" He hadn't held the daisies moments ago. She was quite sure of that fact.

"Nash arranged for the delivery. They just arrived. Kid came rushing in with them while you were locked in place and relentlessly rethinking all of your life choices."

The white petals on the daisies looked so soft, while the yellow centers of the flowers were like a burst of happy sunlight.

"Nash ordered them while you were on the plane coming to Vegas. Said you liked them or some shit, so, yeah, you get daisies for the wedding bouquet." He squinted at her. "You are still not moving. What is it?" His eyes widened. "Dammit, are we missing the list? Do you think it's some bad mojo? Is that what's holding you back?"

Ryan had lost her. "What list?" She brought the daisies up to her face. The petals were incredibly soft against her skin. Nash had remembered how much she liked daisies? After all this time? The thought had a pang sliding through her. Her gaze darted back to him.

He waited at the end of the aisle, next to a man in a black suit. The man in the suit had to be the officiant at the Love Heart Chapel. A cute white chapel on the outskirts of Vegas that promised "the wedding of your dreams."

Since her last wedding had been a straight up

nightmare, she was hoping more for the dream version this time.

Nash's intense stare was on her. She could feel the impact of his penetrating gaze throughout her entire body.

"There's always a list that goes with a wedding," Ryan informed her, pulling her attention back to him. "Everyone knows this." Spoken with complete authority. "I'm pretty sure you're supposed to have like...something old and new. Borrowed and blue." He scanned her body. "The sweater is blue. The daisies are new. That's two of our four." He shoved his hand into his pocket and pulled out a silk handkerchief. Because while she and Nash might be in jeans, Ryan was in a suit. Looking stylish and handsome. He wrapped the handkerchief around the base of her bouquet. "There. Something borrowed. Three of four done."

"What is happening right now?" Delaney asked him.

A long suffering sigh. "I'm trying to give you good luck for your marriage. You have to follow the list or I'm pretty sure you're doomed."

"Are you superstitious?" Never, ever would she have thought Ryan followed superstitions.

"I'm minorly stitious."

"What?"

"Not super so, just minorly." Another sigh. Just as long suffering as the first one. "Let's simply say I'd rather err on the side of good luck and not bad. Don't you think you've already had enough bad in your life?"

"More than enough, yes." Her hold tightened on the flowers.

"You still need something old," he muttered. "Can't just have three of four."

Nash began heading toward them. Very determined steps.

The music stopped playing.

Delaney sucked in a sharp breath as she caught the fierce expression on Nash's face. He kept coming forward, only stopping when he was about a foot away from her.

"Change your mind?" he bit out.

"No, dude," Ryan responded before she could. "The woman does not have all the things on the list. Considering the way her last wedding ended, don't you want her to have good mojo?"

Nash cut a quick glance at his brother, only for his stare to immediately return to Delaney. "What is he talking about?"

"He's being stitious. Minorly so. Not super."

The furrow between Nash's brows cut deeper. "Am I supposed to know what that means?"

She was still trying to follow along herself. "Thank you for the daisies," she murmured. "They are my favorite."

"I know." Nash cleared his throat. His head angled toward his brother. "What list are we talking about?"

"Her sweater is blue," Ryan announced. "Her daisies are new. I gave her a handkerchief to borrow, but the woman needs something old or this marriage is just going to be doomed. *Doomed,* I say."

"Heard you the first time," Nash muttered.

"Do you *want* it to be doomed?" Ryan pressed.

It was a fake marriage. Ryan could ease up.

"I want you to be less of a dramatic asshole." Nash shoved his hand into the pocket of his jeans. "I've got something." He inclined his head toward Delaney. "Left hand, please."

She extended her left hand. Her right continued to hold her precious daisies.

Nash slid a gleaming, diamond and pearl ring onto her finger. It was a perfect fit. A truly beautiful ring.

"An engagement ring," he said. "There. Something old. Done."

"Pearls are my birthstone," she managed to say, feeling more than a bit dazed.

"I know."

Her head whipped up. His expression had shut down. Gone so unreadable.

Ryan cleared his throat. "If you just got that from Jez for the cover story, it doesn't count as old. Hate to break it to you, but those are the rules. I don't make them. I just follow them."

Delaney was pretty sure Ryan *was* just making things up as he spoke.

A muscle jerked in Nash's jaw. "I didn't just get it." His Adam's apple clicked. "I've had it for years. Happy, bro?"

"Getting there," Ryan allowed. "Moment by moment. Gotta give this real marriage all the luck it can get."

It wasn't real. But she'd still take any luck that came her way.

Nash remained in front of Delaney. "Are you ready to marry me? Did we check off everything on your list?"

Not everything. Her list was different from Ryan's. Her list mostly contained just one item. Nash hadn't professed undying love to her, and that would be really awesome but...

Fake. Marriage.

But that confession was not going to happen.

"I'm ready," she agreed.

He turned on his heel and strode back down the aisle. The organist resumed playing *The Wedding March.*

Goosebumps rose on Delaney's skin. "I really hate that song," she told Ryan.

"I'm sure Nash would stop the music in a heartbeat, if that's what you want."

There was something about his voice...Her head turned.

Ryan quirked a brow. "How long do you think he had that ring? An engagement ring, with your birthstone? How utterly convenient that it was just in his pocket, am I right?"

Her heart beat faster. "You did the whole thing with the list deliberately." Delaney wet her lips.

"*Moi?* Am I truly that much of a schemer?"

She thought he was.

"I'm just trying to help you have some good luck. Figure you and Nash could use some good mojo this time around."

She wasn't buying his easy words. "You knew that Nash had the ring."

Ryan winked at her.

"You knew, and you wanted me to have it." She took a step forward.

"Well, it was always supposed to be yours, so it makes sense that you should have it. And the guy had it in his pocket, so, clearly, he was going to give it to you today. Don't know why he hadn't already. Hmm. Maybe stage fright."

She stumbled. Ryan caught her arm and balanced her.

From the end of the aisle, Nash frowned.

"What do you mean, it was supposed to be mine?" Delaney had locked onto those words. Hard. *It was always supposed to be yours.*

"I don't like for my brother to hurt. It hurt him when he lost you."

They took two steps together. "He didn't lose me," Delaney denied. "He walked away." That was quite different from losing someone. It wasn't like he'd put her somewhere and forgotten where she was. He had ended things.

Her heart had shattered.

"I think things were far more complicated than you realize." Ryan's voice carried only to her. "I was there when he had to live without you, and it was like he was some ghost. Barely going through the motions. I hated to see him that way. Closed down. Fucking grieving."

She shook her head, an instinctive denial.

"Then he threw himself into the CIA. Took missions that were dangerous and deadly as hell. Scared the shit out of me."

Two more steps.

"And you know I don't get scared. At first, I thought the guy had a death wish. So I had to follow him." Again, his words were low. Just for her.

A few daisy petals fell to the carpet.

"You're holding on too tightly," Ryan chided her. "Be careful with fragile things."

Nash's hands had fisted at his sides as he watched them approach.

"I soon learned Nash wasn't interested in dying. He was interested in fighting. In learning to be the most lethal version of himself possible. He took out targets that other agents thought were impossible to reach. He was relentless. It was like—like he was trying to completely reinvent himself."

More steps. "Why?"

"That is the million-dollar question. It's also a question that you should ask him."

They were almost to Nash.

"While you're asking him that, maybe you should ask him why he had an engagement ring for you, why he never gave it to you, but why he kept the ring all these years. Kept it with him, no matter where the hell he went in this world."

Her head snapped toward Ryan.

"I caught him holding it in Madrid. Saw him staring at it on a beach in Bali. Found him holding it in the middle of a frigid night from hell in Russia. He always had that ring with him. Like he was carrying around a piece of you, wherever he went."

That couldn't be true. Could it? Slowly, her head turned back toward the front.

They were at the end of the aisle.

Ryan took her hand, and he slid it toward Nash. Instantly, Nash's fingers closed around her own. He pulled her closer, and a relieved breath seemed to slide from him.

Her gaze was on his profile. He was staring at the officiant. All of the information that Ryan had just revealed flew through her head. Her heart raced too fast. Adrenaline, fear, and excitement coursed through her veins.

"Does anyone have just cause why these two should not be united?"

At those words, she held her breath. Even found herself jerking around to stare at the closed doors to the Love Heart Chapel.

But the doors didn't come flying open. No one interrupted. And soon the officiant was asking, "Do you take this man to be your husband?"

Her gaze was back on Nash. She knew the whole scene was pretend, but it felt so incredibly real. Too real as she murmured, "Yes."

Nash smiled at her. A smile of such savage satisfaction that alarm bells went off in her head.

"Do you take this woman..."

She didn't even hear the rest of the officiant's words.

"*Yes. Always.*" But she heard Nash's response clearly. He put a ring on her finger. A gleaming, gold ring. And he gave her one to put on his finger, too. She wondered where he'd gotten those.

Surely, he didn't have these two wedding rings for years, too. Surely...

"You may kiss the bride."

It was done. The stage set. They'd be photographed after this ceremony. Word would leak. An announcement would be made. The right people—or, in this case, the wrong ones—would learn about the ceremony. The trap would be sprung.

But in that moment, as Nash's fingers curled under her chin and he tipped her head back, she didn't care about Kurt or any trap. Her lips parted, and when Nash's mouth touched hers, the tenderness of the kiss shocked her.

She'd kissed Nash in many ways over the years. Nervous kisses when she'd been a teen. Desperate, hungry kisses when she'd been older and learned what passion truly meant.

But this...

Gentle.

Almost worshipping.

His lips feathered over hers, and tears stung her eyes. For a moment, Delaney felt like she was truly in a dream. But, no, this was better than a dream. Because he was really kissing her. The weight of the two rings she wore on her left hand was real. He was real.

This time, her wedding had not been a nightmare. Not at all.

Nash swung her into his arms. "I'm not letting you go again," he vowed. Nash began to carry her down the aisle.

Her right arm looped behind his neck. Her left held the

daisies. They'd done it. She and Nash were married. *Pretend* married. He was carrying her toward the chapel's doors.

Ryan beat them to the exit. He swung open one door. Rushed outside. Nash followed. The sun was setting because they'd been in Vegas for most of the afternoon. The CIA had put all of their plans in place. And this was another part of the master plan. They were supposed to be photographed leaving the chapel. A photographer would take shots of her and Nash.

Bam. Bam. Bam.

The blasts caught her unaware. They sounded like fireworks, and for a frantic beat, she found herself looking around in confusion except...

The car racing down the road had a man hanging out the passenger side. A guy with a gun in his hand.

Ryan bellowed, *"Get down!"*

Nash was already spinning with her. Flying with her to the ground and covering her with his body.

Bam. Bam. Bam.

Not fireworks. Those were bullets blasting at them. Delaney was too afraid to scream, and she held onto Nash's shoulders for dear life. She'd dropped the daisies. He was what she grasped. He was what mattered.

And he was covering her with his body as gunfire rained down on them.

Tires squealed as the vehicle raced away.

Nash kept covering her.

"Nash?" A strangled whisper. So many bullets. Terror threatened to choke her as she gasped out, "Nash, are you okay?"

He raised up. Stared down at her with an expression so fierce and dark that her heaving breath froze in her chest.

"Are you okay?" she repeated.

A jerky nod from him. His hands flew over her body, looking for injuries.

"I'm all right. Nash, Nash, *I'm all right.*"

He kept searching her for wounds. His hands touched her arms. Her stomach. Her legs.

"I'm all right, Nash! I promise!" Delaney blinked quickly because fear had her tearing up. She'd married him in one moment and nearly lost him in the next instant. That had not been part of the plan. A photographer should have been there to shoot them. Not someone with a real gun. The CIA had promised they would be safe.

The CIA lied.

"What happened?" A terrified cry from the organist. She stood near the open chapel doors, with the light glinting off her round glasses.

"*Little...help...*" A gasp. From Ryan.

Nash's head jerked to the right. So did Delaney's. Ryan stood a few feet away, with his hand to his left shoulder. As they watched, he shoved out of the suit coat that he wore. He revealed a crisp, white dress shirt. One that was quickly turning dark red all around his shoulder.

"Ryan!" Nash leapt to his feet.

Delaney tried to leap up after him.

"No!" Nash grabbed her. Tossed her over his shoulder. Carried her back to the chapel and shoved her inside. "*Stay in here.*"

"But—"

He pushed her and the organist back. Nash yanked the doors closed, slamming them right in front of Delaney.

"Oh, my dear." The woman's fingers fluttered around Delaney's shoulder. "What happened?"

Every part of her wanted to run outside. She stared at

the wooden doors before her. *Not a dream wedding. Another nightmare.* "I think someone just tried to kill my groom."

* * *

HE CRUSHED the daisies beneath his feet. Nash hauled ass in order to get back to his brother. Ryan had moved toward the side of the chapel, seeking cover, and the blood on his shirt had just gotten darker. Thicker.

"I...returned fire," Ryan grunted. He still gripped his weapon. "It's not as...bad as it looks."

Nash looked for himself. He ripped away Ryan's shirt.

"You should call for backup." Strained words from Ryan. "In case the car comes...back."

"The agents are swarming right now." He'd seen them surging forward. He could hear their footsteps behind him. "No shooter should be here. No one should have gotten to us so soon. *This wasn't part of the plan.*" The bullet had gone in and out of his brother's left shoulder. Nash could see the exit wound when he pulled Ryan forward a bit.

Ryan hissed out a breath. "Someone...you know what it means...someone..."

Nash met his brother's gaze. "Someone at the Agency is working with Wellington. Someone fed him intel. Yeah, I know."

"Yes." Ryan winced when Nash probed his wound. "You can't trust anyone."

He was staring at the only operative he trusted completely, and with this gunshot wound, Ryan was about to be sidelined.

"You looked worried and pissed as hell." Ryan heaved out a hard breath. "An...unfortunate combination."

Sirens were screaming. Had the agents called them? Or concerned bystanders who'd heard the bullets blasting?

"While you are worried about my well-being..."

"Stop talking," Nash ordered Ryan as he applied pressure to the wound.

"I have a confession I have to make. Don't be...angry at an...injured man."

The sirens were screeching louder.

"Don't...be mad," Ryan mumbled.

He pressed *harder* on the wound.

"Remember how...it was supposed to be fake?"

He'd caught sight of two familiar faces behind him. Agents in plain clothes who were coming in fast.

"It's not," Ryan mumbled. "Fuck, that burns like a mother."

"You're gonna be fine." Nothing vital had been hit.

"I know. Been shot before." A wince. "But you are gonna kill me."

A police cruiser screeched to a halt near the sidewalk. The two CIA operatives were less than five feet away.

"Why would I kill you?" Nash's brows climbed.

"It was real," Ryan confessed on a long sigh.

"What was real? The gunfire? Uh, yeah, I get that. You're bleeding all over the place."

Ryan stared back at him, the faint lines near his mouth bracketing.

Oh, hell. "What did you do?" Nash demanded.

"What I...thought you wanted..."

"*Step away!*" A shout from a uniformed cop. Figured that the agents would let the cop take lead. The better not to blow their cover. "Step away from the victim!"

"The victim is my brother!" Nash raised his hands to

show that he wasn't armed. "You're looking for a gun-metal gray Dodge Charger."

"With bullet holes on the back passenger side," Ryan gasped out. He winced. "Don't be mad, Nash. I wanted to help. This is your chance." A rushed mutter.

"What did you do?" But the twist in his gut told Nash the answer. "What was real?" He needed to hear the words.

"You know." Ryan wet his lips. "I...can see it on your face."

"Say the fucking words."

"I...didn't get a substitute officiant for the ceremony. Everything..."

Oh, shit. Oh, damn. Oh, hell.

"Congratulations," his blood-soaked brother told him. "You just married your dream girl."

Chapter Sixteen

Nash scooped Delaney into his arms.

"Wait!" she cried. One arm was behind his head, and her fingers clamped onto his shoulder. "Is this a good idea? The last time you carried me, gunfire erupted."

Nash turned his head to look at her. "We're on a secure floor of the hotel. We're in front of our honeymoon suite." A grim nod. "I'm carrying my *bride* over the threshold because that is how shit is done."

"That's how it's done for real marriages, but there is no one but you and I here to see this. It doesn't matter what we do."

They'd had to stay at the Love Heart Chapel for nearly two hours. The cops had come. There had been questions. So many questions. And they'd had to be incredibly careful with their responses.

Ryan had been taken to the hospital. He'd protested the whole time, but he'd gone. Eventually, Delaney and Nash had been escorted by the police to their hotel.

Now they were on the fifteenth floor. Right in front of the honeymoon suite. All alone. And he did not need to carry her over the threshold. "It doesn't matter," she said again.

His lashes flickered. "It matters to me. Swipe the damn key card."

Her left hand flew out. She swiped the damn keycard.

He yanked open the door with one hand while his other arm held her, and he carried her across the threshold. Didn't act like her weight bothered him at all. Considering all his bulging muscles, it probably didn't. He kicked the door closed.

She expected him to put her down.

He didn't. He went right on holding her. His head turned, and his gaze burned as he stared down at her.

"You can...let me go." Why had her voice gone all husky?

A slow, negative shake of his head.

"I'm sure Ryan will be okay." He'd seemed loud and grumpy as he ordered the EMTs around, so she took that as a positive sign.

"He'll be fine. An in-and-out wound. He'll have restricted range of motion with that arm for a few days, but he'll be back in action in no time."

Good to know. "I'm sorry he was hurt."

"He shouldn't have been fucking hurt." Nash strode forward with her in his arms. "Should have been safe. We *all* should have been safe, but someone sold us out." He'd reached the floor-to-ceiling windows. With his free hand—because he kept holding her with the other—he pressed a button to lower the blinds.

Unease slithered beneath her skin. "You mean someone in the CIA."

His eyes pinned her. "Yes."

"That's not good." A hoarse whisper.

"Sweetheart, it's a fucking nightmare. It means, with Ryan temporarily out of the picture, you can't trust *anyone* but me."

"You could have died on the steps of that chapel." Her unease was getting way worse. More like transforming into full-on fear and panic. "When the bullets started flying, you covered me with your body."

His head tilted to the left. "That's the job."

"No, you dying is not the job. Not in any way. That is nowhere in the job description."

"Sweetheart, I think you're having trouble with the meaning of *bodyguard*."

She twisted in his hold. *Both* of his hands moved to tighten around her. He did not let her go. Breath heaving, Delaney fumed, "I think you're having trouble with the meaning of *don't get hurt for me. Don't risk your life for me. Don't—*"

"My brother was shot. You were sliced with a knife and stuffed in a closet. If you think this isn't personal for me, you're dead wrong."

"Put me down."

He turned away from the window and walked across the suite. He did not put her down. His hold did tighten.

"*Nash.*" Anger hummed in his name.

He took her past the small den area. Into the bedroom. A massive bed waited. One with black, silk sheets that had been turned down. Red rose petals dotted the floor and lead toward the bed. Champagne chilled on a bedside table, while soft, classical music played from a small device beside the champagne flutes.

A room for romance. A perfect suite for a couple in love.

But they weren't in love. They weren't a real couple.

"When you're involved," he bit out, "it's always personal for me." Then he finally put her down. Right in the middle of the bed. Her body slid over the silk sheets. His hands slid over her. Lingered on her, before he jerked them back. His fingers fisted at his sides even as he took a step back. "*You* are personal. You're my wife."

A lock of hair had tumbled over her cheek. She shoved it back. "Pretend wife."

He looked away.

"Where did you get the ring?" Delaney asked as she remembered all that Ryan had told her.

"Jezebel had the wedding bands for us." He yanked his phone from his pocket and tossed it onto the small nightstand. "She sent me the bands."

Jezebel. Someone they may not be able to trust. "I'm not talking about the gold bands. I'm talking about the engagement ring. The one with my pearl birthstone on it."

His stare shot back to her.

"Where did you get it?"

"A jewelry store."

Hardly an enlightening answer. So she'd just ask a different question. "When?"

"You don't want to know. Stop asking these questions."

The hell she would. "If I didn't want to know, I wouldn't ask!" Her legs dangled over the side of the bed. A very high bed. "When did you get the engagement ring?"

He surged forward. His hands slapped down on either side of her. "Eight years ago."

It was a good thing she was sitting on the bed. "Liar."

"The only thing I've ever lied about...*fuck it.* It's not loving you. When I said we were done, when I said I didn't care—*I fucking lied.*"

She felt those words drive straight in her heart.

"I had the ring eight years ago. I wanted to marry you. I wanted to grow old with you. I wanted to live until we were old and gray and be in a freaking rocking chair watching our grandkids play."

Why didn't you? Why. Didn't. You? The words were caught in her throat as pain ravaged her.

"But..." His jaw clenched. He shoved away from the bed. "That wasn't meant to be. You had a life to live. I had to walk away."

She grabbed his arm. "*Why?*"

"You don't want to know."

She jumped to her feet. Their bodies brushed. Anger crackled in the air between them. "If I didn't want to know, I wouldn't have asked! You just put yourself between me and bullets. You kept an engagement ring for eight years. Those are not the actions of a man who does not care." Her hands locked around his powerful upper arms. She wanted to shake him. "Tell me *why*. I deserve to know *why*."

Why he'd wrecked both of their lives.

"You can't take some things back." Gritted. "Once a deed is done, there is no going back. Let the past go, Delaney. *Please*."

No. The past was still ripping her apart. "I want to know what happened."

He looked down. "I still have my brother's blood on me. I need to wash it away." He pulled back. Put several steps between them.

He was heading for the shower. She surged forward, dodged around him, and physically put herself in the bathroom doorway. "Don't you dare take another step until you tell me what happened eight years ago."

He froze in front of her. Torment flashed on his face,

only to be quickly masked. He was so good at doing that. Masking his emotions.

"Something happened. Something that made you leave me. That made you destroy us."

His hand lifted. Pressed to her cheek. "Let it go, baby."

"No." She'd let them go years before. She hadn't fought for him. She'd run away, and she'd wrapped herself up in pain.

His forehead lowered and pressed to hers. "Just let me be a villain in your backstory. That's what I've been for years, isn't it? Let me stay that way."

Yes, dammit. No, no...

You were the man who made me happy. Then the man who broke my heart. Hero and villain all at the same time.

"I had a choice to make." His voice was rougher, deeper, than it had ever been before. "I chose to walk away from you. I am the villain. See that shit."

No, she would not. "I'm pretty sure the villain would be the man who locked me in a closet and shoved a knife in my side."

"*I'm going to kill him.* I am one hundred percent certain of that fact. My very willingness to kill should tell you that I am dangerous to you."

"Not to me. To other people, to the bad guys? Yes. But not to me." A sharp inhale. "What do you think will happen if you tell me the truth? That I'll forgive you for the past?" His touch was sending her system into overdrive. "Or that I won't?"

"Can't we just screw the past? Forget it and go forward?"

Is that what they were doing? Going forward? "You kept the engagement ring for eight years."

His head lifted. "Yes."

"You took it with you, wherever you went." Had Ryan been right about that?

"Yes."

"*Why?*"

His breath heaved out. "I have to wash my brother's blood off me."

Her shoulders sagged. He was not going to tell her. "There are no secrets that I kept from you. I told you everything about my life." She moved out of the way. Headed for the bed even as she wrapped her arms around her waist.

"You *are* my life." His words stopped her. "And I'll be the bad guy a million times over if it means that you get to keep living and that you're safe. I will sacrifice my own happiness again and again because that is *nothing* compared to the fucking darkness I'd feel if I didn't know that you were alive somewhere in this world."

What? She whipped around.

Too late.

The bathroom door clicked shut.

* * *

DAMMIT.

Nash stripped. He tossed his bloodstained clothes into the trash. Yanked on the hot water in the shower and heard the thunder as the stream poured into the massive tub.

He glared at his reflection in the mirror. He hated keeping secrets from Delaney. He wanted to be able to tell her everything but...

I am still trying to protect her.

Even from himself.

He stepped into the water. It was on full blast, and the

surge hit him hard. Steam began to rise around him, drifting tendrils in the air.

The thunderous shower drowned out everything around him, so he didn't hear the bathroom door open. But he was staring straight through the fogging glass of the shower door, and he saw Delaney when she crept toward him. He watched the blurry outline of her body as she stripped. And then as she reached for the shower door. She opened it, sending more of the steam pulsing out and stretching toward her.

His gaze drank her in. His beautiful, heartbreaking Delaney. Those high, curving breasts. The tight nipples that he longed to feel against his tongue. Her curving waist. Her flaring hips. The bare sex that he needed against his mouth.

His dick surged toward her. Hard and eager. He wanted in her. He wanted Delaney. He wanted *his wife*.

"You got to touch me last night," Delaney told him, her sexy voice stroking along every inch of his body. "I think I should get to touch you."

He started to back up. "Bad idea."

"Because you're a bad man?" She entered the shower. The space felt even tighter. "You told me that already. Guess what? I don't buy it." She reached out and turned down the steaming water. Softened and cooled the flow.

Then she lowered to her knees in front of him.

Very bad idea. "Why are you doing this?" Did she want him to be completely insane?

Her fingers curled around his dick, pumped from base to head, and a shudder worked along the entire length of his body.

"Aren't you tired of *why?*" Delaney asked.

She'd wanted to know *why*. He'd been so afraid to tell her. To hurt her.

Some truths could shatter a person. He did not want her shattered. Not ever.

"I'm tired of why," Delaney said. "Screw why."

The water hit his back. Steam drifted around them.

"I'm tired of hurting." Her hand pumped his dick. A long, slow stroke. "How about we both just feel good for a little while? Where is the sin in that? What is so *bad* about that?" Then her mouth closed over the head of his eager dick.

One of his hands flew out and slammed into the tiled wall of the shower. The other hit the glass of the door. His breath shuddered in and out.

She teased him. Took in just the broad head of his cock. Her tongue snaked over him. Then she pulled him in a little deeper. Opened her mouth a little wider. He stared down at her, completely lost, because it was Delaney. *His* Delaney. Taking his dick into her mouth. Sucking him. Licking. One delicate hand still curled around the base of his cock as she guided him to her. Pulling him in. Driving him insane.

It wasn't like his control had ever been the greatest where she was concerned. Did he get points for *trying*? He'd tried to do the right thing. Maybe not been sweet and gentle or soothing but...

Fuck, fuck, fuck. My dick is in her mouth.

All rational thought fled after that.

He grabbed her and lifted her up. "*Delaney.*" A primitive snarl.

She tossed back her hair. Her eyes were dark, the hazel shifting deeper. "I wasn't done."

"I'm not done, either." He would *never* be done with her. His mouth crashed onto hers as the water poured down. His tongue thrust into her mouth even as his hand covered one breast. She moaned into his mouth, and he teased her nipple, squeezing it between his fingertips.

Not enough.

His mouth tore from hers. He kissed a path down her throat, lifting her higher, holding her easily.

"Nash!"

His mouth closed over the breast he'd touched. He licked her taut nipple. Sucked. Her nails bit into his shoulders.

She pushed against him. "More!"

His same thought. Because this was *not enough*.

His mouth went to her other breast. His tongue lashed her. Her legs curled around his hips. His dick shoved against her as he angled his body and pinned her against the tiled wall.

Then...

Into her. The head of his dick shoved into her. Tight. Hot. Everything that he'd needed. Everything he'd missed.

She gasped out his name.

He pushed deeper. Because it was *not enough*. Her inner muscles flexed against him, tight, so tight, and he wedged a hand between them so he could stroke her clit and get her to open up for him. She'd always needed care when his cock drove into her because Delaney was so small and he was definitely fucking not.

Nash froze. He blinked at her as the water trickled down his face. His dick was in Delaney. Not balls deep, not yet, but that was where he wanted to be. All the way in her.

"Don't stop." Her wet hair clung to her shoulders. "I need you."

He'd needed her his entire life. "I'm bare, Delaney." Hard, savage words. Words that should have been a warning.

Instead, he said them, and he pushed deeper into her core. *Heaven. Hell. Pleasure and torture.* Pleasure because she felt so good. Because this was his Delaney. Torture because he had to stop. He couldn't do this. He didn't have on a condom.

"I'm on birth control. I...I wasn't lying when I said that I didn't have sex with Kurt. I haven't been with anyone in over two years."

What the fuck?

"I want *you.*"

His teeth snapped together. "I haven't been with anyone in two fucking years, either."

Her eyes widened.

"Don't like fucking anyone else." The words were ripped from him. He was not going to be able to hold back. Could not. "*They aren't you.*"

Then he was strumming her clit and driving hard and deep into her. Delaney let out a gasp, and a moan, and then her hips slammed against his.

The water pounded.

The steam drifted.

Their bodies collided.

Over and over. There was no slowing down. There was no restraint. A beast had been unleashed inside of him, and Nash was relentless. He could not get close enough to her. Could not get deep enough.

Her body was soft and sensual. Her sex tight and hot. She grasped him greedily, possessively, and he felt the clenching of her body even as she gave a fast, sudden cry.

He watched the pleasure sweep over her face. He kissed her because he wanted to taste her pleasure. Nash wanted to taste every single bit of her. His thrusts became even harder. Faster. *Delaney.* He was with his Delaney again.

Fucking her.

Taking her.

Loving her.

Once would not be enough. It would never be enough to satisfy him.

The climax hit him. He held her too tightly. Kissed her too hard. And came inside of her on a relentless surge of the best pleasure he'd felt...

Since the last time he'd fucked her.

* * *

Kurt drove by the Love Heart Chapel. Yellow police tape fluttered near the front doors. He hadn't arrived in Vegas in time to stop the wedding.

The fucking wedding.

But he'd given orders for the groom to be taken out. If you died right after the wedding, did it matter that you'd said the vows?

Only the groom hadn't died. He had lived to escape and to, no doubt, fuck Delaney.

The limo cruised slowly past the chapel. The shooter hadn't been caught yet. He would not be caught. At least not by the cops. Kurt had given orders for the bastard to be eliminated right after the screwup on the drive-by.

Simple instructions should be followed, after all. Kurt had ordered for the groom to be murdered.

You fucked up my wedding. I'll fuck up yours.

His orders had not been carried out properly. Failure wasn't tolerated. If you tolerated failure, then you looked too weak.

Kurt was not weak.

And, unfortunately, the man he now knew to be Nash Quinn was not dead.

But the shooter who didn't get the job done is.

"Take me to my casino," he ordered his driver. The privacy window was down so he could easily address his driver, Vino.

"Which one, sir?"

"The one in the building right next to my fucking bride." Except, she wasn't his bride, was she? Because she'd married Nash Quinn. "Bliss," he gritted. "The Bliss Casino."

Nash Quinn. He'd gotten intel on the man. Nash had a history with Delaney. The two had been hot and heavy years ago, only for the relationship to crash and burn. Nash should have stayed the hell away from Delaney after that moment. Had he?

No. The fucker had come running to take her away from Kurt. *On our wedding day.* Nash had spirited Delaney away, and when he'd taken her, he'd taken the entire inheritance that came along with her.

"Sir." Vino cleared his throat. "Sir, I'd like to say again that I think this is a bad idea."

"Don't remember asking for your opinion."

"Sir, we have intel that he's CIA. You *know* this."

Yeah, he fucking did. Because he had power and connections and knew people who would sell out their own mothers for the right payday. So when he'd started digging and trying to figure out who the hell the mystery man was who'd taken Delaney away, he'd reached out to his contacts with the Feds. And with the CIA. He'd had a few photos of the guy, shots of the bastard hauling Delaney over his shoulder as he'd run from the church with her in North Carolina. He'd gotten his contacts to run the photos through facial recognition and with Kurt's CIA contact, he'd hit pay dirt. *He called to tell me that Nash was a red flag. To tread carefully. And with that warning, I knew what was happening. I knew.*

Delaney's ex was a spook. A spook in love with Kurt's bride.

With the right pressure, Kurt had been able to find out exactly where Nash Quinn had traveled. Nash and Delaney had boarded a public flight in Nashville, Tennessee, and they'd flown to Vegas.

Where Nash had scheduled a wedding. With my Delaney.

"It's a trap, sir," Vino told him. "He's CIA. He married her deliberately, no doubt to bait you. You need to step away. Forget her. She's not worth all that you could lose."

"Pull over, would you?" Kurt asked him. Vino had been with him for years. Three years, to be exact. Vino wasn't just a driver. He was a bodyguard when the need arose. Also, a fixer.

Vino had been in the church on the day of Kurt's wedding. He'd been the one to pull out his gun, only to have it ripped from his fingers by Nash Quinn.

Vino drove off the road. The limo eased into the parking lot of a strip mall. The windows in the vehicle were tinted, giving them perfect privacy.

"Sir, you're making the right decision by stopping this pursuit—" Vino's words ended in a choked gasp. Maybe a gurgle.

Because Kurt had just leaned forward, and he'd driven his knife into Vino's throat. "This is your fault," Kurt whispered. "If you'd just *shot* the asshole when you had the opportunity, I'd still have Delaney. I'd have *everything* I needed by now." He yanked the knife to the left.

Another gurgle.

"You think I don't get that this is a setup? I have fucking intel that lets me know exactly what sort of man I'm up against. I don't need your fool ass giving *me* advice."

Vino's hands had lifted. They were shaking. Curled like claws.

Kurt yanked the knife to the left. "You don't walk away when another man steals your bride. That shit makes you look *weak*. Understand this, there is no world in which I don't go after Nash Quinn and kill him."

Vino's hands never touched his neck.

"I will never, ever be weak." He left the knife in Vino's neck. Kurt pulled his hands back into the rear of the limo. Nodded. Kurt straightened his tie, and he climbed from the vehicle.

His head tilted back as he stared up at the sky. It was too bright here to see the stars clearly. Vegas was always too bright for you to see the stars when you were in the city. But you go outside the city, you travel just far enough, and it was like a whole new world.

He knew, because he'd often traveled out of the city. It was easier to hide bodies out there.

Kurt put his phone to his ear. "Gonna need a new ride." Or, at the very least, a new driver. Then he'd be going to collect his wife.

And kill CIA operative Nash Quinn.

Not like it was the first time he'd killed a spook. Not the first, not the last. But it did take more skill to eliminate someone with Nash's training. Skill and the right distraction.

Luckily, he had the perfect distraction.

And her name was Delaney.

Chapter Seventeen

The water thundered down on them. Delaney's legs were still wrapped around Nash's waist. Her hands clung to his shoulders even as her nails bit into his skin.

She should probably move.

She *would* move, as soon as the aftershocks of pleasure stopped careening through her body. Until then, her sex squeezed around him. Around his very much hardening cock. Because his cock was getting bigger, already. *Again.*

Her eyes opened. She stared up at Nash. His face appeared brutally handsome as he gazed back at her. Blazing eyes. Locked jaw. Sharp cheekbones.

"I need you again," he told her. "Can you handle me?"

Deliberately, she squeezed him once more, holding him fiercely with her inner muscles.

"Fuck," he breathed.

Yes, wasn't that what they were doing? Fucking in the shower? As the water poured around them and steam settled into the air?

He pulled his dick back. Not out completely. Leaving

the head inside of her. The broad, thick head, and then he drove back inside.

She sucked in a breath.

He kept watching her.

He pulled his dick back. Again, just leaving that broad head inside of her. She was so sensitive, her body on edge, and when he drove deep inside of her again...

A moan tore from her. Her nails sank into the muscles of his arms.

His eyes never left her face. He watched her as if memorizing every feature.

His cock withdrew. Pushed deep.

Back. In.

Her hips arched toward him. She gripped him as fiercely as she could. He'd been fast and frantic before. She'd been the same way. As if the lust had taken over and the only thing that mattered had been feeling the maelstrom of their release. But this time...

He withdrew.

Eyes on her, he thrust deep.

This time, it was slow. Deliberate. She didn't speak. He didn't, either. Too intense for words. Need pulsed in the air, but it was different. Silent but savage. Just as consuming as before, but still, different.

A slow withdrawal of his dick.

Then that thick, hard thrust.

Her thighs trembled around him. Her entire body trembled. She was so close to coming again. So close, and he was going to watch her. Going to see every single moment.

One of his hands still wedged between their bodies. His fingers raked over her clit.

Her head tipped back against the wall. Her eyes began to drift closed as the climax reached out to take her.

"I need to see, Delaney." Growled. "I need to see every moment of your pleasure. *Look at me.*"

She did. The orgasm hit her even as her eyes locked with his. She couldn't breathe. Couldn't speak. Could only feel as the release seemed to ravage every cell in her body. Pleasure didn't pulse. It consumed. It claimed. It *owned*.

"So fucking beautiful," he rasped. He'd gone still as she climaxed. That hard dick was lodged fully inside of her, and he had to feel her squeezing him. Greedy. Hungry. Squeezing and taking and taking.

"Fuck." A muscle jerked along his jaw.

He poured inside of her. Locked together, her eyes on him, she watched the pleasure sweep over him. The release had her holding him ever tighter, and the way his eyes seemed to go blind, the way his features sharpened even more...

Yes, fucking beautiful.

The water pounded down on them.

* * *

"Guess if the ceremony had been real, we would have just consummated the marriage, huh?" Delaney had no idea why she said those words. Maybe to break the heavy silence that had followed the amazing sex in the shower.

He'd carried her from the shower, dried her off, and carefully checked her wound. He'd assured her that she was healing well, and he'd put a fresh bandage on her cut. Then...

Silence.

She wore a white, fluffy robe. Nash had jerked on a pair of jeans. They were in the bedroom, the windows were covered, the classical music kept playing, and it should have been an incredibly romantic scene, but something was just off now. That *off* made her worry.

"Fuck," Nash said.

He said that a lot.

She peered at him and saw that he'd just squeezed his eyes closed. Delaney frowned. "Is something wrong?" She knew it was.

A jerky nod.

"You...you regret what we did?" Her fingers pressed to her heart. Catching the movement, she immediately dropped her hand.

His eyes opened. His face was still way too hard. A fierce mask. "I will never regret fucking you. That is just not humanly possible for me to do."

"That's good to know." She wet her lips. "I, um, certainly don't regret being with you, either. You're the best lover I've ever had."

He stalked toward her.

Her stomach did a little flip. Her thighs were still trembling. She wondered if he was coming across the room to grab her, to passionately sweep her into his arms. Maybe he'd toss her onto the bed, and they'd slam their bodies together again in a wild frenzy of lust. Maybe that would happen.

Or maybe not.

His hands slapped against the wall behind her. "I don't *like* to think of you fucking anyone else."

Not like she loved the thought of him with anyone else, either. "I wasn't in cold storage after our breakup." An important point. "*You* chose the breakup." She'd just tried to learn how to live without him. Tried so hard that she'd been forcing herself to marry a man she didn't even love. A man who wanted her dead. So, obviously, that had worked out well.

Nash's eyes narrowed. "You are the only person I ever want."

"Look, don't pretend that you weren't with other people in the last *eight* years!" Because she would not buy that story.

"When I closed my eyes, they were all you."

She did not have a comeback for those words.

"But when I opened them, they weren't. You weren't there, and I was fucking disappointed every time. Disappointed, and I hated myself because they weren't *you.*"

Enough of this. Enough, enough, enough! "*Why did you do this to us?*"

"I thought you were over the why questions."

She had been. She was. She... "Damn you." Real anger. Anger that had been inside of her for a long time. "Are you just playing a game with me?"

"*Never.*" His nostrils flared as he kept caging her between him and the wall.

"Then don't lie to me. Don't ever lie to me again." She hated lies. "Kurt was nothing but a liar. I don't want to be kept in the dark about anything. You have a secret? Tell me. Share it with me. No holding back. No worrying about hurting me. Just *tell me.* I can handle anything that you throw at me." She wasn't some delicate flower that would get battered by too much rain. Couldn't he see that?

He leaned in closer.

She thought he was going to kiss her.

"We're married," Nash said.

Her breath huffed out. "I know, Nash. I was there for

the ceremony, remember?" She put her hands on his chest. His bare chest.

Such a bad idea because sensual awareness immediately surged through her body. Delaney's gaze dropped to his chest, and she frowned because there were so many marks on his skin. On him.

In the heat of the moment, in the steamy shower, she'd been focused on pleasure. Hers. His. And she hadn't stopped to notice the changes that had occurred to his body in the years that they'd been apart. "Oh, no." Sadness. Horror. Her hands began to fly over him. "You have so many scars." Her fingers slid over a slash on his stomach. A rough ridge on his side. A trio of cuts across his abdomen. "*Nash.*"

His hands caught hers.

Her head lifted. She blinked away tears. "How did this all happen? You were supposed to be a doctor. What changed?"

"I changed." Deep. Dark.

"Nash—"

The ringing of a phone cut through her words. A shrill, fast cry. She jerked at the sound.

He pulled in a deep breath, and he stepped back. One step, then another. He grabbed for the phone that was on the nightstand, and she had zero recollection of him putting that phone on the nightstand. When had he even done that?

"Have to take the call. Could be about Ryan. Could be about the mission." His finger swiped over the screen. He pressed down with his thumb to put the call on speaker. "Hello?"

"You're supposed to be attracting attention." Jezebel's voice.

Nash's gaze never left Delaney's face. "Figured we had

his attention, seeing as how Ryan took a bullet not too long ago."

A quick inhale. "You blame me for that, don't you?"

"Someone in the CIA leaked the location of the chapel. Or maybe someone deliberately fed that intel to Kurt in order to *attract attention*. Tell me, Jez, will it be easier to convict Wellington if he's tied to the murder of two agents? Me and Ryan?"

"I didn't do that." Sharp. "I did not give up your location at the chapel. I would not put you straight in the crosshairs. Yes, yes, dammit, I believe there is a leak. Which is another reason why I want Wellington stopped. But I am not selling you out. I'm doing my best to protect you—you and Delaney. That's why I've called in new backup."

His brow furrowed. "Just who is this backup?"

Delaney's hands twisted in front of her.

"A Fed you know. Grayson Stone. Seeing as how he's tight with your brother, I thought he'd be good to step in since Ryan has been temporarily sidelined."

Grayson Stone. The name meant nothing to Delaney, but she saw Nash's shoulders relax so she took that as an extremely good sign.

But Nash said, "You're territorial, Jez. Why are you just inviting a Fed to step into your case?"

"Because I'm not sure who I can trust in my own ranks," she retorted, voice lowering. "And I need to know that you have someone *good* at your back."

Okay, so, this Grayson Stone was someone good. Someone Nash trusted. Two points for him.

"He'll stay in the shadows," Jezebel assured Nash. "You won't see him, but just know he's there in a pinch."

"Does Gray understand that Delaney's safety is priority?"

"He understands that Kurt Wellington has to be taken down. That we are gathering enough evidence to put Wellington away forever."

With those words from Jezebel, Nash's shoulders were back to being just as tense. "He needs to understand that Delaney's safety *is* priority." His stare burned into Delaney's. "Make that clear, Jez. She. Is. Priority."

"I don't believe you are supposed to be giving me orders," Jezebel murmured.

Delaney took a hesitant step toward Nash.

"I can make her vanish," he said, never taking his eyes off Delaney.

Her heart raced.

"I can take Delaney, and I can make her disappear in less than ten minutes." His stare pierced straight to Delaney's soul as he promised Jezebel, "You won't find her. The CIA won't find her. You can be left to deal with Wellington on your own."

"You're bluffing," Jezebel charged.

"No. I'll do it. I will take her far away from here if I think that you are risking her life for this case." With every word, his penetrating stare didn't leave Delaney. He didn't so much as blink.

Delaney believed what he was saying. And she thought that Jezebel did, too.

Jezebel cleared her throat. "Ahem. Fine. Fine. I'll make sure Grayson understands that, should anything happen to you, Delaney is to be protected."

"Nothing should happen to Nash," Delaney blurted. "That's part of the deal, too."

"Or what?" Jezebel threw at her. "You'll make him vanish?" Doubt layered the words.

"I'd vanish with her in a heartbeat if that was what Delaney wanted," Nash stated, voice flat.

Her own heartbeat sped to a double-time rate. *He means it.*

"Let's all take some deep breaths, shall we?" Jezebel's tone had turned soothing. "You're both going to be just fine. You'll survive this mission, and the bad guy will be locked away."

"Nash needs to be protected, too." Delaney was adamant.

"That's why I have Grayson rushing in. To make sure *everyone* involved will be protected." A brief pause. "Don't worry so much about Nash," Jezebel assured her. "I'm starting to think he can survive practically anything." A sigh. "Now get your asses out of that honeymoon suite." No longer soothing. More like a barked order. "I need evidence. I need Wellington brought into the open, and I need that done *now*."

But Nash didn't move. "Pretty sure honeymooners are supposed to want to stay behind closed doors and fuck like crazy."

Delaney blushed. An automatic reaction to *fuck like crazy.* They, um, had been. In the shower. She could feel the heat staining her cheeks.

"This is not a real honeymoon," Jezebel snapped back. "But her ex is a real killer so...*get the hell out there. Get him focused on you.*" Jezebel hung up.

Nash tossed the phone onto the bed. "Judging from the gunshots earlier, I thought he was focused on me."

She rocked onto the balls of her bare feet. "Who is Grayson Stone?"

"Gray." Nash rolled back his shoulders. He also turned and headed for the bag that waited at the foot of the bed.

His luggage. Delivered while they'd been at the chapel so the suite would be ready and waiting for them. "Gray Stone is a very powerful figure at the FBI. He was Agnes's boss, and Gray also is close with Ryan. They served together in the Marines. *Semper Fi*."

"You trust him?"

He shouldered into a white dress shirt. "I do. Gray has gone to the mat for me and my family before. He's a good man. And he's not afraid to get his hands very, very dirty."

That was reassuring. Mostly. A wee bit scary, too.

If Nash was getting dressed, then she needed to ditch her robe, too. Time to paste on a smile and go catch a killer. That was the goal, after all. Not to fall in love with Nash again. Not to have wild passionate sex with him.

The goal is to catch a sadistic killer.

Her knees almost buckled at the thought.

And at the whispering thought of...

I am falling for Nash, all over again.

Or perhaps she'd just never stopped loving him.

* * *

SHE WAS sexy as hell in the red dress and the strappy, two-inch sandals. The elevator was too small. She smelled too good. And he wanted to fuck her into oblivion again.

Instead, they were off to catch the attention of a killer. Even though Nash was pretty sure they already had the man's attention. *He sent a shooter to the chapel. If that wasn't catching his attention, then what the hell is?*

Her eyes were on the floor numbers as they appeared on the small screen above the elevator doors. She'd swept her hair back into some sexy twist, painted her lips red, and sprayed on the perfume that held the heady scent of jasmine.

And he was about to take her out and wave her around like a red flag in front of a bull.

You picked the dress deliberately, didn't you, Jez? Because the CIA had been the ones to prepare their luggage. To have everything delivered. Delaney was literally a walking red flag, and Nash hated this shit.

His hand flew out, and he stopped the elevator.

"Nash!" Horror. Some shock. "What did you just do?"

He took a step toward her. "The CIA is monitoring the elevator. Agents have eyes on us through the security system right now." Which meant some operative was watching everything that minute. And as much as Nash might want to grab Delaney, lift her up against the elevator wall, and fuck her in that sexy red dress...

Not gonna happen.

Her gaze cut to the small security camera on the control panel, then her eyes darted to him. "Why did you stop us?"

"Because...I've got you."

A little furrow appeared between her eyebrows. "Excuse me?"

"I know you don't trust me completely, not after the way things ended with us before. But I have you." He nodded. "I will take a bullet for you. I will fight any threat. I will kill if it means keeping you safe."

The furrow deepened. "You're wrong."

Nash shook his head. "I'd do it in a heartbeat. You need to know that. Whatever is coming, whatever happens, I will be there for you. One hundred percent."

"No, I meant—look, I trust you completely. If I didn't, I wouldn't have fucked you."

He blinked.

She pursed her lips. "Any other big, important disclosures that you'd like to make to me? While our elevator appears to be stopped between floors?"

Nash swallowed. "We're married."

She rolled her eyes. "Nash, we are fake married. We have been over this."

He shook his head. "Delaney—"

"*Sir, is there a problem with the elevator?*" A disembodied voice drifted through the speaker, cutting across the jazz music that had been playing.

Shit. "No problem."

"Then the elevator should restart," the voice told him. "Prepare for it to restart within the next ten seconds."

Delaney watched Nash with wide eyes.

His hand slid under her chin. "We are married," he said again.

"I know the cover story. I won't forget it."

The elevator began to descend again. Her lips were right there, and his time with her was running out. Nash knew it. Dammit, he didn't want their time to end.

He wanted for Delaney to choose him. To stay with him. To love him. "I'm sorry," he said. Words that he should have said a very, very long time ago.

Her long lashes fluttered. "For what?"

"For hurting you. Hurting you is the biggest regret that I have in my life. If I could take away every bit of pain that you've ever felt, I'd do it." He needed her to understand this. "I am sorry."

The elevator dinged. The doors began to open. He edged back.

She grabbed his shirt and hauled him toward her. Her lips pressed to his. A hot, passionate kiss. Her tongue dipped inside his mouth. His hands closed around her hips. He dragged her closer.

"*Ahem.*"

Dammit. Dammit to hell and back.

Nash raised his head and glared over his shoulder.

A frowning man with a goatee stared back at him. "People need this elevator," the man huffed. His white hair was swept back from his high forehead, and his right hand gripped a cane.

"Oh, Lawrence, stop!" The woman beside him sent Nash a merry smile. "Have you forgotten what it's like to be in love?" She wrapped her hand around *Lawrence's* arm. "Once upon a time, you couldn't keep your hands off me!"

Lawrence huffed again.

Nash bobbed his head toward the couple. "We're newlyweds. And you're right, I just can't keep my hands off my wife." His hands curled around her waist right then as he escorted Delaney from the elevator.

He was surprised to see that red flashed on Delaney's cheeks.

They hurried from the elevator and walked into the lobby. Their hotel fed directly into the attached casino, so it was only a short walk until the sound of slot machines filled the air. Voices rose and fell. Some with excitement. Some with dismay. Waitresses bustled around, handing out drinks like candy. In a place like this, the customers always gambled a bit more when the drinks flowed freely. Tipsy customers made for better business.

"All right, sweetheart." He kept her tucked against his side, and Nash bent so that his words whispered into her ear. "It's showtime. So stay focused. We're going to take a stroll through the casino, see and be seen, and then we'll venture to our next stop."

She stiffened. "Agents are watching us?"

"Lawrence and his wife Frannie *are* agents." Agents in careful disguise.

Her head whipped toward him. She nearly clocked him in the chin. "What? That couple waiting for the elevator?"

"Welcome to the spy world. What you see is not always what you get." Not even close. "Time to let the games begin."

Chapter Eighteen

"OKAY." A DETERMINED NOD FROM DELANEY. "Noted."

She was handling the whole situation surprisingly well. No way could he not admire her. But, then again, he'd always admired Delaney. Mostly, he'd wished that he could be as kind as her. Her heart had been so big when she'd been a kid, and it had just stayed wide open and generous when she'd become an adult.

Back when she'd been a teen, Delaney had been the one to organize the group who volunteered at the local food pantry. Delaney had been the one to get other high schoolers to spend Saturdays walking dogs at the animal shelter. Delaney had been the one in charge of coat drives, shoe drives...hell, had there been a drive she hadn't been involved with?

And he knew plenty about the work she'd been doing in Milan. Yeah, fine, he liked to keep tabs on her. Sue him. She'd gone to design school, and from all accounts, Delaney was a fabulous costume designer, but in her free time, she worked with local kids in their theater productions. She designed all the costumes for them, and he knew she did it for free.

Now that she had her grandfather's fortune, he didn't think Delaney was about to become some spoiled, pampered princess. That just wasn't her. In fact...

He brought her hand to his lips as they began to walk through the casino. His gaze swept the scene, taking in every threat. His body was alert and ready to attack at any moment. "What are you going to do?" Nash asked her.

Her body drifted toward the right. He, of course, drifted with her.

"Do?" Delaney repeated. Her eyes were on a massive slot machine. One that had to be over fifteen feet tall and had a handle that was easily the size of Delaney's head.

"With your grandfather's money. The houses. The fortune."

Her head turned toward him, and her cute nose scrunched. "Pretty sure that's all ill-gotten gains."

His lips twitched at "ill-gotten gains" because no one in the world but Delaney would actually use that phrase.

Her gaze darted back to the massive slot machine, then returned to him. "I figure at this point, the CIA will probably seize everything, won't they?"

Probably. Yes.

"I'll just go back to living my life the way I did before I met my grandfather."

He tensed. *I was there before. Will you go back to me?* "But what if you did get to keep it all? What would you do?"

"I'd set up some charities. Actually, I'd love to do this sort of innovation tank program." Her eyes lit up. Brighter. Golden. "I read about this online. You find these great people with ideas but no backing. People who just need a little help. If I had that money, I could help." Easy words.

I could help.

Words he'd heard before.

When he'd been a dumbass high school teen. Older than Delaney. And his damn truck had broken down. Delaney had casually strolled up and paused by his ride. She'd frowned at the steam coming from beneath the hood. *I could help.* Her words. *If you want.*

He'd started to dismiss her, his pride hurt because his little sister's gorgeous friend was offering to help him. But Delaney's dad had owned the best garage in town, and she could, in fact, help. She could. She had. She'd changed his whole world that day.

Delaney had loved her dad so freaking much. She used to spend hours and hours with him in that garage. And...*she doesn't know that her grandfather had him killed.*

Nash swallowed.

"What's the plan?" Delaney leaned toward him. "I know you have a whole master plan, and I think I should be clued in on it, don't you agree?"

"The plan is to see and be seen. To attract attention." She'd be attracting plenty of attention in that killer red dress.

"How?" Delaney asked. She glanced around the casino. "Everyone is playing. No one is looking twice at us."

So wrong. The men were doing double takes at Delaney. Annoying. He glared at one guy who hurriedly glanced back down at the cards in front of him. The joker needed to be playing blackjack and not staring at Delaney's legs.

"How?" Delaney repeated. She was back to staring at the massive slot machine. The pale, white lights at the top flashed and rolled, and chiming music spilled from the machine every few moments.

"We'll play at the tables. Win big or lose big, but the result will be the same. One of Kurt's casinos is right next door to this place."

Her head whipped toward him. "Right next door?" A squeak.

"Yeah, so I'm betting someone here…" Probably a few someones. "Someone will have ties to Kurt. A plant that he has in place to watch the competition. Those eyes will find you. Me. And we'll go from there." *Once we are spotted, that intel will be reported to Kurt right away.*

"Okay." Her shoulders squared. "Okay."

Again, she was handling the whole situation surprisingly well. "Maybe you're in the wrong business." He wanted to see her smile. "Forget costume design. You could have a career in the spy world."

No smile flashed. "I don't think so. I hate lies."

Fuck.

"How did you know I have a career in costume design?"

Nash swallowed. "You always loved design. Figured you stayed with it."

Her stare was breaking his heart. No, breaking *him.* She'd just said she hated lies. So, screw it. He'd give her the truth. "I found you," Nash admitted.

"I don't follow."

"I would check on you. Seek you out. Make sure you were safe."

"You…stalked me?"

"Stalk is such a negative word. Can't we say I *looked out* for you?"

Her mouth was wide open. Gently, he slid his finger

beneath her chin and pressed up. "I wanted you to be safe. I didn't interfere."

Her hand rose to curl around his wrist. "You know I'm a costume designer because you've been watching me."

Yes.

"Why didn't you ever approach me?"

"Because I thought you hated me." Partial truth. "Because it wasn't safe for me to be in your life."

Her thick lashes fluttered. "Why wasn't it safe?"

He didn't speak. Voices drifted around them.

"I looked for you, too," Delaney confessed.

His fingers lingered beneath her chin.

"But you weren't there. You were never there."

Yes, I was. I was watching you. So many times. He leaned forward, and his lips brushed against hers. They needed to look like the besotted couple. Considering that he was besotted, it was an easy enough role for him to play. He eased back. Cleared his throat. "Let's go play."

"We are going to finish this conversation later. You will explain why it wasn't safe."

He'd spent years hoping to make her life *safe.* Only to find out that her freaking fiancé wanted to kill her. *Maybe she is only gonna be safe with me.* Or maybe Nash was just telling himself shit he wanted to believe.

Delaney inched toward the massive slot machine. "This is going to sound crazy but, um, I've never gambled before." Another little inch toward the machine as it chimed loudly. "And I think I'd really like to start with this guy."

With the biggest slot machine in the whole casino? One that was so huge just because it was a tourist trap? "Delaney, you aren't going to win there." He hated to disillusion her. Hell, wasn't that the whole reason he clung so tightly to his secrets?

"I never really thought life was about winning. Thought it was about being happy." Her eyes were on the machine. "Yanking down that ginormous handle and watching the numbers spin will thrill my little heart." A determined nod. "Seriously."

He swiped his card over the machine. *You had me at "thrill my little heart."* When he had it in his power, he would do anything to make her happy. "Go for it."

"Nash, you just put one hundred dollars on this machine."

"Yeah, well, I wanted your heart to be thrilled."

She laughed.

He took a step back.

Delaney frowned. "Nash, what's wrong?"

He could not speak.

Her brows rose. "Is there danger?" Her gaze flew around the crowded casino. "Some sort of threat?"

Fuck, no. He would never step *back* if there was a threat. He frowned at her. Then he put another hundred in the machine as a credit.

"What are you doing?"

He'd been hoping to hear her laugh again. Because it was a sound he'd missed far more than he'd ever realized. "You want more money?"

"No!" She pushed his hand away from the machine. "This is more than enough. In fact, it's too much."

The woman was an heiress. Granted, she was the heiress to a crime fortune, but an heiress nonetheless. Two hundred dollars was not too much in her world.

"Do I have to play it all?" Delaney fretted. "Can we get some of it back?"

A guy in khaki pants and a polo walked by, his gaze sliding down Delaney's legs.

Nash moved into his path. "Really? You gonna stare at my wife like that with me right the hell next to her?"

All of the color fled from the man's face. He turned and practically ran away.

"Nash!"

Right. Dammit. Jaw locking, he looked at his wife. His real wife. He'd told her, twice, that they were truly married, but she hadn't understood. Should he go for a third time?

"Nash, can we get some of the money back?"

Screw the money. "Play it all."

"All? At once?" She nibbled on her lower lip. "That feels like a lot."

"There are max and minimum bets. You don't have to play it all. But if you want to, have the hell at it." He scraped a hand over his jaw. Felt the stubble there and realized that he needed to shave soon. Especially if he was planning to get close to her delicate skin again. And he was. Definitely planning that.

She crept closer to the machine. "Do I just pull this big lever?"

"You can. Or you can just hit this button." He pointed to the button near the front of the machine.

Her nose scrunched again. "Why would you hit the little button when you can pull this giant lever?"

She did pull the giant lever. While on the max bet. Because he didn't think she understood how to change the amount she was betting. She pulled the lever, let out a gasp of actual delight even though they were on a mission that should have terrified her, and, for that brief moment, as she scooted back and her body brushed against his, as she grabbed his hand and they watched the screen spin on that massive machine, Nash felt normal. Like, it was all real.

They were honeymooning, and Delaney was happy. She was holding his hand, and she was *his* again.

A loud alarm blared, cutting through the entire casino. The lights weren't a pale white at the top of the big machine any longer. They were rolling in a bright red, continuous wave.

And...

Holy hell.

All eyes were on them because the machine was going *wild*. Wild because Delaney had just won.

"What is happening?" Delaney bounced. "Did we win? We did, didn't we? How much did we win?"

His jaw was on the floor.

She hugged him. "We won!" Delaney waved to the people who were rushing to gather around them. A whole lot of people. "We won!" Delaney hugged Nash again. Her body pressed tightly to him.

Over her shoulder, he surveyed the crowd. She'd won. As impossible as it should have been, Delaney had just won *big*, and she'd certainly succeeded in attracting everyone's attention.

His arms curled around her as he lifted her up against him. More of her delighted laughter spilled from her. It was beautiful and warm, and it filled the cold, empty places that had been inside of him for far too long.

"*Sir*." An insistent tapping on his shoulder. "Sir, you will need to come with me."

Keeping his hold on Delaney, Nash looked over his shoulder.

Two men stood behind him. Both dressed in black suits. Both with earpieces.

"Casino security, sir," the man to the right said. A blond. "Gonna need you both to come with us."

The people around them were offering congratulations. But these two men...

"*Now*," the blond added, in a tone that brooked no argument.

As battle-ready tension hummed through him, Nash realized that Delaney had caught more than just the crowd's attention. She might have put them dead center for their target's attention, too.

He lowered Delaney to the floor. Nash wrapped an arm around Delaney, kept her close at his side, and ordered, "Lead the way," to the blond. As they exited the casino and headed upstairs, toward the private office area, Nash got ready for the fight that he knew was coming.

"Nash?" A faint hitch in his name as they ascended a spiral staircase.

He winked at her.

She shivered.

*　*　*

"How the hell did she just do that?" Jezebel demanded as she watched the security footage. It had been an easy enough matter for her team to hack into the security feeds at the casino. Child's play for the techs who worked under her supervision. So, thanks to that hacking and the video feeds that she could watch on the screens before her, she'd had a perfect view of Delaney and her big win.

"I think she was lucky," the hacker to her right said. Thin, balding, with gold hoops in his ears. A guy who did not see field work but spent the majority of his time with his fingers poised over a keyboard and ready to steal every secret that the tech world possessed. Dominic "Dom" Blay might not look intimidating, but that was part of his appeal. The man was a CIS master.

"I don't believe in luck." She also didn't believe in giant slot machines. But…

Her players were on the move. Heading up to the big offices upstairs. And they were being escorted by two security men. Men currently being run through facial recognition software courtesy of Dom.

Her phone rang. She kept her eyes on the screen—screens—in front of her even as she put the phone to her ear. "This had better be good."

"I'm out of the hospital," Ryan Quinn informed her. "Real dick move trying to bench me. Not cool."

Jezebel grunted. "You were shot. That means you're staying benched."

"I am never benched." He seemed insulted. Probably because he was. Typical Ryan. "I *am* still in the field, very usefully so, might I add. Because I'm the one calling you about a scene I just left."

What? "I thought you'd just left the hospital."

"Um."

Um was very noncommittal. That was why it was one of her favorite responses. Ryan had picked up her habit of using that lovely noncommittal sound. "Ryan…"

"So, thought you'd like to know that a dead body was just found in a limo about two miles away from the Love Heart Chapel."

Her back went ramrod straight. "You have my attention."

"Thought I might. The poor driver had a knife lodged in his throat. Cops haven't traced down the owner of the vehicle yet because they're a wee bit overwhelmed here in Sin City, but I've got the tag info and you've got the insane access that you have, so let's see what magic you can uncover, shall we?" He rattled off the tag number.

With Dom's help, she got the match in moments. "That limo traces back to Kurt Wellington. Wellington Enterprises." Seriously sloppy work. Which meant...A wide smile curved her lips. "He's losing control."

"Uh, Jez, he *just killed a man*. Because from what I saw —don't ask me how, you don't want to know, let's just say I charmed and got up-close access—the blood spatter was all over the steering wheel and the dash. The attack came from behind, as in, the person in the back of the limo decided to kill his driver. Don't know how long the vic was dead before someone actually approached the vehicle and discovered him. Windows were tinted so it could have been moments or it could have been hours."

Which meant that Kurt Wellington could currently be *anywhere* in Vegas. "Give me the location. I want to try and access street cams."

He gave her the location. She had him on speaker by then, so Dom instantly went to work accessing the info. She held her breath.

"It's going to take a while to work through the footage," Dom warned her. "Especially if we are talking hours and not minutes since the killing."

Fine, yes, she understood that. But excitement fired her blood. If they had just *gotten* Kurt Wellington at the scene of a murder, if they had footage that could tie him to the kill, it was like a prosecutor's dream come true. "He's making mistakes." Jezebel nodded. "This is exactly what I hoped would happen." He'd just needed to be manipulated and pushed to the absolute edge. In her experience, men were best manipulated when they were fighting jealousy and rage. And hurt pride. *Delaney hurt you, didn't she? You thought you were in control, but she ripped that control away from you.* "He's working on instinct. Emotions."

"So his instinct is to kill and his emotion is rage." Ryan's voice was tight. "Uh, huh. *Not* what I want to hear when my brother is the one standing beside Wellington's runaway bride." Ryan was worried.

She was, too, but... "We have eyes on him."

"Someone is a double agent." Flat.

She did not deny the charge.

Dom's fingers paused over the keyboard.

She cut a glance his way. "There a problem?"

"No, ma'am." His fingers went back to flying.

She and Dom were the only ones in that Vegas hotel room. A hotel room one floor beneath the honeymoon suite that had been given to Nash and Delaney. Instead of bringing in normal luggage, she and Dom had made sure they were equipped with the best tech imaginable.

"You know someone is feeding intel to Wellington." Ryan's tone had turned considering. "Otherwise, the chapel would have been secure, and I wouldn't be sporting a new bullet wound."

"I have the situation under control," she assured him. Ryan wasn't normally the type to need reassurance. This was not a normal case. "Stand down," she ordered him. "You are injured and are no longer part of this mission."

"Nash is my *family*. I'm always part of a mission that concerns him."

Nope. Not the way things worked. "Stand down," she repeated. "I have the situation under control."

Silence. Then, "If anything happens to my brother, I will fucking burn down the entire CIA to find the traitor."

Sweat trickled down her back. With Ryan, there were never idle threats. People at the Agency often thought Nash was the greater danger. He was a bit bigger. More intense. While Ryan was the charmer. The chameleon who could fit in easily with anyone, anywhere. Nash never tried to blend. Didn't socialize.

Ryan was always the life of the party. Fun. Flirtatious. Smiling and joking.

Only he'd still be smiling and joking, and he'd be *fun* when he killed you.

Ryan is more dangerous than Nash. Jezebel knew that truth. She'd always known it. Ryan had been born to be a predator. Nash had been forced to become one due to circumstances. In another life, Nash would never have been a killer.

But he'd had to change. Because of Delaney Daniels. Did the woman have any clue what Nash had sacrificed for her? Probably not. Jezebel suspected Nash would sooner cut out his own heart—which he'd done for the woman before—than cause more pain for Delaney.

"Your friend Grayson is on site," she informed Ryan.

"Yeah, Gray's on site because I told him to get his ass to the casino. He was already in the area. Man has his hands in every damn thing. I'll seriously owe him, but I know Gray will have Nash's back in a heartbeat."

Now she bristled. The FBI always made her tense. "I have CIA operatives watching Nash."

"And I trust Gray. His allegiance will one hundred percent be to my brother. See, when all the dust has settled, I want Wellington locked away. Just like you do. But I also want my brother to *walk away*. Do you hear what I am saying?"

"Nash's safety is paramount."

"No, Jez. I want him to *walk away*."

Her heart thudded into her chest. She'd always

wondered just how much Ryan truly understood about the situation with Nash. Brothers should tell each other everything, but Nash did enjoy his secrets.

"Stand down, Ryan," she ordered again.

Dom typed steadily on the keyboard.

"Hey, look at it this way. At least you'll still have me as a consolation prize."

"Ryan, go rest. Recover from your gunshot injury."

"Rest is boring. I like the action too much for that." A little hum. "You're welcome about the tip on the limo. Oh, and FYI, the Dodge Charger involved in that drive-by at the chapel? A friendly cop just told me the vehicle was at impound. Two dead bodies found inside. Hell of a busy time for the Vegas PD."

Her breath whispered out. "I was aware of the vehicle's discovery."

"And of the two dead bodies?"

She did not reply. But, yes, she'd known about them.

"Is my brother aware?" Ryan pushed. "Is he fully cognizant of the fact that Wellington has gone completely off the rails and is eliminating people left and right here in Vegas? Does my brother know that the danger on this case has just spiked one thousand percent?"

Her gaze remained on the surveillance screens. One of the guards who'd been escorting Nash and Delaney had just opened a black door. Nash and Delaney were crossing the threshold and heading inside an office.

"Goodbye, Ryan. Follow my orders." She hung up. Motioned to the surveillance footage. "Do we have access to security cameras in that room?"

Dom squinted. The light hit his glasses. "I don't think there are cameras in that room, boss." His fingers tapped again on the black keyboard in front of him. "No, no, that's the office of the casino's owner. No access."

Her expression remained the same, but her heart rate increased even more. "Get the other agents to pull in closer."

The two guards followed Nash and Delaney inside the room. And right before the door shut, one of the guards pulled out his gun.

If anything happens to my brother, I will fucking burn down the entire CIA.

No, Ryan never made an idle threat. In her experience, he just made promises. She could almost smell the smoke.

Chapter Nineteen

NASH DIDN'T WAIT FOR THE DOOR TO CLOSE FULLY before he attacked. He lunged for the blond guard, caught the jerk's hand in a savage grip, and halted the rise of the weapon that the man had clearly been pulling.

Nash whirled the guard to the side, slammed him into the wall, and he twisted the man's wrist even as the fellow howled in pain.

"*Stop.*" A low, hard command.

Nash didn't particularly feel like heeding the command. So he drove his head into the blond's, and he snatched the gun from the falling creep. Spinning, Nash brought the gun up and aimed it at the second guard, a man who was already trying to snatch out his own gun.

"Don't," Nash told him. "Or I'll have to shoot you." He sidestepped. Two sidesteps. And he made sure Delaney was shielded behind him. "Is this really any way to greet a winner?"

Mocking laughter. Not from the guard. But from the man behind the big, mahogany desk.

"Get out of here, Tobias, Luke. Now." An order from

the person who was clearly in charge. The guy with the white t-shirt and battered jeans. He strolled from behind the desk, crossed his arms over his chest, and quirked a brow at Nash. "I believe we have business to discuss."

The blond guard groaned as he tried to rise.

A sigh and an eye roll from the boss. "Luke, help Tobias. Take him to a medic. Make sure something is not broken."

"Oh, I don't believe I broke anything," Nash allowed. He cast a critical eye at Tobias. "Probably a wrist sprain. Someone just can't handle his pain well." He returned his focus to the real threat in the room.

"What are you?" the guy in the t-shirt asked. "A doctor?"

Nash smiled at him. "And what are you? An asshole criminal?"

Luke hauled Tobias out of the room. The door closed behind them.

The man in the white t-shirt rested his hip against the side of the desk. "My name is Logan Sterling, and I own this casino." A pause. "And the hotel where you're staying."

"Considering the hotel and casino are connected, I figured you had to own both." Nash had turned the gun toward Logan Sterling. As if he didn't know who the man was. Before they'd arrived in Vegas, he'd done recon work on their destination. He knew who owned the location. Just as he knew he was staring at a man who supposedly hated Kurt Wellington. *Mortal enemies,* if the gossip was correct.

Logan's gaze was on Delaney. Or, rather, he was trying to put his gaze on Delaney as he attempted to peer around Nash's body. "Are you her human shield?" Logan mockingly asked Nash.

"Yes." Not mocking at all. Dead serious.

Logan wiggled his dark brows. "And here I thought you were her husband."

"Pretty sure that's what a husband's job is—to protect his wife from any and all threats in the world."

Logan cocked his head. "Do I look like a threat?"

Did Nash look like an idiot? "Your dumbass guard just pulled a gun so...yes."

"*Ahem.*" A delicate throat clearing from Delaney. "Is this meeting about our winnings? Because it does not feel that way. I've yet to hear the word 'congratulations' and there is an awful lot of gun play happening here."

Logan smiled. "This meeting is about the fact that I have CIA operatives running wildly through my property. A big annoyance, if you want the truth."

Nash kept his gun aimed. He also kept his body positioned protectively in front of Delaney.

"You think I don't know who you are?" Logan shook his head. "In my business, knowledge is always power. And my tech team here at the Sterling Casino and Hotel is actually pretty good. I believe in hiring skilled workers. You get what you pay for in this world."

"Wouldn't know that based on Tobias," Nash pointed out. "Unless you deliberately paid for a shitty guard who doesn't know how to hold on to his weapon."

Logan pushed away from the desk. "He's new. The team that runs my tech is not. They are fully aware that the CIA has tapped into my security feeds and are treating themselves to an all-you-can-watch showing of my facilities." He paced toward Nash. "I'm assuming all of this was done without warrants. How very *illegal.*"

"You really want to talk about *illegal?*" Nash challenged him.

Logan laughed. "Fair enough." He held up both hands. "I'm unarmed. And I need to talk to the bride."

"Just because you don't have a weapon in your hands, it doesn't mean you're unarmed."

More laughter from Logan. "Fair enough. How about this? I have no intention of hurting the bride in any way, shape or form. How about that? Better? Does that satisfy you?"

Nash felt a tap on his back. One tap. Two.

"I have a name," Delaney declared quite loudly. She gave him a third tap. "I don't particularly enjoy being called 'the bride.' Makes me sound like I'm with Frankenstein's Monster."

Logan's eyes gleamed. "Noted." He stared straight at Nash. "How about you step to the side?"

Nash did not move. Not yet. He needed this message understood. "I *am* a fucking monster. Try to hurt her in any way, and you'll have a bullet between your eyes."

"Aren't we the protective one?"

"We are."

"And a bit violent?"

Nash smiled. "More than a bit."

The tapping on his back became even more insistent. "You're not a monster," Delaney snapped.

Sure, he was.

But he did ease to the side. He kept his body partially in front of her, though, and he stayed poised to attack.

"Hello, there," Logan murmured. "I have been quite curious about you."

"Don't refer to him that way," she ordered. "Don't ever call Nash a monster again."

A considering nod. "Ah, someone else who is protective.

Aren't you two just adorably alike? Do accept my humble apologies. It was a slip of the tongue."

Nash did not like Logan. Or his BS apology. "Why did you have us hauled up here?"

Logan shifted to get a better view of Delaney. "To congratulate the lovely lady, of course. She's a big winner."

"Was the win fixed?" Nash demanded bluntly. "Did you arrange for her to win just so you'd have a reason to pull us into your office?"

"Oh, how insulting." Logan put one hand to his chest. "Are you suggesting that my establishment is not one hundred percent above board?" A faint smile teased at Logan's lips. "Hurtful."

"I will show you hurtful in about five seconds if you don't get to the point." Not a threat. A promise from Nash. He did not like this situation. His internal alarms were shrieking.

"I'm keeping the money I won." Delaney edged to Nash's side. "There are a lot of people who can be helped by that kind of cash."

"Oh." The smile vanished from Logan's face. His lips pulled down. "You're one of those. Disappointing."

"Those—what?" Delaney wanted to know.

"The do-gooder type. You make my head hurt."

"The five seconds are up," Nash snarled.

"Right. And you are *not* the do-gooder type. Much easier to handle." Logan rolled back his shoulders. "The enemy of my enemy is my very best friend in the world."

"What in the world are you talking about?" Nash had zero patience left. He was also still holding a gun, so the dick in front of him should not be playing games.

"An old proverb," Delaney murmured. Her shoulder

brushed against Nash because she'd stepped closer. "Pretty sure he's suggesting a team up."

Logan laughed. The man seemed to do that far more than was necessary. "Indeed, I am. You see..." His face hardened. "I fucking hate Kurt Wellington. The man has been cutting into my business for far too long, and there is nothing in this world that would make me happier...than if Wellington was no longer a problem. Not for me. Not for the bride—"

"Delaney. My name is Delaney."

"Yes, but you were supposed to be Kurt's bride. I recognize your face from the surveillance photos I have."

"Surveillance photos?" Nash latched onto those dangerous and telling words. "Just what game are you playing?"

"The one where I win, of course." Pure cockiness from Logan. "The house always wins."

"Ahem." From Delaney. "Excuse me, but I'm pretty sure I won downstairs. Unless your casino is completely crooked."

Logan gasped. "You don't just *say* shit like that about a person's casino. Not in this town." Logan shook his head and pointed at her. "Though your ex sure runs the most twisted games there are. I know for a fact that he's been cheating his ass off for years."

"Probably because Kurt is laundering a ton of dirty money." Nash had no intention of lowering the weapon any time soon. Nothing Logan had said so far reassured him.

"I want him shut down." Logan's hand dropped and shoved into the front pocket of his jeans. "I want him out of Vegas. I want him out of my way." His right hand rose, and he gripped a key between his thumb and index finger. "This is to a storage unit on the outskirts of town. You'll find plenty of my...surveillance work inside."

"And you think your surveillance is better than mine?" Better than the CIA's?

"I think I may have access to info that you don't." A smirk. "And I think you'll go look to see what's waiting for you. Curiosity is a dangerous beast, isn't she?" He gave the address of the storage unit without batting an eyelash.

Still gripping the gun with one hand, Nash's other hand swiped the key. "Thanks. I'll be sure to pass this along to the right individuals."

"Right ones. Wrong ones. Whatever works." Logan's attention had shifted back to Delaney. "Do you have a thing for bad guys?"

"No." An immediate reply from Delaney.

"Sure about that? You were marrying the worst of the worst. Thought you might go for that killer edge. Then I heard you left Kurt holding his own balls at the altar." His eyes gleamed. "That shit made me laugh for hours, just so you know."

"He wasn't holding his balls." Prim. She sniffed.

"He was flat on his ass," Nash supplied. "Went down without a fight."

"Ah. Bruised pride. You beat him and took his bride." Logan nodded sagely. "Probably one of the many reasons he wants you dead so badly. There is a major bounty on your head right now, FYI." His pose was completely relaxed. "The bounty makes the prize that the bride won downstairs look like small change."

"*Delaney. De-lane-ee.* Why is it so difficult to use my name?"

Logan's stare raked her. "A man can tell when a woman loves someone else."

Delaney pressed closer to Nash.

"You think Kurt didn't know? Trust me. He did. Probably something that made you unattainable in the first place. A challenge. He wanted to win you. Dumb bastard might have even believed that he had, and then you ran off with this guy." An incline of his head toward Nash. "Not just ran off with him, but you instantly went to Vegas to marry the dude who'd stolen you." A low whistle. "I'd say you have a death wish, my new friend—"

"We are not friends," Nash assured him.

"—but, clearly, you're just trying to drive Kurt absolutely insane. What's the idea? That insane men make mistakes?"

Logan Sterling was an interesting individual, Nash would give him that. "You know where he is," Nash charged.

Logan didn't respond.

Nash took that as an affirmative.

"He's planning to kill you first. Get you out of the way." Logan motioned toward Delaney. "Then he'll go after her."

"Thank you for the obvious. We're aware of his intent." Nash shrugged. "I just don't plan on dying."

"Well, I'm sure her father didn't plan on dying, either," Logan said.

Wait. Fuck, no, stop!

"But shit happens. Her grandfather just bided his time, he hunted him down, and then he took her father out right in front of her mother's eyes."

"*What?*" Delaney's absolute shock.

Logan frowned. "Come now. You're married to the CIA operative who spent years trying to annihilate your grandfather's empire. Of course, you know all of this."

"Shut your fucking mouth," Nash fired out.

Instead of shutting, Logan's mouth dropped open. Shock flashed on his face. "You...she..." His stunned gaze zeroed in on Delaney. "You really didn't know? Who did you think had executed your father?" Then his stare flew right back to Nash. "You married her. Why in the world wouldn't you *tell her?*"

Logan had way too much intel. He was an unknown, and Nash hated dealing with unknowns. But...

Jezebel. She would not have put them in that particular location unless she thought it was secure, and that meant that Jezebel knew Logan Sterling. Was he a CIA plant? An operative? The web was too tangled.

"Nash?" Delaney grabbed his arm. Her grip was hard as she pulled him even closer toward her. "What is he talking about?"

"Delaney..."

"He's lying." Delaney's desperate words. "Tell me that he is lying."

Nash locked his jaw.

"He's not lying?" Whispered. "And you knew?" Her stunned gaze searched his. "How long did you know?"

"Oh, your new husband *knows* a whole lot more than just that." Logan wouldn't shut up. "Don't you, Agent Quinn?"

Nash put down the gun. Very deliberately. He pocketed the key. He turned toward Logan, and he drew back his fist so he could beat the hell out of the smug bastard.

Delaney stepped in front of Nash. "My grandfather killed my dad?"

His hand immediately dropped.

"How long have you known this?" Tears weren't in her eyes. But plenty of rage was.

Years. "We need to leave this room, Delaney. Now."

"*What else do you know?*" she cried.

He reached for her hand.

She jerked back. "You were trying to take down my grandfather's empire?"

"Yes," he gritted out the confession.

"That's how Jezebel knew...when we talked at the cabin in Tennessee. She knew my grandfather was a criminal."

"Oh, darling, *everyone* in the right circles knows that." Logan leaned in to purr at her ear.

"Get the hell away from her," Nash ordered. "*Now.*"

"Right circles. Wrong ones. Whatever, like I said before—"

"*Get away from her.*"

Logan took a step back. "No need for the rage at me. I'm trying to help. I'm not the one leaving a trail of bodies in Vegas. That would be her ex."

She whipped around to face Logan. "What trail of bodies?"

"Has your new husband told you *nothing?* Seriously? How does he expect you to be prepared for the danger if he keeps holding back with you?" A sigh. "I would have told you from the beginning. Lies are just so unnecessary. Here you go, let me help. Your ex Wellington? His limo driver was found not too long ago, covered in blood and with a knife sticking out of his throat." He pointed to his own throat. "Quite the horrific scene. I personally hate gore. Unnecessary."

What. The. Hell?

"And the shooters at the chapel where you two said I do? Both dead, too."

"How do you know all of this?" Delaney's hands had fisted at her sides.

"Certain cops in this city understand how much I value

intel, so I get news very quickly." Logan raised his brows as he peered at Nash. "Were you not aware of these developments? Was I truly informed faster than the CIA? That's just sad." He *tut-tutted*. 'Unless, of course, you are deliberately being kept in the dark."

"Delaney, let's go." Nash extended his hand toward her.

She peered at his palm. She did not take it.

"Delaney." Tossing her over his shoulder and running out with her was not a good plan. He had to mentally repeat that to himself three times. "Delaney, we need to leave."

Tossing her over my shoulder and running out is not a good plan.

Fine. Four times.

"You are answering my questions," she snapped at him. "You are going to tell me everything. No more lies. No more secrets. I am *suffocating* because of them." She stared at him with betrayal in her eyes, and the look gutted him. "I always thought a robber killed my dad. Someone who broke into the garage. Took all of the money from the safe."

Because that was how her grandfather had set the scene.

"You're saying my own grandfather did that? In front of my mother?" Her lower lip trembled. "Why?"

"Not here," he rasped. He could feel her pain, living and breathing around them, and he hated it.

"When did you learn this?" Delaney's voice rose.

Logan curled his hands around her shoulders.

She flinched.

"Oh, I can help with that. Me, me. Pick *me*." Logan Sterling was a complete asshole.

Nash glared at him. A *shut-the-hell-up* glare.

Logan did not heed the message. "He learned it when your grandfather paid him a visit. Carmello came to him in person. Years ago," Logan purred. "Back when you were in college, I believe. Your groom might have been in med school, if I remember correctly."

The prick had too much knowledge. That much intel—*fuck, he can't be trusted.*

"Get your hands off her," Nash commanded him flatly, "or every single finger will be broken."

Logan snatched his hands back. "The possessive type, got it. Forgive me for not realizing it, but when you let her walk away for eight years, I just wasn't sure how involved you really were. My mistake."

Eight years. The smarmy sonofabitch had intel that he should not possess. *Who the hell is Logan Sterling working for? How does he know so much?* "Consider me highly involved."

Delaney spun to face Logan. "Did you know my grandfather?"

A nod. "Not well. You don't want to know men like Typhon well. You want to stay out of their way."

Fucking hell. Nash's teeth snapped together.

"What?" A hard, negative shake of Delaney's head. "My grandfather was not Typhon. *Kurt* is Typhon. I heard Kurt get called that by a man he shot. A man he killed!"

Enough of this. Logan was too much of an unknown, and this scene was done. It had already exploded in Nash's face enough. Nash grabbed Delaney. Tossed her over his shoulder. She was sharing far too much with a man who Nash believed was their enemy, and as for Logan, Nash didn't trust him for a second.

"What in the hell are you doing?" Delaney yelled at him.

"Carmello Ricci *was* Typhon," Logan said with complete certainty. He didn't even quirk an eyebrow at seeing Nash toss Delaney over his shoulder. "That's why your husband here—and his boss—worked so hard to bring Carmello down all those years. Why they stalked him. Carmello was very, very big game in the spy world."

Nash spun for the door. But it was too late. Logan had revealed too much.

Delaney kicked him, hard. "*Don't you dare.*" She twisted and shoved in his hold. "Let me go. Now!"

He held her tighter.

"When Carmello died," Logan just kept right on dropping classified intel that he had no business possessing, "Kurt wanted to inherit everything that your grandfather left behind. That meant the property, the criminal enterprises, and the title that went along with it. The title of *Typhon*. But in order to get all of that, Kurt really needed you, Delaney. You were the key."

She stopped struggling against Nash. "Put me down, Nash." So much pain and anger in her words. It was the pain that got him.

Fuck. He'd grabbed her purely out of desperate instinct. He'd wanted to run and carry her out of that office before Logan Sterling could shatter her world.

Our world.

"Congratulations," Logan told Nash. "Guess you beat Kurt to the punch. You married her. Does that mean that you're now the king of all fucking monsters? Are you the new Typhon?"

Nash slowly lowered Delaney until her feet touched the floor. He stared at her face, and he hated the agony and betrayal that he saw in her expression.

"Is it true?" she whispered.

Fuck.

But she nodded, as if she'd seen the answer. Then, "Did you break up with me because of who my grandfather was?"

Dammit—

She sucked in a breath, and he knew she'd seen too much yet again.

Rage and desperation twisted inside of Nash. "Delaney, I *will* explain." But not there. Not with Logan watching everything.

Nash caught her wrist. The wrist that still bore a mark from the ropes that Kurt had put on her. He eased Delaney behind him even as he snatched up the gun he'd put down moments before. Once more, he aimed the weapon at a seemingly unconcerned Logan. "Who the hell are you working for?"

A roll of one shoulder. "Myself. I'm strictly freelance."

"You have way too much intel for someone who is freelance."

"I don't work well with others. Can't take orders for shit. Despise a chain of command." Another partial shrug. "What you see is what you get."

Nash didn't buy that lie. Not with the intel this man possessed.

"*You should have told me.*" Delaney's coldly furious voice.

Logan winced. He leaned forward, conspiratorially. "I hate to be the bearer of bad news…"

All the guy had done was share bad news.

"But it sounds like the bride is furious."

"*I'm going to punch him in the face,*" Delaney declared. "*De-lane-ee.* Say it with me."

"No one likes betrayal." Logan sighed and shook his head as if in sympathy. "Secrets are the devil's favorite weapon."

Nash believed he might just be looking at the devil.

Delaney tried to surge past him and get close to Logan.

Nash locked one arm around her waist and hauled her back against him. "We're leaving," he told Logan. "Are you picking up the phone as soon as we exit to let Kurt know exactly where we are?"

"Why would I do that? We both understand that he already knows." His gaze flickered to a struggling Delaney. "You'd better protect her," he warned.

As if Nash needed to be told how to do that job.

"The best way to do that," Logan's eyes gleamed, "isn't for Kurt Wellington to be locked in a jail cell. It's for him to be buried in the ground."

Nash hauled Delaney toward the door.

"Fun talk," Logan called after them. "Pleasure meeting you both. Sometimes, reality does not live up to the hype, but you two are delightful."

"Piss off," Nash snarled at him.

"I'll send champagne to your suite. My treat."

"Stay the hell away from me and Delaney." Nash yanked open the door. They stalked out. He kept the gun. Hell, yes, he was keeping it. Always good to have an extra weapon.

"Nash..." Delaney began.

His head whipped toward her. "*Not until we are alone.*" An elevator bank waited to the right. He double-timed it that way, not letting go of her for a second.

Her beautiful face was furious. Her body tight with her rage.

And he just kept thinking...

I'm going to lose her. I didn't tell her the truth because I wanted to protect her. And I'm still going to lose her. There was never a way to win. The odds were always stacked against me.

* * *

"WHAT HAPPENED IN THAT OFFICE?" Jezebel leaned toward the screen. "Something bad," she muttered beneath her breath. "Because they both looked pissed."

They'd met with Logan Sterling. Logan, a man who *should* have been playing nicely with the CIA. Unfortunately, the guy didn't like cooperating with anyone, and he tended to be far too much of a maverick for her liking.

But they'd needed his hotel and casino. They'd needed his cooperation. He'd *said* that she had it. Only now, Jezebel wondered if Logan had sold out her team.

Delaney and Nash were rushing to a nearby elevator bank.

Nash appeared to have a death grip on Delaney. The elevator doors opened. They jumped inside.

"Elevator footage, now," she ordered Dom.

His fingers tapped on his keyboard.

She saw an image of the elevator's interior appear on the screen to the right. A little grainy, but she could make out Nash and Delaney. Unfortunately, she could not hear them. "Sound," she blasted. "Give me *sound*."

More tapping.

The elevator doors closed.

"Delaney," Nash began.

Yes! She had sound.

"I know it's a lot to take in..." Nash was oddly halting. So unusual for him.

What's a lot? What happened in there? Jezebel's eyes were locked on the screen.

Delaney wrapped her arms around her stomach as the elevator began to descend. "My grandfather was Typhon? And you knew?"

Oh, no. Jezebel stopped breathing. She leaned closer, desperate to hear Nash's response.

But the entire screen before her went black. "What's happening?" She lifted her hand and tapped on the side of the screen, as if that would magically bring back the image. "Why did we lose them?"

Then she heard the scream. Delaney's terrified scream. A scream that was abruptly cut off.

Chapter Twenty

DARKNESS. ONE MOMENT, THE LIGHTS WERE ON IN THE elevator, and Delaney could see Nash's handsome, betraying face perfectly. And then...

Black. Everything around her went pitch black, and there wasn't even any emergency lighting. Before she could ask what in the hell was happening, the elevator dropped.

She felt it. A sudden, sharp drop, and her body flew *up* in response. Her feet left the floor, and a horrified scream broke from her. This couldn't be happening. It wasn't real. It wasn't possible. *This couldn't happen.*

But her body was now hurtling toward the floor, and Nash was grabbing her, trying to twist and pull her against his bigger form. Trying to shield her, but there was no time.

The cables must have snapped. She'd seen something like that in a movie once. The cables snapped and the elevator plunged down but...but they hadn't even been that high up and—

She hit. Landed on top of Nash. Sprawled over him. Her heart raced in her chest. Her hands slammed against him as she shot up. "Nash!"

"*Fuck me.*"

Not the time or the place. "Are you okay?"

"No, I'm fucking furious." His hands locked around her waist. "How are *you*?"

Terrified. Shaking. Alive. "I'm not dead. So that's a win."

"Yeah, baby, let's keep up that winning streak of yours."

Darkness was all she saw. Her head whipped to the left and the right as she continued to straddle him. "Why are there no emergency lights?"

"Better question. Why the hell did our elevator just fall?"

Yes, that was an extremely good question. "Maybe..." She swallowed to ease the dryness in her mouth. "Logan Sterling has shoddy safety standards?"

"Or maybe he sold us out to Kurt Wellington."

She still straddled him. Her dress had hiked up. Her knees shoved into the floor of the elevator, positioned on either side of Nash's body. Delaney was sure the skin had been ripped off her knees because they ached and throbbed. Her hands pressed to his chest. "We didn't fall far."

"Lucky for us, there wasn't far *to* fall." He lifted her up. Off him. But his hands remained around her waist.

One shoe had fallen off. She didn't bother searching for it in the dark. She just kicked off the other shoe.

"You're okay?" Nash's gruff voice. "You're sure?"

Her body wouldn't stop trembling. "Well, other than the fact that you knew my grandfather killed my dad, that you hid that important news from me, and, oh, yes, you knew my grandfather was *Typhon*—"

"Typhon is like a freaking title. The mantle went to someone else when Carmello died. The CIA suspected it had gone to Kurt, we just couldn't conclusively prove it, so that wasn't a lie. What I told you about Kurt *wasn't* a lie—"

"*Did you ever even love me?*" A desperate cry that broke from her as she tore through his words.

Except she should not have let the cry out. Wrong time. Their stupid elevator had just plummeted. She was probably lucky to be alive. This was not the time for her to be raging at him and asking if he'd ever loved her. Did she even truly want to know the answer? "Forget it. Let's just find a way out of here." Since it was so dark, the doors had to be shut, but maybe they could pry them open and get out.

His hold on her waist tightened. "I have never loved anyone the way I love you. Doesn't matter if it was eight years or eight days or eight minutes ago. I love you the same now as I did before. I will love you until I die."

The elevator groaned. A hard, heavy sound. Fear raced through her.

"The doors are opening," Nash rasped as a sliver of light cut through the darkness. "I dropped the damn gun." He let her go. He bent down.

She started searching frantically in the dark.

The doors cracked open more, sending a bigger stream of light inside the darkness.

* * *

"Get me a picture!" Jezebel yelled. She grabbed for her phone. "I'm calling in backup, now—"

"No, you're not." A gun muzzle pressed to the side of her head.

Jezebel knew it was a gun because she'd had a gun pressed to her head three other times in her life. Three other, very unfortunate times. *You never forget the feel of a gun muzzle pressing into your skin. Especially when some bastard is threatening to blow your brains out.*

"You're not calling in backup." Dom stood beside her. Several inches taller than her and with his *gun* at her head. "You're not calling anyone. Nash and Delaney are vanishing."

Her gaze cut toward him. "Dom, you don't do well with field work." A gentle reminder. She could practically smell his fear. Plus, the gun was trembling against her.

"I'm doing just fine." His voice cracked on *fine*. "Will be doing even better when I get my payday."

The first time that a gun had been pressed to her head, she'd pulled a hidden knife on her attacker. She'd driven that knife into his throat before he'd had the chance to pull the trigger.

"They are going to disappear from this building." More cracking in his voice. This time on *disappear*. And more trembling of the gun. "Nash will never be seen again."

The second time a gun had been pressed to her head, Nash Quinn had come rushing in to take out her attacker. Interestingly enough, that had been Nash's first kill. He'd still been a green agent at the time. He'd tried to save the creep that he'd been forced to shoot.

"I'm assuming Nash will die quickly?" Jezebel's voice remained calm.

"I don't care if he dies f-fast or if he dies slow. I get the same amount of money either way!"

The third time a gun had been pressed to her head, a lover had been the one holding the weapon. A man she'd never fully trusted. She'd known all of his weak spots, so she'd been able to take him down. He was still rotting in a prison cell. Every few months, he would request to see her. Every few months, she'd refuse that request.

"Nash dies." Jezebel kept her body relaxed. Unthreatening. "And what of the woman? What's gonna happen to Delaney?"

"I guess she'll be a widow."

A soon-to-be dead widow. That gun still pressed against her. Still trembled. "You're the leak at the CIA." *I knew there was one. I just had to get the mole to show himself.* "You told Kurt Wellington that Nash and Delaney would be at the Love Heart Chapel, didn't you?"

"Oh, I told him plenty more than that." Smug. "His team has pics of every agent here. Your little trap is going to explode in your face. I know all the players. Kurt knows all the players. You are *screwed.*"

The hotel room door opened behind him. A door that should not have opened because only Jezebel and Dom had keys. But the door swung open, and, as Jezebel cut her eyes in that direction and Dom partially turned toward the door, Ryan Quinn strolled inside.

"I will not be benched," Ryan began.

Shock flashed on Ryan's face as he took in the scene before him. Then, in a heartbeat's time, he was reaching beneath his coat and grabbing for a gun that she knew had to be there.

Dom wrenched his weapon away from her head and aimed it at the new threat.

Jezebel grabbed one of the computer screens that had been set up on their table. She slammed that screen into Dom's head as hard as she could.

Dom didn't get off a shot. The traitor lost his grip on the gun. It skittered across the room even as he slammed toward the carpeted floor. Groaning, Dom shoved his hands against the carpet and started to lever himself up.

Only for his eyes to lock on the gun that Ryan had pointed dead-center at him.

"This is why you aren't cut out for field work," Jezebel crisply informed him. She dropped the screen. Deliberately let it slam into Dom's back. "You are such a disappointment."

"Jez..." Ryan's voice held worry. "Tell me what's happening."

"Dom here sold us out. I think Kurt already has a crew in the building, and I think they are making a move against Nash and Delaney right *now*." A fast exhale. "I'll contact all of our on-site agents. They're wearing earpieces, and I'll get everyone to swarm—"

Dom's laughter drowned out her words.

Ryan crouched before him. Put his gun to Dom's forehead. That move stopped Dom's laughter. "What did you do?" Ryan asked with zero emotion in his voice.

Ryan was an agent who happened to be made for field work.

"I cut the comms. No one will be communicating through those links." A smug response from Dom. "She can't reach any of the agents here. They can't reach her. Nash is alone in the dark. That's how he's going to stay. That's how he's going to die."

The hell he was. Jezebel grabbed her phone and sent out frantic texts. So the comms didn't work. Freaking normal texts *did*.

"He's not alone," Ryan responded in a voice layered with ice. "Delaney is with him."

"Then he'll die in front of her." Still so smug.

"If my brother dies..."

From the corner of her eye, Jezebel saw Ryan's finger tighten around the trigger.

"Then you die, Dom. Only your death will be a thousand times more painful. So you had better start talking. *Now*. Who is here? What's the plan?"

Dom opened his mouth and laughed again.

Ryan shoved the muzzle of his gun into Dom's open mouth. "I'm sorry." Not a real apology at all from Ryan. "Did I stutter?"

"*Ryan*." She rushed at him.

"I don't think I stuttered. And I don't think you fully understand the situation. Your brains will be all over the computer screens in this hotel room if you don't *talk*."

Tears leaked from Dom's eyes. Someone wasn't smug any longer.

"He can't talk with the gun in his mouth," Jezebel pointed out.

"Right." Ryan eased the gun out of Dom's mouth, but he kept it pointed straight at Dom's face. "I love my brother. I will do anything for him. Including torturing you until you beg for mercy." A tense beat. "You are now properly motivated to talk, aren't you?"

Yes, he was. Dom started talking. Every secret he had spilled from his lips.

That was the thing about Ryan. People didn't understand quite how deadly he was, not until it was too late.

* * *

HE'D DROPPED the gun that he'd taken from the annoying guard, Tobias. But that certainly had not been Nash's only weapon. As if he'd work an undercover mission with no weapon. So even as the elevator doors began to crack open,

Nash bent and grabbed for the gun that he'd strapped to his ankle before leaving the honeymoon suite.

The doors opened a bit more, slowly. "You folks all right?" A warm voice called out. "I think something is wrong with this elevator shaft. I got a call in to maintenance right now."

Nash's eyes narrowed. The door had only opened a few inches. He couldn't clearly see the figure out there, but a southern drawl dipped in the words, and he could just make out the gray uniform that he'd seen several of the janitorial staff wearing in the building.

"We need help!" Delaney cried. "The elevator just fell and please, please open the door all the way for us so we can get out!"

The doors began to open more. Looked like there were a few different hands *prying* the doors open.

"Get back, ma'am," the warm voice instructed. "We're coming in."

We're.

Nash saw the gun muzzle sliding between the opening doors. "Delaney!" Nash roared. He leapt in front of her even as he fired his weapon.

But the man with the southern accent rising and falling in his voice had fired, too. Wild shots because he wasn't aiming well. There was too much darkness in the elevator.

Delaney screamed.

Nash felt one bullet rip across his left thigh. Felt another burn against his right shoulder.

Dammit.

The doors opened more. The light was behind the bastard outside of the elevator. Correction, *bastards.* With all that new light, Nash could aim and fire perfectly.

He did. One bullet took out the shooter firing wildly.

The second hit the jerk with him who was reaching for his gun.

Nash knew he and Delaney were sitting ducks in that elevator. They had to *move*. He grabbed her wrist, pulled her forward, and they jumped over the figures slumped just outside of the elevator. He was going to get her the hell away from that scene.

"Freeze!"

Or, maybe he wasn't.

Because there were five more men out there. Different ages, races, heights. All wearing the gray uniform of the janitorial crew. All holding guns on Nash. He positioned his body in front of Delaney.

One of the fuckers smiled and said, "Perfect."

"No!" Delaney broke free of his grip and jumped in front of Nash. "Don't shoot him!" Delaney shouted.

He'd already been shot, twice. Correction, grazed twice. No bullets were in him. yet.

"You have orders, don't you? What are they?" she asked frantically. "To take me back to Kurt? How about you take *us* both back? Don't kill Nash. *Don't!*"

He could take them all down. Well, he could take out at least three of them. The other two might get shots off. And...

Delaney, sweetheart, I'm not so sure they care whether or not you die. They were firing blindly into the elevator. Those blasts could have killed you. I don't believe we are looking at the best and brightest here.

No matter what, she was not going to stand between him and the enemy. Time to start attacking.

"I'll come without a fight." Delaney stepped forward.

The hell she did.

"But Nash doesn't get shot."

Again, he'd already been shot at, and the woman who absolutely owned his heart was just offering herself as a shield. Screw that. "You guys all have ten seconds to put down your guns."

Laughter.

He shoved Delaney behind him.

Delaney grabbed at his shoulder. "What are you doing?"

"Giving them a chance to live. Ten seconds." He nodded toward the men. "The clock is ticking for you idiots." As for his wife, "Delaney, *run*." His backup wasn't there. His backup should have been there.

"*What?*"

He shifted his focus to their attackers. The fools were laughing. He wasn't. "I lied," Nash informed them. He'd never planned to give them ten seconds. He'd just needed to get Delaney out of the line of fire.

Nash started shooting his gun.

One target down.

Two.

Delaney wasn't running. A frantic look showed him that she was—she was raising a gun. Aiming it at the men in the gray uniforms. She fired and hit a man in the stomach. He dropped to the ground, howling. She turned her weapon at another attacker. Shot at him. She missed, but he ducked for cover.

Nash took out another perp. Then Nash lunged for Delaney. "You found the gun in the elevator?" He hadn't even realized that she'd had it.

"Got it right before the doors opened and they began firing. Hid it behind my dress." Her breath shuddered out. "Did I kill him?"

The man was currently howling at the top of his lungs,

so, no, he was very much alive. For the moment. "Let's *go*." There was still no sign of his backup, and this shit wasn't good. They were too vulnerable. Nash locked his hand with hers and rushed through the parking garage. That was where they'd wound up when the elevator decided to drop them—the parking garage. Which meant they'd fallen about four floors? They needed to get to the stairwell exit because this scene was clearly a coordinated attack.

Before they could reach the stairwell, bright lights flashed at them. A black van barreled toward them, like a beast that had just been waiting to attack. It came at them hard, and Nash fired his gun even as he shoved Delaney out of the way.

His bullets blasted through the windshield. But the driver didn't stop. The front of the van plowed into Nash, and his ass was tossed into the air. Tossed toward one of the concrete columns. His head cracked into the concrete, and he heard Delaney scream.

Chapter Twenty-One

"I think the first time I fell in love with you, you threw me out of the path of an oncoming vehicle." She gently slid her fingers through Nash's hair, being careful to avoid the wound at the back of his head. The wound he'd gotten when the van hit him, and Nash flew through the air and slammed into a concrete column. "You yelled at me and you told me that no turtle was worth my life. Then you kissed me." She leaned down, and her lips brushed over his. Tears stung her eyes. "Hey, Nash?" A whisper against his lips. "I'm not worth your life." Her head began to rise.

But his hand flew up. He caught the nape of her neck. Pressed his mouth against hers and held her there for a timeless moment before, "You fucking *are*. You *are* my life."

Her breath shuddered out. "Nash?"

He let her go, and as her head lifted, he stretched slowly, as if testing his body.

"Where the...hell...are we?" Gruff. A little groggy.

"From what I could tell, we're in some shack, in the middle of a Las Vegas desert." After the attack in the parking garage, they'd been tossed into separate vehicles.

Nash into the rear of a black SUV. Her into the backseat of a Jeep. A gun had been pressed to her side for the entire, terrifying ride. She'd been so afraid that Nash was dead in the SUV. That she'd never see him again.

Then...

They'd arrived in hell. Or, whatever this little shack was. A storage shack? Maybe it had been, once. From what she could tell, the windowless place now held only dust and cobwebs. She'd been ordered inside. Nash had been dumped in there. Then the door had been closed.

They'd been locked in darkness.

His unconscious body had been tossed inside the shack or shed or whatever it was, even as she'd yelled at the abductors to be careful with him. They had *not* been careful. As soon as she could, Delaney had tenderly put his head on her lap in an attempt to provide a cushion for him.

Groaning, he sat up. "Sonofabitch." His voice was stronger.

She bit her lower lip. "You have blood on your leg and your shoulder, too." Blood she'd seen in the parking garage and felt in the darkness of the shack as she tried to assess his injuries.

"Screw that. *Are you okay?*"

"You could have a skull fracture. You hit that column really hard." She'd heard the thud of impact. "Or a concussion. Or—"

"Yeah, my head is freaking splitting open. I'm *sure* I have a concussion, but I don't give a shit at the moment. *Are you okay?*" His hands slid over her in the dark. His turn to assess for injuries.

"I'm okay." The only light came from a small sliver beneath the one door in the shack.

His hands curled around her shoulders. "*Delaney.*"

"They took us out to the desert. Locked us in this place." She wet her lips. "I'm pretty sure they are just waiting for Kurt to arrive. Then they are going to dump your body out here. And, probably, eventually, mine, too."

His grip tightened. "When was the second time?"

"What?" He'd lost her.

"I heard you talking," he growled. "You said 'the first time I fell in love with you' just a minute ago. When was the second time? Because you made it *sound* like there was a second time."

He was focusing on that? When they were about to die? A half laugh, half sob broke from her. "They brought us out here to kill us. There is no sign that the CIA is going to arrive with guns blazing. We are on our own. The bad guys searched your body. They searched mine. They took all the weapons that you had hidden on you. We have nothing to use against them."

One hand rose to curl under her jaw. "I didn't want you to know the truth about your grandfather."

"Oh, no." She sucked in a breath. "You're finally going to confess all because you think we're both dying. You think this is it. The end for us." Unfortunately, he was probably right. This was it. She knew it, too. "So, what, we're supposed to get everything off our chests now? You want to give me the truth before you die?"

"I never wanted you to know the truth." His fingers rubbed lightly along her jaw. A soft caress. "I could have knocked the hell out of Logan Sterling for telling you about your grandfather."

His touch was so gentle. "You have a concussion." By his own admission. "You probably have no idea what you're saying."

"I'm saying that I never stopped loving you. I sent you away because it was the only choice I had."

She blinked quickly. Those were beautiful words. Words she'd dreamed of hearing so many times. *But not here. Not now.* Not when she thought he'd be executed in front of her, and she'd be crying over his dead body at any moment.

Why couldn't he have told her the truth a year ago? Two years ago? *Eight* years ago? Why couldn't they have gotten a chance to enjoy some happiness together? Instead, she'd *just* gotten him back in her life. Now he was going to die.

So was she.

"We always have choices," Delaney murmured. "You could have told me what was happening. We could have worked it out together." Now there was no time left to work anything out.

"The truth is..." His thumb brushed over her lower lip. "I was not strong enough to protect you back then."

She didn't believe that. Nash was the strongest man she knew. He'd been taking out those guys in the parking garage like it was nothing. She and Nash had been escaping. Until he'd been hit by a van.

Another gentle brush of his thumb. "But I am now. I am strong enough now."

"Uh, Nash, I hate to break it to you, but we are locked in hell." As close to hell as she could get. "We have no weapons. You're injured. We've been taken to the desert to meet up with Kurt. I am ninety-nine percent sure that he plans to finish you off and dump your body out here where it will never be found."

"I'll kill him first."

Okay, so maybe being delusional went along with a concussion?

"I'll kill them all," he promised.

Her eyes closed.

"I just need you to stay back. I need you to be safe. When I start attacking, don't fucking jump in front of me again. Stop doing that shit. I'm saving you, sweetheart."

"Yeah, cute, *concussion,*" she reminded him. "How about we figure out a way to save each other?" Her eyes flew back open. All she could see was a shadowy outline of him.

"Your grandfather came to my apartment." Low. Flat. "I had no idea who he was. Even told him that I thought he might be at the wrong address. And then I saw your mother, standing behind him. She had tears on her cheeks."

Goosebumps rose over her skin. Odd because it was warm in that little building.

"They came inside. He introduced himself. Said his name was Carmello Ricci and that he was your grandfather." A pause. "I told him that I loved you. Hell, I was *happy* to meet him at first. I didn't understand..." Nash's words drifted into silence. A soft exhale. "He said if I loved you, if I really loved you, I would get to prove that love."

Her chest burned. She'd asked him for the *why* behind their breakup so many times, but, in that terrible moment, she didn't want to hear the explanation. Maybe it would be better to die without knowing. Did that make her a coward? Yes.

Dammit.

"Carmello said he had plans for you. Very, very big plans. That you were going to cement his dynasty. He told me that your mother had disappointed him. She'd run, tried to escape, and he'd hunted her down. He'd punished the man who'd taken her from the life that Carmello had planned."

A tear leaked down her cheek.

"He killed your father, Delaney. He confessed to me. Just said it like it was nothing, and I remember thinking... this can't be real. But it was."

No. "My mother—she would have said *something to me!* She wouldn't have just let me go and live with a man who had killed my father!"

"She was sick, Delaney. Physically sick back then. You didn't know it, but she'd already been battling cancer for a while. She was weak, and I think that he was offering her treatment."

"*Paying* for it, you mean," Delaney corrected. Because wasn't that what her grandfather had done in Milan? Paid for treatment? Extended her mother's life by precious years?

"Your mother was a pawn in the game he played," Nash revealed. "A pawn who fell in love with a man your grandfather hadn't picked, and she fled her home to be with him. Later, I'd learn she fled because she knew your grandfather was Typhon. That she didn't want to be part of his criminal world. She wanted better for herself. For you. But despite her efforts, she didn't get to permanently escape."

Her mother had cried for days when they first arrived in Milan. Now Delaney understood why.

But Nash wasn't done. "He told me...Carmello said I didn't fit in the plans he had for you. *I* told him to fuck off. *You* were my only plan."

Another teardrop rolled down her cheek.

"Then he put a manilla file in front of me. Told me that, inside, I would find information on my biological parents. I had wondered about them my whole life. Always wanted to know why they gave me up. Why they walked away. He was offering me every answer. Right then and there. All I had to do in exchange for that information was walk away from you."

A weak nod. "So you did."

Another gentle slide of his thumb over her lower lip. "No, baby, I told him to fuck off again. They were my past. You were my future."

A sob slipped from her.

"Carmello said that was an unfortunate decision on my part. He made a phone call. Right in front of me. Told someone to shoot and..." A ragged breath. His hand began to fall away.

She grabbed his wrist. "*Nash?*"

"Your mother was crying. Your grandfather left with her. Before the door closed, he told me to look inside the manila file, then to be sure and check the news."

Her heart beat wildly in her chest.

"*He had her killed, Delaney.* He ordered the hit right in front of me. My mother's photo—her name, her address— they were right in the file. I checked online for news happening in her city. It was there—her death. Her death showed within hours on the local news outlets in her area. He had her killed because I wouldn't follow his orders."

Horror twisted inside of her. "I'm so sorry." She let him go. *How can he touch me? Nash has to hate me.*

"You have *nothing* to be sorry for! You didn't do it! That bastard did! I went to the police. I stormed to the local PD, and he was *there*. Waiting for me. Smirking. He put me in the back of a limo, and, as he sipped champagne, Carmello told me that he could wipe out everyone I ever loved. My biological father was still out there—he could eliminate him with a phone call. He could take out Ryan. Agnes. *Everyone in my family.* The family that had taken me in and loved me for years. The family that had given me a home. He was threatening to kill them all. Told me that he'd kill every single one of them, and then he'd kill me. Because one way or another, he was going to get you back. He wasn't going to lose you the way he'd lost your mother."

That little shed was as silent as a grave after those words. Grief and rage battled inside of her.

"Carmello promised me that he would give you the world. And that he'd give me death. If I tried to stay with you, if I didn't send you away, then he would leave a trail of bodies around me. I didn't know what the hell to do. I was in way over my head, and I just knew that when I stared into his eyes, I was staring straight at evil."

Her grandfather had always been so cold. So withdrawn. She'd known that her mother feared him but...

I never knew this. How could she have possibly known this?

"Carmello swore that you would be safe. Told me that you would have an army around you. That you'd want for nothing. He could give you everything. I could give you— well, he said I would be dead before I could give you anything at all but pain and grief." Anger rolled in Nash's words. "I asked him why the hell he didn't just kill me right then and there. Death would be easier than losing you."

Death would be easier than losing you.

She shook her head, frantic. It felt as if her heart had been ripped from her chest.

"Carmello sipped his champagne and said he'd killed the man his daughter loved, and that every time she looked at him, he could see the pain in her eyes." Delaney caught the faint click of Nash's swallow. "Carmello didn't want you looking at him that way. He didn't want you to ever see a monster. So he was giving me a way out. You were never supposed to know. I was never supposed to reach out to you again. I would get my life, along with the cash to pay for the rest of medical school and to cover the training for surgery and the start-up of my practice, and you'd get a life with him."

The pain in her heart would not stop. "You didn't become a doctor."

"No, sweetheart, I didn't."

"But you walked away from me." *Because what other choice had there been?*

"I couldn't protect you back then. I didn't have the means. Or the skills. So I found a way to change."

Every word battered at her. They didn't have time for this. They should be looking for a way to escape. But maybe...maybe he couldn't escape. Maybe he was too weak from his wounds and trying not to show her how desperate things were. Spoiler, she knew it was bad.

The blow to the head. The blood on his shoulder and his thigh. Maybe Nash knew death was coming, and the idea gutted her.

"Jezebel Jenkins," he whispered.

She wished Jezebel would come rushing to the scene.

"She found me the day after Carmello left. The day after I lost you." A press of his lips to her temple. "She'd been following him. Not like she could say too much because it was classified and I was a civilian, but I saw an opportunity with her. A chance to become the man you needed."

He'd always been what she needed.

"I traded in doctor's scrubs for spy school. I became the most lethal predator that I knew how to be. And, in return for taking the most dangerous operations out there, I had eyes put on you. Jezebel knew your protection was what mattered to me. Agents would check in on you. *I* would check in on you. We kept tabs on you to make sure you were safe over the years." A careful brush of his lips against her cheek. "Full confession? I didn't need Agnes to call me and tell me to stop your wedding. I was already on my way to you."

She grabbed for the front of his shirt. Her fingers fisted around the material. "We are going to die."

"No, baby, I am going to *kill*. When that door opens, I am going to kill for you. We are going to make it out of here, and you are going to tell *me* all about the second time that you fell in love with me."

Delaney wished she could see his face clearly.

"I'm sorry that I left you before." Emotion scraped in the words. "I will never do it again. I only wanted to protect you. It's all I've ever wanted."

"All I wanted was for you to love me."

"*I do. I have. I will. Always.*"

She could hear voices outside. The men who'd taken them, coming back. Or maybe even Kurt, coming to finish them off. The CIA had wanted to catch him in the act. They'd wanted to have enough evidence to bury him.

Instead, it looked as if she and Nash would be buried. "The second time," Delaney began as she heard the squeak of the door begin to open. "It was when you gave me daisies at our wedding." In the faint light from that opening door, her mouth found his. Her lips pressed lightly to his. Softly. Sadly.

A male voice snarled, "*Stand the hell up!*"

She wasn't sure Nash could stand.

But what she was sure of...Delaney was sure that when she took her last breath, she'd still be loving him.

Chapter Twenty-Two

HE DIDN'T HAVE A GUN. HIS KNIVES HAD BEEN TAKEN. Nash knew because he'd done a quick pat down on himself to see if the jerks might have overlooked a few of his favorite tools.

Unfortunately, they had not. Thorough pricks.

He'd been stripped of weapons. He was in a hot, musty shed in the middle of the desert, and the creeps coming in the door wanted him dead.

But Delaney still loved him. So, hell, yes, he had a reason to keep living.

His head hurt like one right bastard. Pounding and throbbing and aching in the back where he could feel the wetness of blood. His shoulder burned, and his thigh still trickled blood. All things considered, though, he was in pretty good shape.

Delaney still loved him.

And he was about to annihilate every threat around her.

Slowly, he rose. He hadn't faced the enemy yet, he figured that he looked bloody as hell from the back. He could feel the wetness of blood on his shirt. Dripping down his back from his head wound. That was the thing about head wounds. They bled and bled.

His enemies would think he was weak. They'd underestimate him. That was exactly what he wanted.

One called to Nash, "Hey, bastard! Guess what you're gonna get to do?"

Slowly, deliberately stumbling, he turned toward the men. Two men in the doorway.

"Boss wants you to dig your own grave." He tossed a shovel at Nash's feet.

A shovel.

Seriously?

Nash had been thinking he'd have to use his belt to strangle these morons, and then they go and throw a shiny weapon at his feet. Weren't they the generous idiots? He bent to scoop up his new, precious gift.

"No, no! *Do not kill Nash!*" Delaney's desperate cry. "I want to see Kurt! I want to talk to him—*Nash can't die!*"

She loves me. It was hard not to be freaking shouting with joy, but he had a job to do. He picked up that shovel, making sure to look nice and weak and injured as he did so. The fact that his blood kept drop, drop, dropping around him really helped set the scene. For just a moment, though, his head turned toward her. *Trust me.* He mouthed those words to Delaney.

One of the bastards bellowed, "Get your ass out here! *And start digging!*"

He shuffled toward the door. Delaney stayed behind him. When he got outside, more darkness waited. A million stars glittering overhead. But he didn't really care about the stars. His focus was on the men who thought they were going to bury him.

The two perps who'd come into the shed. A third man who stood near the front of a dark Lexus, and...

"Well, well," Nash muttered as his grip tightened on the shovel. "I did not think I'd see you again."

And the motel clerk who'd sold him and Delaney out to Kurt Wellington ambled toward him. Beneath the glow of the moon and the stars, Nash could see that the kid's face was swollen and bruised. Nash grunted. "You look like you got the hell beaten out of you."

The kid surveyed him. "Same, man. Same." He whistled. His hands were shoved into the baggy pockets of his pants. "This is not personal. Like, it's about survival, you know? I am all about my own survival." He pulled out a knife. He pointed that knife at Delaney. "I'm gonna need you to come here, lady."

Oh, hell, no.

"I have a job to do," the kid continued. But he wasn't really a kid, was he?

"Tell me your name." Nash maintained his hold on the shovel.

"You're about to be dead, man," the guy told him. "Why does my name matter?"

"It matters." Then, deliberately, he said, "*Trust me.*" But those two words weren't for the little creep who should not have been there. They were for Delaney. His signal that he was about to attack and that she was not to get anywhere near that jerk.

"Charlie," the punk mumbled. "Name's Charlie." He gestured with his knife toward Delaney. "Come on!" Louder. A shout. A desperate one. "He's gonna be here soon!"

A car door slammed. The rear door of the Lexus. The headlights of that Lexus turned on, firing right at Nash. The driver had turned on the lights while the man who'd just exited the vehicle casually strolled forward.

"Hate to break it to you," Nash tipped his head to the left, toward the approaching figure, "but I think he's here already."

Sure the hell enough, Kurt Wellington was strolling toward them. Cocky, confident. Soon-to-be dead.

"Why isn't he digging a hole?" Kurt's annoyed voice carried easily through the night. "I believe I gave an order. The man was supposed to dig his own grave." He reached their small group. "And then I am going to shoot him and send his ass to hell so he can fall into that grave."

"Kurt, stop this!" A frantic plea from Delaney. "Let him go!"

Kurt's head swung toward her. "Hello, darling. I missed you."

Charlie lowered his knife and edged back nervously.

The two goons with the guns kept them aimed at Nash, but their attention was divided now, as well. The boss was there, and his presence seemed to make everyone nervous.

Good.

"I'm about to make you a grieving widow." Kurt seemed happy to deliver this bit of news to Delaney.

"Nash and I are not really married," Delaney fired back. "The ceremony was staged. *Everything was faked.* You're surrounded by the cops, and they are about to swarm and take you into custody."

Insects chirped in the distance.

Kurt glanced around. "Is the swarm going to happen anytime soon?"

More chirping. No swarming.

"That's what I thought." Satisfaction purred from Kurt. "See, I happen to have a mole at the CIA. I've been steps ahead of you the whole fucking time. No one is coming. Nash Quinn is dying, and then I will be taking everything that belongs to me." He took two, hard steps forward.

Not quite close enough, but almost...

"Carmello promised that I would get everything," Kurt snapped. "I was his errand boy for *years*. I did his dirty work. I paid my dues. I bided my time. I moved up through the ranks. I was supposed to take over the throne when he passed."

"I don't think there was a throne." Nash felt duty bound to point this out. "Just a whole lot of crimes." *And prison time. A whole lot of prison time just waiting in the wings.*

"You interfering ass! I did *everything* that Carmello ordered! Drug deals, smuggling, hits—I took out his enemies, and I never blinked. He said that I'd get everything in the end. That I'd get what I was owed. He swore that I was the heir to his empire." Kurt pointed at a silent Delaney. "Then he brought you home. When you arrived, he wanted me to stay in the shadows until the time was right. I thought, sure, fine, Carmello is old freaking school. He wants me to marry into the family. So I kept playing his game. Waiting, waiting..."

A hot wind seemed to blow against Nash's skin. He wanted to look back at Delaney. Instead, he kept his head bowed, his shoulders slumped, but his eyes remained on Kurt.

Kurt wanted to talk, so Nash would let him. Confession was supposed to be good for the soul, wasn't it? It was also good for the CIA.

"Then one day, that SOB Carmello says that—that maybe I'm not right for his precious granddaughter. That maybe she should have been with someone else. The old guy starts talking about second chances and bullshit and

how he needed to go see his maker with a clean conscience."
Rough laughter. "*A clean conscience?* After everything he'd
done? After what I'd done for him? No way. No freaking
way. He didn't get to change the plans. I killed that bastard
then and there, and I—"

"*You killed him?*" Delaney's ragged voice.

"Don't pretend you care," Kurt mocked. "No one cared
about Carmello, and he cared for no one. All that mattered
was his stupid blood line. He was going to use you to pump
out kids so that he'd have great-grandsons to carry on his
name. His attack of conscience would not last. I didn't buy
that second chance crap he was peddling. *There are no
second chances.* So I eliminated him, and I stepped in to
take what was waiting. The whole dynasty, the fortune, the
world that was waiting for me."

Okay, well, that felt like a full confession to Nash.
"Sound travels at night."

"What?" Kurt waved his hands angrily. "What in the
hell are you mumbling about?"

Nash lifted his head. "Sound travels at night. Especially
if you're the CIA and you have the best listening devices
and sound amplifiers imaginable."

Kurt stomped toward him. "There is no one else out
here, you arrogant ass!"

Perfect. Now his prey was close enough. Nash slammed
his shovel right into Kurt's face. Bones cracked. Smashed.
Some teeth might have shattered, too. Nash didn't stop to
check. He was already spinning and ramming his shovel at
the men with the guns. One took a hit to the stomach. The
shovel plowed hard into him. Even as that one was falling,
Nash whipped the shovel around and pounded it toward
the hand of the other gunman.

The gun went flying out of that jerk's grip. And then

the shovel collided with the side of his head. Goon number two hit the ground right next to his buddy.

"Get her, Charlie!" Kurt bellowed as he spat out blood.

"Run, Delaney!" Nash thundered. *"Run!"*

The driver of the Lexus had jumped from his vehicle and was sprinting for Nash. Nash swung his shovel again. It *clanged* when it drove into the driver's head.

Charlie lunged for Delaney. "I'm sorry, I'm sorry, I'm sorry," he chanted as he came at Delaney with his knife.

Done with the driver, Nash surged for Delaney, but Kurt threw his body against him. They collided, hitting the ground, and that tricky bastard Kurt pulled a gun on Nash. "You're dying!" Kurt screamed at Nash. "You are *dying!*"

Nash rammed his elbow into Kurt's throat.

Kurt's gun went off, but the bullet was wild, and it didn't even come close to hitting Nash. His elbow struck Kurt a second time, the jerk lost his weapon, and then Nash reached out to grab his trusty shovel once more. He leapt to his feet, and then he brought that shovel rushing down toward Kurt's throat.

"Stop!" A cry from Charlie.

The edge of the shovel pressed to Kurt's Adam's apple. Nash wanted to plunge the weapon down. Brutal. Bloody. Violent.

But his gaze jumped to Charlie. A Charlie who was racing after Delaney.

Kurt began to laugh. "You're...gonna lose her."

Nash's gaze whipped down to Kurt even as the shovel pressed deeper into his prey's throat.

"Picked him...deliberately. Delaney—that heart of hers was always too soft. You think...you think she's gonna try and hurt someone who looks like a kid? He'll slice her throat, and she won't even be able to call for help."

Nash's grip tightened on the shovel. "You're the dead one."

"She'll never love a killer." Kurt smiled at him. "We both know that, don't we?"

"It's a chance I'll take." He—

"Freeze!"

Fuck. The cavalry had arrived. But then again, he'd known they'd arrive sooner or later.

"Nash, get the hell away from him!" Ryan thundered.

But he wanted to kill the man who'd tormented Delaney. Nash's body tensed. It would be so easy to drive the shovel down. One brutal plunge of the shovel was all that he'd need to do. Just one strike.

"Nash!"

* * *

HE WAS COMING at her with a knife. Nash had told her to run, and the kid from the no-tell motel was chasing her.

Distance is key. A lesson that Nash had taught her. She wasn't supposed to let her attacker get too close, but the guy was far faster than she was. He was barreling toward her, and she needed a weapon, desperately.

Grab whatever is nearby. More words from Nash. Instructions he'd given her when she asked how to defend against a knife attack. *A lamp. A picture. A pot. A freaking pan. Whatever you can find, use it.*

She slipped in the dirt. Her feet were bare, and her ass went down, hard. Like an unfortunate heroine in a horror movie, she just tumbled right down. Her fingers grabbed at the dirt.

"I'm sorry, I'm sorry," the guy chanted as he closed in on

her. *Charlie. His name is Charlie.* "But I have to do it! I have to prove I can!"

Delaney staggered to her feet. He was almost on her. Definitely within striking range. So she threw the handful of dirt that she had right at him. It hit him in the face, in the eyes, in his mouth.

"Bitch!" Charlie yelled as he spat out the dirt and lifted a hand to automatically rub his eyes. The hand that held the knife. Since it wasn't pointed at her and he was distracted, Delaney threw her body at him, as hard as she could.

They slammed into the ground, tumbling, and the knife dropped from his fingers. He grabbed her.

So much for following the distance-is-key advice. Maybe throwing her body into his had been a bad idea. She should have kept running.

His fingers tightened around her throat, cutting off her air.

"*I'm sorry!*" Charlie cried again. But his fingers tightened. He was apologizing as he killed her.

Her fingers stretched and closed around the handle of the knife. *Your attacker is going to overwhelm you.* Nash's voice was so clear in her head. *They'll start slicing and won't stop.*

She couldn't breathe. He was closing off all her air. But she'd just touched the knife. She had a weapon. His young face was above her. He was apologizing. Voice cracking. But hands hurting.

She sliced out with the knife. Cutting at his arms. His hands. Again and again. Fast, frantic stabs. *They'll start slicing and won't stop.* Something else Nash had said. But her attacker wasn't the one slicing. Delaney was.

She didn't stop.

He screamed. Let her go.

She kept slicing.

It was her life or his.

I have to fight. I have to survive. I have to get back to Nash.

"Delaney!" Arms curled around her and hauled her back. "Let me, baby, let *me!*"

Nash. His arms were around her. He was pulling her away from Charlie. He was taking the knife from her and surging back toward the guy who'd attacked her. He was killing—

"*Nash, stop!*" Ryan. Ryan was there, too. Only he wasn't alone. Some big guy with a gun gripped in his hands was beside him. An intense man with...was that a badge clipped to his belt?

"We have him!" The man with the badge yanked out handcuffs. "We have them all, buddy. So just stand the hell down, would you?"

But Nash let out a primal roar and tried to charge at Charlie.

Charlie whimpered.

Ryan jumped into Nash's path. "*Stop! Look at her. Look. At. Her!* Delaney is safe!"

Nash sucked in a shuddering breath. His body whipped so that he faced Delaney.

"I'm okay," she managed. She was. Adrenaline poured through her. Fear quaked in her blood. But she was alive. "I'm safe."

"*I'm not!*" Charlie shrieked. "*I think she cut off my pinky finger!*"

She might have done that. She'd been very stabby at the time.

"You're safe." Nash took a step toward Delaney. He dropped the knife. "You're okay."

Delaney threw her body against his. Her arms wrapped around him. She held on for dear life.

"Fuck." The man with the badge crouched next to a sobbing Charlie. "She did cut off his finger. See if you can find it, will you, Ryan?"

"Damn, Delaney." Ryan seemed impressed. "I did not think you had it in you."

Nash's arms locked around her. He shuddered against her.

"Ryan, *search*," the man blasted.

"Gray, chill," Ryan tossed back. "He can survive without a pinky finger. Not a big deal."

Her eyes squeezed closed. *Gray.* The man with the badge had to be Grayson Stone. The FBI agent that was supposed to be watching their backs. Gray was there. Ryan was there. Nash was holding her. So Kurt...? "What happened to Kurt?" Delaney asked. The last image she'd had of him—the edge of the shovel had been against his throat.

Nash's head lifted. "Jezebel has him. I wanted to kill Kurt. I wanted to destroy him. I wanted—"

She shot onto her toes. Yanked him toward her. And kissed him. Because all she wanted in the entire world was Nash. For Nash to be safe. For Nash to live. For Nash to survive.

And he had. He'd lived. They'd both survived.

And, as she'd boldly told Kurt, the cops were swarming.

This time, it looked like the good guys were going to win.

Chapter Twenty-Three

"I want a lawyer!" Kurt Wellington slammed his cuffed hands on the small table in front of him.

Jezebel burst into laughter. The hard, rolling kind that started in the pit of your stomach and just exploded from your mouth. The kind that just made a woman feel fabulous.

Her laughter also made Kurt pound his hands all the harder. "I. *Want. A. Lawyer.*"

"*I. Don't. Care.*" She pounded back. Then shook her head. "Who do you think I am? Some beat cop? Typhon, you are talking to the CIA right now. If I want, I can have you tossed into a deep, dark hole, and you will never be seen again."

He stopped pounding. He'd stopped when she said *Typhon*. Ah, the magic word.

"Um, do I have your attention now?" Jezebel reclined in her chair. Ryan Quinn was in the room with her because, injured or not, she knew the man had her back. Ryan had come in with his friend, FBI Agent Grayson Stone. Not *just* an FBI agent, though, because Grayson was

270

practically running the Bureau. Jezebel hoped that she and Grayson didn't enter a pissing match on this case. Typhon belonged to the CIA. The Feds needed to settle down. Though she *had* appreciated their assistance out in the desert.

"I want a deal!" Kurt thundered. But that thundering voice held the faintest hint of desperation.

More desperation would be coming soon, Jezebel was certain of that fact. "Do I look like I'm offering a deal?" Her head turned toward Ryan. She found him glaring at the prisoner. She cleared her throat.

Ryan's gaze briefly darted to her, then back to his prey. The rage on his face was concerning, and she understood his fury. Truly, she did. Kurt had taken Ryan's brother. Had tried to kill Nash. Ryan would never forgive that particular sin. When it came to family, Ryan had a zero-tolerance policy. Zero tolerance as in, you messed with his family, and he'd destroy you.

"No deal," Ryan rasped. His hands remained clenched at his sides.

Grayson edged a little closer to Ryan. Probably because he was afraid the other man might attack the prisoner at any moment. The Feds tended to frown over things like that. Grayson even curled a hand around Ryan's shoulder, as if he thought he might have to physically hold Ryan back.

Unnecessary, of course. She trusted Ryan.

And she currently had a deal working with him. Ryan had saved her ass—though, really, she'd had things under control. She'd simply been waiting for the right moment. Jezebel could have disarmed Dom in her sleep. Still, Ryan had been there when it mattered, so she'd make sure he got what he wanted.

Nash walks away.

"You don't understand the connections I have!" Kurt cried.

Her head turned back toward him. "Of course, I do. You were shouting about them out in the desert. I believe that Nash warned you, sound travels."

"Especially when you're using high-tech devices to pick up that sound," Grayson added.

She smiled at Kurt. "We had a tail on Delaney and Nash from the moment they were driven from the parking garage." The elevator incident had not been part of the plan. Dom had arranged for that unfortunate situation. She hadn't realized that he'd been able to get total control over the elevator banks. A serious security flaw that Logan Sterling would be correcting.

Logan Sterling. Such a very tricky individual. He'd wanted Kurt Wellington removed from the Vegas scene. And...wish granted. The storage facility that he'd turned over to the CIA had been full of all sorts of useful evidence that she planned to use against Kurt. More nails in his coffin.

But Logan bothered her. The inside intel he'd gotten, the things Nash had reported that Logan knew about were... *concerning.* She would be watching Logan Sterling very, very closely in the future. Despite the cooperation that he'd given to her and to the CIA, she did not trust the man. A man with too much knowledge should never be completely trusted. Perhaps she'd send an agent in to get close to him. To find out where Logan's allegiances truly belonged.

But that was a job for the future. For the present, she was taking down Typhon. Eliminating the last of his empire. This particular goal had been on her to-do list for quite some time. Sort of a life goal.

Goal achieved.

But that success had almost come at too high of a price. If Nash had been killed, she never would have forgiven herself. She liked the man, admired him, and, hell, he and Ryan were as close to family as she had.

The elevator incident should never have occurred. When the monitoring screen had gone black and Delaney had screamed, real fear had flooded through Jezebel's veins. That fear and distraction had allowed Dom to get too close with his weapon.

Dom had overridden the safety protocols and sent the elevator surging down four floors at rapid speed. *It's a good thing that Nash and Delaney weren't higher up. If they had been...*

Well, no sense lingering on that particular thought.

Nash and Delaney had survived the elevator drop. They'd been loaded into waiting vehicles. Whisked from the scene. But, luckily, Grayson had caught a visual of their fleeing prey. He and Ryan had tailed their targets. They'd been joined by the other agents Jezebel had texted and ordered into action.

They'd followed the perps out to the desert. Set up a full operation around that little shack, and then they'd just waited for Kurt Wellington to appear. They'd been recording, watching every moment. Hearing every detail.

Most civilians didn't understand just what sort of equipment the CIA used in their everyday operations. Then again, most civilians would have no clue that their friends and neighbors were secret agents. Spy games meant the best tech, the kind that would put those seen in the movies to shame. Spy games also meant constant lies and deceit to the people you loved the most. Such was life.

"You killed Carmello Ricci," she charged. Time to cut to the chase. "You were his flunky. You worked for him ever since you were a dumb college kid who found himself in Milan over the summer. A kid who made your way into Carmello's world."

"*I can tell you everything about his operation. Let's make a deal.*"

"It's your operation now, though, isn't it, Typhon?" Jezebel raised her eyebrows. "You killed Carmello. Took over. You've probably killed dozens of people over the years."

A faint smile came and went on his lips.

Sick bastard.

"Me?" A shake of Kurt's head. "You have the wrong man. I just wanted to get back my lost love. Nash kidnapped her, and I was trying to rescue Delaney from his clutches."

"Really? We're going with that story?" Why? To bore her? "Delaney has already given a sworn statement about you. She told us all how you shot a man in front of her before your wedding, how you tied her up and locked her in a closet when she wanted to get away from you, how you *stabbed* her when she balked at walking down the wedding aisle with you." A shake of her head. "She also told us that she *willingly* left the church with Nash because she was so desperate to get away from you."

His chin lifted. "Delaney is confused. Traumatized."

"Yeah, because of you, asshole," Ryan snapped. "You traumatized her."

Jezebel leaned forward. Her eyes did not leave her prey. "I think Delaney is quite the strong individual. She put her life on the line when she agreed to act as bait in order to nail your sorry carcass to the wall." A smug smile. "And she did a fabulous job, don't you think? She got you to confess your crimes. She got you to be directly linked to the abduction and attempted murder of both herself and of Nash Quinn. Plus, well, you're such an idiot that you took us straight to your dumping grounds."

One blink from him. Two.

She could smell the blood in the water. This jerk was going *down*. "You wanted Nash to dig his own grave. Stupid move, by the way, giving a man like Nash a shovel." Mocking laughter. "What did your goons expect him to do with it? Did they truly think he would just meekly follow their orders?" A roll of her eyes. "I suppose, though, they were used to dealing with victims who were terrified and beaten down. Men and women who did start shoveling." This part made her chest ache. "We've already uncovered seven bodies." And it had only been twelve hours since the dramatic scene at the shack in the desert. "My investigators tell me that there are more bodies out there." Plenty more. She swallowed. "I'm betting you were sloppy with your victims. All sorts of DNA and evidence will probably be uncovered in those graves. I'll tie you to so many crimes that you will never see the light of day."

"I want to see Delaney!"

"Not happening. Not ever again. But she is seeing you." Jezebel waved toward the one-way mirror on the right. "She's watching you right now. Delaney, and her husband, Nash. They both wanted to see the look on your face when you realized that *you* will never see freedom again. No deals. No escape. Just the end for you." An end she'd worked a long time to achieve.

Typhon.

Yes, she knew that Typhon had originally been Carmello Ricci. She'd approached Nash in the very beginning after Carmello had visited the young medical student. Curiosity had compelled her to interview Nash, but once she'd met him and learned his story, then Nash had become a weapon she could use.

He'd wanted to bring down Carmello. To make the man pay for murdering Nash's biological mother. *A mother he'd never had the chance to meet.* He'd learned her identity and then she'd been killed.

Nash had wanted to prevent more deaths. He'd wanted to protect his family. He'd wanted to protect Delaney. In order to do that, he'd become someone completely different.

Nash walks away.

Her gaze darted to Ryan once more. She knew what he'd meant by those words. Ryan wanted his brother to get his old life back. And it was never too late for a second chance, she fully believed that. Nash could finish medical school. He could start saving lives.

Start *living* his life.

"The marriage wasn't real," Kurt snapped.

She pursed her lips even as Ryan snorted. "That's the part you want to latch onto right now?"

"It wasn't real. She's not going off into the sunset with that jackass. It doesn't end that way."

Ryan shrugged off Grayson's hold. "I'm not going to attack him," Ryan muttered. "Maybe." He sauntered closer to Kurt. Then he smiled. "It was real. She's the only thing my brother ever wanted. You think I wouldn't do everything I could to make sure he got a bit of happiness? *It. Was. Real.* As real as the handcuffs on your wrists. As real as the fact that we have you dead to rights."

There was no more swagger from Kurt. He seemed to fold in on himself as Ryan loomed over him.

"Thanks for helping us root out our mole," Jezebel told Kurt. "I'd known a traitor was with us for months. So nice to have that problem solved."

"The FBI thanks you, too," Grayson announced, the first time he'd spoken since entering the room. "We were able to track down the rogue agents who fed you intel. I always love cleaning house."

Kurt's gaze jumped from Grayson to Ryan to Jezebel. "I—I have intel you can use...I want a deal. *I want a deal!*"

"Oh, we will be taking your intel. We will take everything from you. But there is no deal. There is only your *cooperation*. And you want to cooperate with the CIA, don't you?" Jezebel asked him sweetly. "Because the alternative to that..." A delicate pause. "The alternative will truly be hell."

Sweat tricked down Kurt's temple. His head turned, and he stared at the one-way mirror to the right.

* * *

KURT STARED AT HER. Or, he seemed to stare at her, but Delaney knew he couldn't really see through the glass. He was cuffed. As Ryan had just said, the CIA had him dead to rights. Kurt would never be a free man again.

And... "Our marriage is real?"

She turned away from Kurt. He didn't matter any longer. He wouldn't scare her. He wouldn't threaten her. He would not hurt her.

Her gaze fell on Nash. A Nash who was not looking through the glass. Instead, his eyes—those beautiful, incredible eyes—were on her.

"Yeah. *Ahem.* About that..." Nash tugged at his collar. "I tried to tell you. At least twice. Ryan did it. *I had no knowledge beforehand.* We were supposed to get a substitute officiant, and the paperwork was supposed to be BS but..." Nash stopped.

"But it wasn't?"

"It wasn't." His shoulders fell. "Baby, I am so sorry."

She threw her arms around him, being very, very careful of his injured shoulder. A bullet had grazed him there, and Nash liked to act like it wasn't a big deal, but an injury was an injury, and she never wanted to hurt him.

His hands curled around her waist. "Delaney?"

She buried her face against him. "I love you."

"Delaney, I know it's not the wedding you wanted. You wanted a beach, you wanted daisies, you wanted—"

Her head whipped right back up. "You remember all of that?"

"I remember everything when it comes to you."

Her heart seemed to swell in her chest. "It was never about the beach. Or the daisies. It was about *you*."

"I want to give you the world," he told her, voice gruff. "I am so sorry for the pain I caused you. I am so sorry for the years we lost. You are all that I've ever wanted. You are my life."

"The past is over." They could not live in the past. Pain and regret? No, she was done with that. "I want you to be my future."

"You're mine. My future. All I want. All I ever wanted."

She didn't glance back through that one-way mirror. What was the point? Everything she wanted—everything that Delaney had ever needed—waited right in front of her.

Nash's head lowered.

She kissed him.

Chapter Twenty-Four

"THE THIRD TIME IS THE CHARM." RYAN PATTED Delaney's hand as the waves crashed into the shore. "That's the idea behind this marriage, isn't it?"

Not another marriage. More like a final ceremony. Because Nash had insisted. He'd said that he wanted to do things right.

They were on a beach. She was carrying fresh daisies. Nash's family was there. His parents beamed at him from their spot in the front row of the carefully arranged line of chairs. And Agnes had actually already headed down the aisle, sniffling and dabbing at tears as the matron of honor made her way across the sand.

Delaney wore a dress she'd designed herself, one very similar to the long-ago dress that she'd sketched out when she used to fantasize about marrying Nash and having a happily-ever-after with him.

The sun had drifted low in the sky. The golden hour was upon them.

Nash waited. A smile curved his lips as he stared at her.

She couldn't help but smile back as joy filled her. "He insisted," Delaney replied to Ryan.

It had been two months since the nightmare in Vegas. Two months since Nash had been told to dig his own grave, and, instead, Kurt had gotten locked away for life. Delaney had turned over all of her grandfather's assets and holdings to the CIA. The agency was still ripping away at the fabric that had been Typhon's world—both when Typhon had been Carmello Ricci and when Kurt had been ruling the criminal empire.

She'd grieved for her father. Her mother. She'd gone with Nash to visit the grave of his biological mother. They'd even met Nash's biological father, a man who had never known about Nash's existence and who'd cried when he'd met his son. His bio dad was at the ceremony, too. Watching. Smiling with everyone else.

Time had passed. The physical wounds they'd all suffered had healed. Now...

Nash wanted her to marry him at the ceremony of her dreams. A renewal ceremony, technically, since they were already legally husband and wife.

No organist played. *The Wedding March* didn't drift through the air. She could smell the crisp scent of the ocean and hear those wonderful, pounding waves.

But before she moved down the aisle, her head turned toward Ryan. "Thank you," she told him.

"For what? Tricking you into a real wedding back in Vegas?" He winced. "I need to apologize for that, don't I?"

"Thank you for always protecting Nash."

"He's my brother." Simple. "I'd die for him."

She knew that was true. But, "How about you keep living? How about we all do that?" Delaney pressed onto her toes and brushed a kiss against his cheek. "You got him out of the CIA. I know you did."

He patted her hand once again. "It wasn't the life he should've had."

She eased back. "What about your life?"

A wide grin curved his lips. "Haven't you heard?" He looked particularly debonair and James Bond-like in his tux. "I live for danger."

There was more to life than danger.

"Nash is waiting." Gruff. His grin had faltered. "I hope you're both happy."

She was happy. "I want you happy, too." Maybe one day Ryan would find someone who was a match for him. Someone who could handle his danger and see past his charming grin to the real man he hid from so many people in the world.

The real man...The one who loved his family. The one who never backed down. The one who would face any threat head-on.

Her shoulders straightened. Delaney pulled in a deep breath as her head angled back toward Nash. He stood patiently near the edge of the beach, right where the waves rushed up to tease the shore. The golden light hit his dark hair.

She began to walk toward him. Not in high heels. But in bare feet that brushed over the sand. Agnes still sniffled from her position near Nash. Sniffling from happiness or pregnancy hormones or from both—it was hard to tell for sure what caused her tears. Agnes's husband stood beside Nash. A rather intense, somewhat scary fellow. His eyes were locked on his wife, and the expression on his face...

Even intense and scary fellows could apparently worship their wives.

Grayson Stone was in attendance, too. Holding the hand of his wife, Emerson.

And, of course, the ceremony would not have been complete without Jezebel Jenkins. Jezebel was currently dabbing at her eyes with a blue handkerchief as she huddled next to Nash's parents.

Blue.

Delaney smiled. Ryan had been handing out blue handkerchiefs to everyone in attendance. Even though it was technically a renewal ceremony, he'd made sure she had everything on her lucky wedding list.

Something old...she still wore the engagement ring that Nash had bought for her so long ago.

Something new...the dress she'd designed.

Something borrowed...Agnes had loaned Delaney the wedding veil that she wore. Agnes had used it in her own wedding, not too long ago.

Something blue...that would be the handkerchiefs that Ryan had supplied to everyone.

Yes, she had all the items on her list.

Delaney stopped in front of Nash. *He* was her most important item. The husband who loved her. The spy who'd fought for her. The man who owned her heart.

"I love you," Delaney said.

Nash bent down and kissed her.

"*That's not supposed to happen yet,*" Ryan muttered, because he was still close. "Dude, it's like the second time you've done this with her. You know the drill."

And Nash just continued kissing her.

* * *

HE CARRIED her over the threshold, and this time, Delaney didn't argue about it. She kept one arm locked around his neck. He was kissing her as they crossed the threshold, and somehow, Nash actually managed to slam the door behind him.

A honeymoon suite. One right on the beach at their five-star, tropical resort.

Delaney loves me. She's mine. She's safe.

He didn't want to stop kissing her. He never wanted to let her go. Some days, it felt as if he'd lived a lifetime without her, and when Nash thought of all the years they'd been apart...

Never want that again. Only want her.

Slowly, very, very slowly, he let Delaney slide to her feet. Her body brushed against his. She still wore the wedding dress that she'd made. To him, she looked like some sort of fairytale princess. The most perfect vision he'd ever seen.

She smiled at him. Her hands went to the back of the dress, and he heard a low hiss.

The zipper gave way. The fabric pooled at her feet. And Delaney...

"Fuck." That was pretty much all he could manage. Delaney had not been wearing any underwear beneath her wedding dress. Her pert nipples thrust toward him. Her curving hips tempted him, and that sweet, sweet paradise between her legs promised him the best pleasure of his life.

"Yes, I thought we'd do that. At the first opportunity." She stepped out of the dress. Kicked it to the side as if she hadn't spent hours and hours painstakingly making the dream gown. "I would very much like to fuck my husband."

He reached out. Caught her left hand. Brought it to his

lips and kissed her knuckles. "Make love," he corrected. "It's always love with you."

She smiled at him. Her smile made him want to take on the world.

He picked her up again. She laughed, and her legs curled around him. Her bare sex pushed over the front of his tuxedo pants. His eager cock shoved against her, and he wanted nothing more than to sink into Delaney. To get lost in her again and again.

He carried her to the bed. Champagne chilled on the nightstand. Just as it had chilled in their Vegas honeymoon suite.

But this scene was so different from Vegas. There were no more threats. No more fears. He had Delaney. She knew all of his secrets. She loved him.

He lowered her onto the bed. His hands trembled faintly as he touched her. Carefully, tenderly, he put her on the edge of the mattress. Then he began to strip. Her eyes drifted over him as he tossed away his tux coat. As he unbuttoned his shirt.

His thick cock ached with need.

My wife. I want my wife.

There was no one in this world he would ever want more.

He ditched the rest of his clothes in record time. Yet before he could reach for her, Delaney rose. Naked, she reached for the champagne. She poured him a glass. Poured herself one.

He took one champagne flute from her hand.

"To forever," Delaney said.

Hell, yes.

Their glasses lightly touched. He drained his

champagne. It was good. Light. Sweet. But he knew something even sweeter. And he would be tasting *that*.

She took a few sips from her drink. Even as she was putting the flute back down, he was tumbling her into the big bed. His hands were hungry and eager. His mouth demanding and caressing at the same time. He kissed her breasts. Licked her nipples and sucked hard, savoring every single bit of her.

My wife.

Down, down he went. Pushing her thighs wide as he slid between her legs. But...

He stopped.

"Nash?"

He reached for her champagne flute.

"What are you doing?" Delaney asked.

He poured a little of that champagne between her thighs.

She gasped. "Nash!"

He poured a little more champagne. Dropped the flute beside the bed and bent to taste his prize. Yes, the champagne was sweet, but she was even better. He lapped her up, licking and sucking every single drop of drink— every single drop of *Delaney*. Tasting her again and again even as his fingers thrust into her. One finger, then a second. So tight. So hot.

So sweet.

He savored every single bit of her. Relentlessly took and took as she arched against his mouth. Her nails bit into his shoulders. He licked her clit. Sucked it. *Hard*.

She came. A wild cry broke from her lips, and he kept tasting all of her as she climaxed against his mouth.

Then he was surging up. His body lifting. His dick

pushed against the entrance to her body, and he sank in deep. As far as he could go in one long, hard thrust. She was still coming around him. Her muscles squeezed and pumped him.

He rolled on the bed, moving her on top of him. Her knees pushed down onto the mattress as she straddled him. Nash's hands caught her hips. He lifted her up, down. Faster. Harder.

"Touch yourself, baby," he growled. "Touch yourself for me."

Her breath heaved. One small hand pressed to his chest as she balanced herself. The other slid between their bodies, wedging down. But she didn't touch herself as he'd ordered. She lifted up, and her fingers curled around the base of his dick. She squeezed him. Tightened her grip so deliciously.

His hips flew off the bed as he pounded into her.

Her fingers broke from him, and, *yes*, she stroked her clit. Her head tipped back as she moaned and that was the end for him.

He blasted his release into her even as Delaney came again.

It should have been tender. It should have been sweet.

It wasn't.

The climax ripped through him and a guttural roar poured from his lips.

* * *

"There's more champagne."

Nash cracked open an eye.

Delaney was reaching for the champagne bottle.

"I am so thirsty," she said.

But…

She didn't reach for a flute. She brought the bottle over him. Over his dick.

Both eyes flew open. "Delaney!"

She poured a little of the champagne on him. Nash hissed out a breath.

"Cold, isn't it?" she murmured. "I noticed that, too." She put down the bottle. "But don't worry, I know just how to warm you up." Her mouth closed around him.

He fisted the sheets.

Fuck, fuck, fuck.

His wife definitely knew how to warm him up.

* * *

"Are we going to talk about it?" Delaney asked as she rolled toward him.

They were in bed. The balcony doors were open. The sun was rising.

He curled an arm around her and marveled at the softness of her skin.

My wife. There was no world where he would ever grow tired of thinking about her that way. There was also no world where he would *ever* stop loving her. But the love of his life had just lost him with her question. "Talk about what?" Nash asked. Had four times been too many? Or could she take him again?

"About the person who caught my bouquet."

A smile teased at his lips.

She gave a thoughtful hum. "I was so sure the flowers were going toward Jezebel…"

Yeah, it had certainly looked that way to him, too, but

then a powerful gust of wind had taken those flowers straight to someone else. They'd actually slammed into the head of that someone else.

And Ryan had been given no choice but to grab the flowers that had hit him.

"But then Ryan snagged them," she finished. "I know he's only *minorly* stitious but..."

He blinked. Twice. "What in the hell is stitious?"

"Some people are *super*stitious. Ryan assured me he was minorly stitious."

Nash shook his head against the pillow. Laughter poured from him. "Bullshit. He's the most superstitious man I've ever met." A grin lingered on his lips. "I've seen him throw entire saltshakers over his shoulder."

She sent him her beautiful smile. "Well, then."

Just that. "Uh, well, then...what?"

"When do you think he'll be getting married?"

"He's going on another mission. Somewhere in Europe." Nash didn't know more than that because the job was classified. Seeing as how Nash was officially no longer part of the CIA, he didn't get access to classified intel. "He's not going to fall in love. He's going to fight bad guys. Ryan is off to save the world."

But her eyes gleamed at him, catching the rising sunlight. "Who says that he can't do all of the above? This *is* your brother. Pretty sure he's a multitasker."

Yeah, Ryan was a multitasker. It wasn't Ryan's future wife who interested him, though. Nash was focused on his own wife. His beautiful Delaney. The glow of the rising sun turned her skin a gorgeous gold. Nash forgot about his brother and the bouquet and focused on the only task that he wanted to complete. "Can you take me again?"

"I can take you...always..." Husky. Breathy. Tempting.

Nash leaned toward her. His lips pressed to hers.

My wife.

He was such a lucky bastard.

"Always, Nash," she promised. "Always."

THE END

Ryan's book is up next! So if you are in the mood for another Protector & Defender Romance, be sure and check out WHEN HE LIES.

Their paths collide on a mission. He's working undercover. So is she. But they are on two very different sides of the law.

A top operative at the CIA, Ryan Quinn is used to hunting down the worst of the worst. Manipulation is the game. And he is exceptionally good at the game. His latest case involves him playing the role of a wealthy and bored businessman as he sneaks into the inner circle of some very dangerous individuals. The tool he uses to get into that circle? The lovely and innocent Simone Sailor.

Fun fact…She's using him. Men always

underestimate her…Too bad. That's their mistake.

Simone has a job to do, and nothing will stop her from achieving her goal. She has some trinkets to retrieve for a very upset family. *Retrieval specialist*–yep, that's her. She thinks that title sounds so much better than say…thief. So she lies, she pretends, and she gets the job done. *One hundred percent success rate.* Playing innocent and fooling her marks? *Please.* That's something that she can do in her sleep. Except this time, she finds herself getting a little too close to one of her targets…the gorgeous and seemingly clueless Ryan. A bored but way too sexy billionaire. A man who has a touch that sends wildfire racing through her veins.

She's distracted during her heist. *He* distracts her, and she gets caught in the act of *retrieving* property. And death is the punishment. For her…and for Ryan.

Uh, oh. Simone *may* have underestimated the danger in her latest job. When she and Ryan are suddenly kidnapped, she realizes that, for the first time in her life, she could seriously use a hero…and turns out, Ryan is not the useless rich boy that she assumed. He's smart, he's incredibly dangerous… and Ryan just killed someone without blinking in order to save her life. Oh, and also…he's saying that she's under arrest. That he has to keep her close, twenty-four, seven, and that there is now an exceedingly large bounty on her head.

She's his prisoner. His leverage. And...his absolute obsession.

Simone is not innocent. She is not sweet. She is going to drive Ryan absolutely and utterly insane. He crossed lines with her–so many complicated lines. He's killed for her, and he will do whatever it takes to keep her alive. She's now a very important witness, and the CIA intends to leverage her knowledge of the international crime world. But...Ryan just wants *her*. And the longer they are together, the hotter the desire between them blazes.

But liars aren't supposed to fall in love.

Too bad because Ryan is pretty sure that he's falling hard for gorgeous Simone. Now, if he can just keep her alive, if he can capture all the bad guys who want her dead, and if he can prove to her that, for the first time in her life, she's finally found someone that she can truly trust...then maybe this spy will have a chance at a happy ending with the pretty thief who may have stolen his heart.

Author's note: Simone never thought that she'd need a protector, but now, her life is on the line, and a *good guy* is the only one who can keep her alive. On the run, thrown together in close confines and chaos, with their enemies fast on their trail...she has no choice but to rely on Ryan. As for Ryan, he's about to prove to Simone that this *good guy* knows all about playing dirty, fighting hard, and burning down the world in order to protect the woman who was meant to be his.

Author's Note

I love a happy ending! And I hope you do, too!

Thank you so very much for taking the time to read WHEN HE LOVES. It is such a treat for me to write the "Protector and Defender Romance" series. Over the top romance, alpha heroes, determined heroines, suspense, action, and just—fun. These books are so much fun for me to write. I am usually typing with a smile on my face because these books truly bring me joy, and my wish is that they will provide you with some joy and escapism, too! We all need our happy endings and our fun. We need our romances!

If you have time, please consider leaving a review for WHEN HE LOVES. Reviews help readers to discover new books—and authors are definitely grateful for them!

If you'd like to stay updated on my releases and sales, please join my newsletter list. Did I mention that when you sign up, you get a FREE Cynthia Eden book? Because you do!

By the way, I'm also active on social media. You can find me chatting away on Instagram and Facebook.

Again, thank you for reading WHEN HE LOVES. Ryan's book (WHEN HE LIES) is up next, and I have so many twists and turns planned for that CIA operative! It's definitely time for him to meet his match.

Happy reading!

Best,

Cynthia Eden

cynthiaeden.com

More Books By Cynthia Eden

Protector & Defender Romance
- When He Protects
- When He Hunts
- When He Fights
- When He Defends
- When He Guards

Ice Breaker Cold Case Romance
- Frozen In Ice (Book 1)
- Falling For The Ice Queen (Book 2)
- Ice Cold Saint (Book 3)
- Touched By Ice (Book 4)
- Trapped In Ice (Book 5)
- Forged From Ice (Book 6)
- Buried Under Ice (Book 7)
- Ice Cold Kiss (Book 8)
- Locked In Ice (Book 9)
- Savage Ice (Book 10)
- Brutal Ice (Book 11)
- Cruel Ice (Book 12)

- Forbidden Ice (Book 13)
- Ice Cold Liar (Book 14)
- Ice Cold Christmas (Book 15)

Wilde Ways

- Protecting Piper (Book 1)
- Guarding Gwen (Book 2)
- Before Ben (Book 3)
- The Heart You Break (Book 4)
- Fighting For Her (Book 5)
- Ghost Of A Chance (Book 6)
- Crossing The Line (Book 7)
- Counting On Cole (Book 8)
- Chase After Me (Book 9)
- Say I Do (Book 10)
- Roman Will Fall (Book 11)
- The One Who Got Away (Book 12)
- Pretend You Want Me (Book 13)
- Cross My Heart (Book 14)
- The Bodyguard Next Door (Book 15)
- Ex Marks The Perfect Spot (Book 16)
- The Thief Who Loved Me (Book 17)

The Fallen Series

- Angel Of Darkness (Book 1)
- Angel Betrayed (Book 2)
- Angel In Chains (Book 3)
- Avenging Angel (Book 4)

Wilde Ways: Gone Rogue

- How To Protect A Princess (Book 1)
- How To Heal A Heartbreak (Book 2)
- How To Con A Crime Boss (Book 3)

Night Watch Paranormal Romance
- Hunt Me Down (Book 1)
- Slay My Name (Book 2)
- Face Your Demon (Book 3)

Trouble For Hire
- No Escape From War (Book 1)
- Don't Play With Odin (Book 2)
- Jinx, You're It (Book 3)
- Remember Ramsey (Book 4)

Death and Moonlight Mystery
- Step Into My Web (Book 1)
- Save Me From The Dark (Book 2)

Phoenix Fury
- Hot Enough To Burn (Book 1)
- Slow Burn (Book 2)
- Burn It Down (Book 3)

Dark Sins
- Don't Trust A Killer (Book 1)
- Don't Love A Liar (Book 2)

Lazarus Rising
- Never Let Go (Book One)
- Keep Me Close (Book Two)
- Stay With Me (Book Three)
- Run To Me (Book Four)
- Lie Close To Me (Book Five)
- Hold On Tight (Book Six)

Bad Things

- The Devil In Disguise (Book 1)
- On The Prowl (Book 2)
- Undead Or Alive (Book 3)
- Broken Angel (Book 4)
- Heart Of Stone (Book 5)
- Tempted By Fate (Book 6)
- Wicked And Wild (Book 7)
- Saint Or Sinner (Book 8)

Bite Series

- Forbidden Bite (Bite Book 1)
- Mating Bite (Bite Book 2)

Blood and Moonlight Series

- Bite The Dust (Book 1)
- Better Off Undead (Book 2)
- Bitter Blood (Book 3)

Mine Series

- Mine To Take (Book 1)
- Mine To Keep (Book 2)
- Mine To Hold (Book 3)
- Mine To Crave (Book 4)
- Mine To Have (Book 5)
- Mine To Protect (Book 6)

Dark Obsession Series

- Watch Me (Book 1)
- Want Me (Book 2)
- Need Me (Book 3)
- Beware Of Me (Book 4)

Purgatory Series

- The Wolf Within (Book 1)
- Marked By The Vampire (Book 2)
- Charming The Beast (Book 3)
- Deal with the Devil (Book 4)

Bound Series

- Bound By Blood (Book 1)
- Bound In Darkness (Book 2)
- Bound In Sin (Book 3)
- Bound By The Night (Book 4)
- Bound in Death (Book 5)

Stand-Alone

- Waiting For Christmas
- Monster Without Mercy
- Kiss Me This Christmas
- It's A Wonderful Werewolf
- Never Cry Werewolf
- Immortal Danger
- Deck The Halls
- Come Back To Me
- Put A Spell On Me
- Never Gonna Happen
- One Hot Holiday
- Slay All Day
- Midnight Bite
- Secret Admirer
- Christmas With A Spy
- Femme Fatale
- Until Death
- Sinful Secrets
- First Taste of Darkness
- A Vampire's Christmas Carol

About the Author

Cynthia Eden loves romance books, chocolate, and going on semi-lazy adventures. She is a *New York Times*, *USA Today*, *Digital Book World*, and *IndieReader* best-seller. She writes romantic suspense, paranormal romance, and fun contemporary novels. You can find out more about her work at www.cynthiaeden.com.

If you want to stay updated on her new releases and books deals, be sure to join her newsletter group: cynthiaeden.com/newsletter.